Gold Bay: An Adam Weldon Thriller

What People are Saying...

"McGinnis's best writing so far! McGinnis pioneered whitewater rafting in California and writing about rafting; now he boldly sails into epic saltwater fiction!"
—Lee Foster, author of *Travels in the American Imagination: The Spiritual Geography of Our Time, Northern California Travel: The Best Options*

"A gripping Bay Area crime thriller suffused with uplifting spirit."
—Becky Parker Geist, Pro Audio Voices

"Clever, authentic and well-done!"
—Jil Plummer, author of *Caravan to Armageddon, Hell's Playground, Remember to Remember*

"Bill McGinnis's new novel Gold Bay grabs our attention as we charge along like a high-speed boat romp through San Francisco Bay. Many of the Bay's unique subcultures and quirky neighborhoods contribute to a desperate race to survive drugs, organized crime, and political corruption. McGinnis has created a thoroughly satisfying sequel to his previous novel, Whitewater: A Thriller."
—Ted Kearn, investor, sailor, surfer, class V river guide

"If you like the idea of being dropped into a high-velocity chase between the most nimble protagonist you could ever imagine and an all-but-invisible and nightmarishly efficient surveillance system—but with absolutely no risk to yourself—then Gold Bay is just waiting for you."
—Scott Parkay, creative writing teacher

GOLD BAY

WILLIAM MᶜGINNIS

Whitewater Press
El Sobrante, California

Gold Bay: An Adam Weldon Thriller
is available in print, ebook, and audiobook from your favorite retailer.

Published by Whitewater Press

Copyright © 2019 William McGinnis
www.WilliamMcGinnis.com

bill@whitewatervoyages.com
(510) 409-9300
5205 San Pablo Dam Road
El Sobrante, CA 94903-3309

Printed in the United States of America
First Edition: October 2019

10 9 8 7 6 5 4 3 2 1

McGinnis, William
Gold Bay: An Adam Weldon Thriller

ISBN: 978-1-7336547-0-8

Library of Congress Catalog Number: 1-7428841171

Book design by Andrew Benzie
www.andrewbenziebooks.com

To the natural wonder that is San Francisco Bay.

I empty myself
To begin

Contents

CHARACTER LIST

Listed in order of appearance

Adam Weldon—Former Navy SEAL, military police investigator, black ops commando. Owner of 70-foot sloop Dream Voyager and Indian Rock Resort on the Kern River

Tripnee—Undercover FBI agent and much more

Peace Weldon—Adam's ex-Zen monk school librarian uncle

Mercedes Montana—FBI special agent in charge of the FBI's San Francisco field office

Judd Wagstaff—FBI agent under Montana

Magdalena Alvarado—Wealthy resident of Belvedere

Black Elk—Wealthy Belvedere neighbor of Magdalena, spiritual leader, head of the Wing Foundation non-profit and Wealth Watch website, etc.

Ben and Jerry—Pilots for Harry Bellacozy

Harry Bellacozy—Billionaire entrepreneur owner of Prophecy, etc., and Belvedere neighbor of Magdalena

General Eisenhower—Right hand man to Harry Bellacozy and head of cyber security and cyber research for Prophecy

Linda—School teacher, follower of Total Embrace

Bob—Follower of Total Embrace

Gaia—Total Embrace guru

Seth, Bo and Fredricka—Low-level La Casa thieves

BC/Billy Calhoun Davis—Tech-savvy black Oakland cop, long-time friend of Peace

Rasheed—12-year-old former La Casa cartel sicario/hitman, friend to Vocab

Vocab—15-year-old former La Casa cartel sicario/hitman notorious for his uncanny accuracy with an AR-15, Very tech savvy

Lakeridge Club Gymnosophists—Peace's Lakeridge friends

Dead-Eye—Security guard for Black Elk

El Dragon—The #2 boss and ultimate enforcer in La Casa cartel

Toast—Adam's military pilot buddy

Admiral Ty Jeppesen—A key mover and shaker in the world of United States espionage.

Valerie Zizmor—Key staffer to a member of Congress in Washington D.C.

El Patron—Head of La Casa cartel

Reamer Rook—FYI: Former head of La Casa cartel on the Kern River, former owner of Indian Rock Resort

Proudfoot—Enforcer in La Casa cartel

Toro Canino—A dangerous, ruthless, coiled dragon of a man who has killed hundreds of Mexican decent, he is the #2 boss and ultimate enforcer in the La Casa cartel

Mack Dowell and Hektor Torrente—La Casa cartel hitmen

The President—The President of the United States.

San Francisco Bay

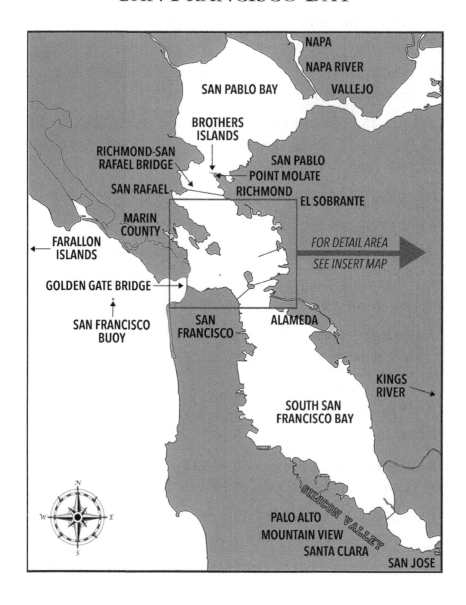

NAPA

NAPA RIVER

VALLEJO

SAN PABLO BAY

BROTHERS ISLANDS

RICHMOND-SAN RAFAEL BRIDGE

SAN PABLO

POINT MOLATE

RICHMOND

SAN RAFAEL

EL SOBRANTE

MARIN COUNTY

FOR DETAIL AREA SEE INSERT MAP

FARALLON ISLANDS

GOLDEN GATE BRIDGE

SAN FRANCISCO BUOY

SAN FRANCISCO

ALAMEDA

KINGS RIVER

SOUTH SAN FRANCISCO BAY

SILICON VALLEY

PALO ALTO

MOUNTAIN VIEW

SANTA CLARA

SAN JOSE

N

W E

S

1. GOLDEN GATE BRIDGE
2. MARIN HEADLANDS
3. HORSESHOE COVE
4. SAUSALITO
5. RICHARDSON BAY
6. BELVEDERE
7. TIBURON
8. MARIN
9. RACCOON STRAIT
10. ANGEL ISLAND
11. ALCATRAZ
12. BAY BRIDGE
13. YERBA BUENA ISLAND
14. TREASURE ISLAND
15. OAKLAND

16. JACK LONDON SQUARE
17. EMERYVILLE
18. BERKELEY
19. BERKELEY PIER
20. I-80 EAST BAY FREEWAY
21. ALBANY
22. ALBANY BULB
23. BROOKS ISLAND
24. EL CERRITO
25. MARINA BAY
26. POTRERO REACH
27. BRICKYARD COVE
28. RICHMOND
29. EL SOBRANTE

CHAPTER 1

INTO THE GOLDEN GATE:

"We're dead."

"What d'ya mean, 'We're dead'?"

"The Bay. All of us. Me in particular."

"Not if I have anything to say about it."

"You're off sailing the world."

"Actually, I'm seven miles from the Golden Gate."

"Yeah? How soon can you get that boat of yours to Horseshoe Cove?"

"I'm making fifteen knots; I can be there in half an hour."

"Meet you there. That is, if I can stay alive 'til then," said Peace Weldon. "Gotta go."

The VHF cockpit transceiver went silent. Suddenly fifteen knots under full sail felt painfully slow. Adam Weldon fired up the two-hundred-horse diesel, and soon seventy-foot sloop Dream Voyager surged forward at twenty knots, slicing through steep rollers at a furious pace.

The fuzzy landscape ahead—San Francisco—the land of Adam's youth—morphed into distinct shapes: Cliff House teetered above Seal Rock; Sales Force Tower stuck up from its surrounding cityscape like a knife jutting from a corpse; and skeletal Sutro Tower stood in a wide stance as though poised for an apocalyptic break dance.

* * *

Six months before, halfway through their round-the-world voyage, Adam and Tripnee had been exploring the Seychelles Islands in the middle of the Indian Ocean. Then Tripnee had gotten an urgent summons from her FBI bosses. With a promise that she would rejoin him on the boat as soon as she could, she grabbed the next flight out of Victoria, the archipelago capital, bound for San Francisco.

For awhile, it was fine having the boat and the vast ocean to himself. Then he missed her—a lot. For a time, her emails had been buoyant, although, per FBI policy, they revealed no details. Gradually her messages became sporadic and strained. Reading between the lines, he knew she was putting a brave face on some tough, dangerous situation. Then all communication stopped. Something was seriously wrong. It was time to race home by the most direct route to find out what was up. That was two weeks ago, when he was far out in the Pacific. He had pushed Dream Voyager hard, crossing the distance in record time. And now, this alarming call from his irascible, normally upbeat, ex-Zen monk uncle Peace!

* * *

Like a great river, the incoming tide picked up speed as it squeezed through the Golden Gate. A wall of fog parted to reveal a massive container ship, floating high and empty as it heaved out to sea against the current, heading back to Asia for another load. The wild mountain scape of the Marin headlands slid past on the port side. Obscured by swirling mist and backlit by morning light, the Golden Gate Bridge soared far overhead.

Adam couldn't help but be moved. Then, just inside the Gate on the Marin side, Dream Voyager swooped down on Horseshoe Cove.

CHAPTER 2

KIDNAPPED

Adam headed into the wind, dropped the mainsail, centered the boom, and turned toward the narrow entrance. His bow penetrated the cove, a pool 200 yards across. To port, three Coast Guard cutters tugged on their moorings, while to starboard, about sixty sailboats and power pleasure boats bobbed in a marina. There, in a parking area straight ahead, Peace pulled up in his Tesla Model S, which Adam had given him several Christmases before. His uncle got out, smiled and waved, and Adam waved back. Wow, the guy— the spaced-out old codger who had taken Adam in at age five after the lad's parents had been murdered on the Kern River— looked quite fit.

Adam brought his yacht to rest alongside the marina's guest dock and quickly secured the mooring lines. What was happening? As he looked over toward his uncle, four short men surrounded Peace. One appeared to stun him with a taser, then they all seized the old man, wrenching his arms behind his back.

Adam leaped onto the dock and raced toward them, but he was too late. The men had dragged Peace into a black truck. The vehicle's engine roared as it took off.

There was Peace's Tesla. His uncle always left the electronic key in his car, so Adam ran to the Tesla and was about to jump in and give chase. But the kidnappers had slashed the tires. Adam's heart sank as he helplessly watched the black truck, with

Peace held captive inside, circle the cove, going south. They were apparently headed for the shortcut that switchbacked up to the southbound lanes of Hwy 101 at the level of the Golden Gate Bridge, far above.

But then the kidnappers stopped, turned around and sped away in a different direction. Ha! Squinting to get a closer view, Adam saw that the supposed shortcut was blocked by a vehicle barrier.

This gave Adam an idea. He dashed back to his boat, pulled out his mountain bike, and set off like a bat out of hell. Within moments, the kidnappers would be on the bridge headed south, but had to take a circuitous route. And maybe, just maybe, Adam could intercept them: although the steep switchbacked shortcut was closed to motor vehicles, it was open to bikes!

Adam's handlebars were soon slick with sweat. His legs burned, and he gasped for air. The one-lane track climbed a cliff directly under the northern bridge approach. There was no time to rest!

At bridge level, he desperately scanned the vehicles headed into San Francisco. It was the morning commute. Traffic was stop-and-go. Was he too late? Wiping away the sweat pouring off his forehead, he searched the lanes. No black truck! He set off across the bridge, redoubling his effort, pedals whirling, his legs screaming. It had to be here! He shot forward past the creeping traffic. Still no kidnappers. Got to keep going.

Suddenly, there they were! Moving aggressively, the black armored truck jumped around, forcing its way from lane to lane, no doubt trying to disappear into the City as fast as possible. But the density of traffic on the bridge allowed Adam to catch up and memorize the license number. What next? How could he stop a truck when he's riding a bike?

Adam considered climbing onto the vehicle. But while that might work in movies, this was real life. He dismissed the idea, passed the villains and pulled ahead. But he was running out of bridge. Beyond the bottleneck of the bridge, traffic would speed up and fan out into the City, and he would lose his chance to rescue Peace.

Suddenly, he saw a way to go. In the outside lane, an eighteen-wheel tractor-trailer rig! Adam got ahead of it, slowed and stepped off his bike, leaving it leaning on the bridge railing. As the semi passed, he jumped onto the passenger-side step and grabbed the door handle. Climbing into the cab, he said, "Cop! Need your truck."

The skinny, bald-headed driver said, "Like hell!"

With a pang of regret that there was no time to win the man's cooperation through gentler means, Adam squeezed the guy's carotid, putting him out cold. Then he shoved the man's limp body aside, got his own feet on the pedals and his hands on the wheel. Checking the mirror for an opening, he swung the rig left, blocking all southbound lanes.

The gangsters, a dozen cars back in the gridlock, could go neither forward nor backward. They'd probably try to make a break for it on foot.

But the determined brutes had other ideas. Surrounded by commuters yelling, cursing and honking, the abductors backed around and began slamming their rear end into the short wall that divided southbound from northbound traffic. The first impact tilted the block wall, the second and third laid it flat, and the fourth sent the black van, with tires screeching, bouncing over the fallen barrier into the northbound lanes, where a massive pileup ensued. The truck limped away from the smash-up, going north, away from the City, its rear end crumpled and dragging.

As the big-rig driver came to, Adam pushed open the passenger door, jumped from the truck and ran to his bike. He dodged through the gridlocked southbound vehicles and took off, pedaling northward, pursuing the kidnappers' truck. Those rogues wouldn't get far with their tires rubbing, their whole left side crushed in, and their rear end scraping grooves in the pavement.

CHAPTER 3

ON THE BAY

Leaving behind a wild scene of mangled vehicles and enraged drivers, Adam pedaled up the empty northbound lanes. For a while, he could still see the limping van, dropping chunks of itself, dragging its tail uphill toward rainbow-festooned Robin Williams Tunnel. Then it disappeared. Must have one hell of a souped-up engine to keep going in its crippled state.

Adam's legs ached. Months at sea had made him soft. But he pushed on—as a horrible sinking feeling spread through his guts. Could he catch the bastards? If they hurt Peace—OK, the guy was dopey, but he wouldn't smash a fly.

Passing through the tunnel, he raced along Hwy 101 as it traversed the hills above Sausalito. Coming to a high vantage point, he paused to catch his breath and study the scene spread out below him. Where the hell was that black clunker? Nothing. Nothing...

Aha! Far below, there it was! Dragging itself along the Sausalito coastline. Adam sped downhill to the freeway exit and then shot along the waterfront. He raced past houseboats and pleasure craft, searching for Peace and his captors. Where the hell were they? Had they driven into a building somewhere? Should he double back?

Then he saw something. Ahead, a low, black motorboat coming in off the main bay slowed and turned toward a rickety dock. A frisson of apprehension slid up his spine. The timing. The look of the craft. This boat was swooping in to meet the mobsters!

He raced around a marsh inlet, through a park, between rows of rusty containers—and burst onto the derelict dock—only to see the black van standing empty and the power launch accelerating away.

Dammit! So close, but out of reach. How does a bicycle catch a boat? Adam again poured on speed, straining to keep the kidnappers' boat in sight. The hijackers tore along the channel parallel to the shoreline, headed out toward where Richardson Bay opened onto the greater San Francisco Bay. Soon they'd be a dot on the horizon. But as long as he had them in sight, there was a chance—a rapidly disappearing chance. Pedaling faster than ever, with lungs bursting, he racked his brain for an idea. They were getting away!

Hey! Ahead was a small powerboat with twin 200-horse Yamaha outboard engines idling, and a guy standing on the dock near the bow hefting an ice chest. Adam braked and, bike in hand, jumped straight into the boat.

"Kidnappers!" he yelled gesturing toward the receding launch. "Gotta use your boat."

After a moment of stunned surprise, amazingly, a knowing twinkle appeared in the guy's eyes, and he said, "No problem, son! Go get'em!" Putting down his ice chest, the guy unhitched the bow line, and added, "Good luck!"

Adam leapt into the phone-booth-sized wheelhouse. As he jammed the boat into gear and gunned both engines, he leaned out of the pilothouse to yell, "Thanks! Name's Adam Weldon. What's yours?"

"Al Capricio," came the reply, barely audible over the roar of the engines.

The boat shot forward and rose up to plane on the smooth

surface of Richardson Bay, strutting its stuff in the warm sunshine. The kidnappers' launch was a small shape a quarter-mile away. Ignoring the harbor's speed and wave restrictions, he kept the throttle wide open, and soon was gaining on the abductors. Got to catch those bastards!

Far out across the central bay, an arm of dense fog filled what local sailors called, "the Slot." One of the most famous and treacherous sailing venues in the world, the Slot was notorious for its high winds, racing tidal currents, speeding shipping traffic, rocks, and opaque, fast-moving fog. But the vast wall of airborne water—the fog—was a couple miles off, and Adam was already barreling down on the perps.

For a moment, he looked back to see the now tiny figure of Al Capricio standing on the dock. Then another shorter man approached Al while pointing wildly at the departing boat and pounding the air with his fists. Hmmm. Maybe this wasn't Al's boat?

Oh, no! A ferryboat! Sliding into Adam's path was a hundred-foot catamaran loaded with commuters. No way could he cut across the bow of this giant hydrofoil about to blast forward, so he swerved to starboard, aiming to cut behind the big craft. At the very moment Adam crossed the ferry's stern, its huge engines kicked on full-blast, sending out a fifty-foot arc of water. The torrent slammed into his wheelhouse and knocked his small vessel onto its side, right onto its beam ends. Water, water, water inundated his wheelhouse, blocked his vision, poured in through the doorway behind him.

Bracing himself in the compact pilothouse, he prepared to roll completely over—but, by golly, the boat wallowed on its side for a moment, then righted itself, with the outboards still running! What a great little craft! Got to thank Al Capricio—or that other guy.

Back upright, the water drained out, allowing the boat to

regain speed, but moisture fogged the windshield. Wiping it with his hands helped, but water coated the outside too. Finally it cleared. Yikes!!

Dead ahead—a flotilla of dinky sailboats! Skippered by sawed-off captains—tiny kids—America's Cup sailors in the making—on a morning race! No way to swerve to miss them—and even if he could, his wake would wreak havoc on these precarious vessels. In a flash he backed the engines. Both transmissions screamed in protest, but somehow made the shift into reverse, sending forth two 200-horse reverse streams of water, rapidly slowing his light boat. But could he stop in time? God forbid he chop up a child in his twin props!!! His aluminum runabout slowed and slowed. And, finally, stopped just yards from the nearest little sailboat—sending a two-foot pulse wave sweeping straight through the diminutive flotilla.

The toy boats—their baby captains' eyes big as saucers—nimbly pointed their bows into Adam's surge wave, bobbed over its crest as it swept through their flotilla, and then swung back onto a broad starboard reach, resuming their race.

Breathing a sigh of relief, Adam scanned the Bay for the torpedo-shaped launch. Damn! It was a half-mile away, a diminishing dot. After steering around the midget fleet, he again cranked his engines wide open and shot off in hot pursuit. Got to catch 'em before they disappear into the fog.

Leaving the shelter of Richardson Bay, he zoomed out onto the wild, exposed, very different world of the main Bay. The temperature plunged. The wind picked up speed, buffeting his boat. The waves grew ever larger. No longer skimming, his hull pounded through the whitecaps. Slam! Slam! Soon he was catching air flying off the crests.

But he was closing in on the fleeing boat, and he'd probably catch it well before it reached the fog. Should he ram it? Force it to stop?

Suddenly, the fleeing launch picked up speed, lifted up on hydrofoils—hydrofoils!—and took off at triple speed. Adam clenched his jaw. Falling behind, desperate for an idea, he racked his brain for a way forward, anything. Then his eyes fell upon a lever half-hidden behind the throttle. Its label read, "Nitro Booster."

Did such a thing even exist? There was one way to find out. He pulled it. For a moment, nothing happened. Then—wow!—the twin engines erupted in a thunderous wail; he was thrown back against the pilot house door; and the boat exploded forward like a guided missile. Ha! He yanked himself back to the wheel as his sweet craft knifed through the rollers like lightning through a storm. Wowee! He was again gaining on the kidnappers.

His speed was astonishing. Still, the black launch was equally amazing—and was getting closer and closer to the cover of thick fog.

He realized he might have a problem. Unarmed, he was chasing ruthless men. At least his aluminum wheelhouse would provide some protection if they opened fire.

Splunk! Splunk! Bullets hit the aluminum skin of the boat's tiny cabin. Dropping to his knees, he hunkered as low as he could get, occasionally lifting his eyes to windshield level just enough to stay on-course. Splunk! Crash! Splat! Some of the shots smashed through the thin metal walls and lexan windows above him.

He tore open a cabinet below the ship's wheel and pulled out a pile of life preserver cushions, then pried up two plywood floor panels and jammed them between himself and the front wall of his enclosure. Just in time! Splaffft. Splafffft! Splunk! Splafffft! The shots zeroed in, searching for him, getting lower, closer, puncturing the wheelhouse wall, burying themselves into the cushions and plywood.

In a lull during the firing, he risked popping up for a quick glimpse. The black launch, gliding on its hydrofoils, more aircraft than watercraft, moved like a demon from hell. Adam was flying through the waves at an even greater speed, no doubt pushing his craft way beyond its design limits. He slowly closed the distance—and felt he would catch them soon. But the pitch-black boat raced on, drawing closer and closer to the fog bank until—damn!—it vanished into the opaque mist.

Determined not to lose them, and encouraged that at least now they were no longer blasting away at him with automatic weapons, he followed their hydrofoil wake into the fog. Standing up, looking out through the opening that had held the windshield moments before, he reduced speed and strained to see a swath of bubbles, anything that might be the kidnapper's slipstream.

Light gray mist enveloped his boat, blotting out the sky, reducing visibility down to fifty feet or so. Was that swath of wash and smoother water their wake? Had to be. He followed it.

Did the fog fill the entire central Bay? Or was there clear air and sunshine not too far ahead? Having gained the fog, would the kidnappers do evasive maneuvers to elude pursuit, or would they simply race straight through to emerge on the other side? Was that shifting swath of foam ahead the kidnapper's wake? Feeling he had no other choice, like a bloodhound with no sense of smell, Adam forged on, doing his best to feel his way, but essentially was running blind.

Finally, he thought he saw something. A thinning of the mist? A lifting of the water. A wave. A big wave! Holy shit! It was the bow wave of a ship coming straight at his port side! Twenty feet high, roaring, spewing spray, cresting forward on itself, pushed up by the oncoming, bulbous, underwater protruding bow of a giant speeding container ship, the wave lifted and rolled his little boat. Instinctively, with his boat sideways on the wave, he jammed the throttle full-on so hard he almost broke the lever. Though the boat was tipped vertical, its propellers were still in the upwelling wall of water, and caught enough to hurl his boat off across the exploding bow wave— and out of the path of the onrushing ship—by a foot or two.

Thrown on its side, minuscule compared to the monster ship, his boat wallowed for a moment on its beam ends, then, like a cork, righted itself—amazing little watercraft that it was! He was close enough to reach out and touch the ship as it raced past. Thank God he wasn't under that massive barnacled hull, getting ground to bits, chopped and diced by its whirling propellers into human-flesh tartare!

Holy shit! That was way too close! Got to stop pushing my luck. Can't help anyone if I'm dead.

Feeling lucky just to be alive, he noticed the fog thinning. Then suddenly he was out of it, skimming over calm water under a clear blue sky. Looking around, the black launch was nowhere to be seen. He found himself over in the East Bay near Richmond. Hmmm. A few miles inland from Richmond was Peace's house in El Sobrante. As he headed that way, Adam dialed the FBI.

Before their world cruise, Tripnee had introduced him to a number of the agents in the FBI's San Francisco field office, so now he went straight to the guy who handled kidnappings: Judd Wagstaff.

When Judd came on the line, Adam explained who he was, and told him about the kidnapping, describing both the kidnapper's boat and the location of the black van. Judd said he'd get right on it. They agreed to meet at Peace's house in El Sobrante.

CHAPTER 4

PEACE'S HOUSE

As Adam rounded the Richmond breakwater and headed up Potrero Reach toward Marina Bay, he found himself flooded with memories of growing up right there along the Richmond waterfront. It seemed like only yesterday that he was sailing that same channel in his uncle Peace's tipsy sailing canoe. Tipsy was putting it mildly—the thing constantly took on water, and once or twice every trip, turned bottoms-up, flipping him into the Bay. Yet he kept going out in that boat, thrilled just to be on the water.

Then there was that insane all-night voyage in an eleven-foot, half-deflated rubber raft. With a flagpole for a mast and a drape for a sail. No running lights. He and three high school buddies had somehow crossed the entire Bay from Marin to Brooks Island just off the Richmond shoreline. Running blind on a moonless night, guided and protected by nothing but dumb luck, they had managed to cross busy shipping lanes without getting run over. He blew out a lungful of air, marveling at how lucky he was just to be alive!

The harbor ahead had once been a key ship-building center during World War II, and later had become a derelict industrial port. Recently, the half-mile-square inner harbor had been transformed into an upscale yacht marina, surrounded by shoreline walking paths, parks, restaurants, condos and townhouses. Adam tied up to a dock on the basin's eastern shore, in front of the Tradewinds Sailing School clubhouse. Inside the clubhouse, he arranged with the owners, who were old sailing buddies, to return and repair Capricio's Sausalito speedboat. Getting out his cell phone, he tapped the Uber app and minutes later, jumped into a red Prius driven by a cranky twenty-something garage-band drummer. Fifteen minutes later, as his ride descended Peace's steep driveway, a rambling wood-frame structure—the home where Adam had grown up from ages five to eighteen—came into view. Once a resort and speakeasy during Prohibition in the 1920s, Peace's property in El Sobrante was an oasis in the middle of the East Bay. Nestled on a bend in San Pablo Creek, the place teemed not only with redwood, oak, bay, apple, orange and lemon trees, but also with wildlife. As the Prius pulled up, a family of deer, which had been feasting on apples, bounded away into the creek's inner gorge.

He unfolded his six-foot-two frame from the vehicle, and filled his lungs with fresh-scented air. When Adam was a little tyke, no doubt more hindrance than help, he and Peace had planted these very trees, including the majestic redwoods that towered skyward over a hundred and fifty feet.

Adam found the key, hidden in its niche under the bronze Buddha by the solid-oak front door—who leaves their key in the same obvious spot for thirty years? The house was the same as always. The rooms overflowed with sturdy furniture that the two of them had made together. Peace's love for flat table space—for writing, trip packing, projects—was much in evidence. Comfortable chairs in conversational groupings recalled times of warm camaraderie.

Plopping down in Peace's favorite chair, Adam found his eyes growing moist. Within reach were his uncle's familiar array of pens and writing tablets, switches for the forest of nearby reading lights, piles of books, and quantities of Dollar Store reading glasses. He felt the deep pleasure of home, but also another feeling. What? A lingering exasperation with the old coot?

Peace had been a monk at the Tassajara Zen Mountain Center near Carmel. After Adam's parents' murder, Peaceful Mountain Weldon, his father's brother, had left the monastery to become an elementary school librarian in order to give tiny Adam a home. His uncle was a Don Quixote, forever battling windmills, somewhat scatter-brained and lost in his own craziness. But the guy had taken him in, had saved him from life as an orphan, had lifted him out of a cold, lonely universe of desolation and abandonment. Thanks to this man, Adam had had a home!

Despite this good fortune, Adam had been haunted all his life by an inescapable sense of traumatic loss. Peace tried, but could never replace Adam's parents, to whom the little Adam had been bound in ways beyond imagining.

Nor could Peace erase Adam's memory of his parents' deaths. It happened at bedtime. His mother and father were bending over five-year-old Adam, tucking him into bed, kissing him, whispering good night and sweet dreams, when a hailstorm of machine-gun fire shattered the window over his bed, riddling his parents with bullet holes—each spurting blood. No bullets reached little Adam—but glass shards lodged in his shoulder, giving him his star-shaped scar.

To the young Adam, Peace's messages about spiritual awareness and embracing life had felt like a non-acknowledgment of his grief. Adam—though he didn't know how to say so at the time—had needed to just feel what he was feeling, for as long as he needed to, to accept himself and his process. Like all human souls, Adam had had to walk his own path—and Peace just hadn't gotten it. But now, the prospect of losing Peace was unthinkable. Now it was time to come through for his uncle.

Adam's investigator training—plus something deeper—kicked in. When facing crisis and chaos, he knew to trust his intuition, to let information and perceptions flow in without having to figure them out right away. Eventually, clues and insights revealed themselves. Often, he found the solution staring him in the face. Oddly, just then he remembered Peace instilling in him this very habit—this way of solving problems by tuning in to what Peace called the higher self.

Adam moved from room to room, scanning walls of photographs, memos, and poetry, and taking in floor-to-ceiling bookshelves jammed with volumes of every description. Perhaps because he had read them recently himself, Adam noticed Michael Gelb's *How to Think Like Leonardo da Vinci*, Nassim Taleb's *Antifragile* and Ann Weiser Cornell's *The Power of Focusing*. A framed Rumi poem read, "Don't you know yet? It is your light that lights the world." A photo showed Adam as a rather sad, serious tyke blowing out candles on a birthday cake displaying a big "6." Another showed a ten-year-old Adam and a youthful Peace atop Mt. Livermore, the highest peak on Angel Island, with San Francisco and the Golden Gate Bridge spread out behind them. Still another showed a teenaged Adam at the tiller of a sailing dinghy in a stiff breeze on Oakland's Lake Merritt.

Adam entered Peace's study, a small room overlooking the creek. A U-shaped desk held an iMac and stacks of books and file folders. On a hunch, he used Peace's cat's name Higher Awareness as the password, and voila! he was in.

Peace's search history and emails reflected his all-too-open mind and far-ranging curiosity. It was just like him to avoid the polarization and name-calling that nowadays permeated civic discourse, and instead empathize with a wide range of perspectives.

What was this? Adam leaned closer. A theme of alarm ran

through many of the emails and searches. Peace had been tracking an explosion of Bay Area kidnappings, drug turf wars and gang violence—much of it performed by child sicarios, or hitmen. One thread, for example, followed the exploits of an infamous fifteen-year-old hitman named Vocab, who was notorious for his uncanny accuracy with an AR-15. In another thread a Berkeley blogger raved about political and judicial corruption, and lamented that a societal breakdown, a terrible scourge of violence and corruption, was devouring the region from the inside out.

Adam read more carefully. At first, Peace seemed to think these declarations were overblown. But just a day earlier, his uncle had received a dire warning from someone named Magdalena Alvarado.

"In general, I look for the silver lining, for the best in people," her email read. "But there is a very bad man—uno hombre muy malo—and no doubt many others—at work. You know who I'm talking about! People are being slammed—and they're afraid. People's lives are collapsing. It's bad! We're facing a breakdown of the social fabric, of law and order. And if it happens here, it's going to spread. The thing is, Peace, you yourself are in danger! You've got to protect yourself. Hide. Go immediately to a safe place, an undisclosed location."

Adam drew in a breath, absorbing this.

Simultaneously, both his phone and Peace's computer chimed. On each one, there it was—the ransom demand: "If you want to see Peace alive: $637 million. Liquidate your assets and pay us within one week. Delay, contact the police or give us trouble, and you, Peace, Tripnee and everyone you care about will die. Payment details to follow. We are watching!"

Messages sent to both devices. How'd they do that? How'd they know so much about him? This rubbed in how far ahead of him they were.

It was uncanny. The ransom amount equaled the entire value of everything Adam owned, including Indian Rock Resort and Dream Voyager. A hard knot formed in his gut. Ever since the resort on the Kern River had come into his hands, he'd enjoyed the options wealth gave him. But material stuff, after all, was just stuff. Selling off his assets in a week was going to be a challenge—and he'd have to start the process immediately. Still, no matter what, ransom or no ransom, people who would do something like this had to be stopped. Permanently. How the blazes was he going to do that?

CHAPTER 5

THE FBI

Moments after the ransom demands arrived, Peace's doorbell chimed. Adam shut down the computer and made his way through the house. On the porch he found the bear-like Judd Wagstaff and a tall, striking woman.

Judd said, "Adam, this is my boss, special agent Mercedes Montana."

They all shook hands and Adam invited them in. Montana moved with long strides, while Wagstaff scurried along behind in a flurry of short wobbling steps that were odd for a big man. Montana's ramrod posture and forward lean exuded strength, and her handsome face seemed to light up with genuine warmth upon greeting Adam.

So this was the much-in-the-news special agent in charge of the FBI's San Francisco field office. What had brought this major honcho to Peace's house? Was it Adam's connection to Tripnee? Was it professional courtesy for an ex-military law enforcement brother? Was there something about this kidnapping that gave it overarching importance?

They sat down at Peace's oak table. Wagstaff started a voice recorder, and Montana, all business, said, "Start at the beginning. Tell us exactly what happened. Include every detail."

Adam described the entire abduction and chase, including his close encounter with the container ship. He concluded, "Their boat was unusual: how many forty-foot, low, black, hydrofoil

23

motorboats can there be in the Bay? If we alert the Coast Guard and deploy agents to check the marinas, someone will have seen them."

"Good points, Adam," said Montana. "We'll follow up."

"How many people can you put on this?" asked Adam. "We need to get moving, track these guys down, and find Peace as soon as possible!"

"We've put a team on this. In fact, they'll be here soon," said Montana. "But, before we go any further, you need to understand something. The FBI will handle this. We are the pros, and you need to stand clear and let us do our job."

"This is my uncle we're talking about!"

"That's just it," replied Montana. "Look, we know you have an impressive military record in combat and criminal investigation. But you're too close to this. Too emotional."

Adam looked at her with disbelief.

Montana, no longer smiling, her jaw set, continued, "I'll be blunt: you're a loose cannon. That stunt you pulled on the bridge could've gotten people killed. You need to stand clear."

Adam shook his head. "We'd be far more effective working together."

Montana said in a low, hard voice, "It boils down to this, Weldon: I won't have you mucking this up, or getting killed on my watch. We're the pros—this is ours. Trust us."

This was weird. Adam looked over at Wagstaff, who seemed smaller than he remembered. Then turned back to Montana. "You're making a big mistake."

Unperturbed, like a tanker grinding over a skiff, the special agent-in-charge scrunched her eyes into slits and said in an even lower voice, "If you don't back off, it's you who'll be making a mistake. This isn't some thriller novel. Rein yourself in, or we'll haul you in."

Not likely! thought Adam, as he glanced at Wagstaff, who, with Montana focused on him, was rolling his eyes.

At that moment, Montana's cell phone went off. With her eyes locked on Adam, she thrust her hand into her pocket and turned the phone off without checking it.

A few minutes later, Wagstaff's cell phone rang. Answering it, Judd listened briefly and his eyes bulged as he blew out a breath. He leaned over to whisper to Montana.

Montana inhaled and stood up. For a long moment, she looked out through a picture window at Peace's idyllic creekside property. Then, turning to Adam, she said, "I've got to go. Agent Wagstaff will personally spearhead this case. We're sealing this house off as a crime scene, so you'll have to leave."

Just then, two black Suburbans pulled up outside the house and a half-dozen FBI agents climbed out. One began stringing crime scene tape around the house, while the others walked in without knocking.

Montana said with a touch of gentleness, "Wagstaff will finish up with you. Look, Adam, you just don't know what you're getting into here. We do. We'll do everything possible to rescue Peace. It'll go better for everyone if you do as I say."

Then she stiffened and said, "Heed my words, or we'll take you in for your own protection. This is bigger than you have any idea."

Standing up too, Adam asked, "What's going on that you're not telling me?"

She calmly stared at him, jaw rigid, saying nothing.

Adam said, "I'll find Peace, with or without you."

With a softening at the corners of her mouth, she looked at him and slowly shook her head. Without another word, she strode out of the room, out of the house, got into her car and drove away, looking back only once, her handsome jaw clamped shut.

Wagstaff talked with the newly arrived agents, and then surprised Adam by offering him a ride back to his boat. They got into Judd's black government-issue Crown Victoria.

After his boss had left, Wagstaff underwent a subtle metamorphosis. He seemed to expand, his shoulders widened, his spine straightened, his gait lengthened. If Montana's mere exit could evoke this physical response in the man, Adam saw a possible way to go.

Tripnee had expressed complicated feelings about this particular FBI colleague. Wagstaff was clever, but there was something off about the guy. The question was: How to get him to cooperate?

Adam said, "I think I got off on the wrong foot with your boss."

"You're not alone," replied Wagstaff.

"She began by pouring on the charm," said Adam, "but when that didn't work, out came the iron fist."

"Oh, yeah," said Judd, "she does whatever it takes to get her way."

"Can't be easy having her for a boss."

"You got that right," said Wagstaff. "She's a royal bitch."

"But she's in control?" asked Adam.

"Oh, yeah! She's in control all right. She's got the power. Entrenched herself like you can't believe. Kisses up to the big fish. But I'll give her this, she gets the job done as she sees it. In most ways she's actually damn good. Scary good. But here with you, Adam, she's making a mistake."

Adam nodded.

"Hell, there's no stopping you anyway, so we may as well help each other." He looked at Adam sharply, "But it has to be on the down-low. You can't let Montana know. It'll really mess me up if you do."

Adam said, "Thanks, Judd. I appreciate it. So, can you fill me in? What's going on?"

"Just between you and me," said Wagstaff, as creases furrowed his broad forehead, "kidnappings are rampant."

Adam pressed for details but Judd stayed vague. He would only say that a number of abductions had hit prominent Bay Area families. All were kept out of the press. Ransoms in the hundreds of millions.

Taking this in as they crossed the Richmond-San Rafael bridge, Adam looked out at the wide, grey, roiling Bay. Shaking his head, he asked, "Why'd Montana dash off? What was that phone call about? "

"That," said Judd, "was Harry Bellacozy."

Recognizing the name of the Silicon Valley billionaire, Adam asked, "Another kidnapping?"

"That, or something else. In case you don't already know, Adam, from the president on down, when the rich and powerful call, we feds jump."

"Including the FBI?"

"Yep. Montana hides it, but she's all about taking care of the super-rich, including you. And, yeah, there are some agents who don't toe the line—a few renegades I won't name," said Wagstaff with a half-wink, his lips curling into a smile, exposing large teeth.

"That reminds me," Judd continued, turning serious, "Tripnee's dropped off our radar. She's undercover, so it's normal for her to be out of touch at times, but I'm concerned for her safety—worried she might be into something over her head."

"I'm worried about her too."

"It's important that you keep me informed. What you're both working on, what leads you're following. So we can work together. So I'll know how to help you if you get in trouble. Again, it's crucial that you keep this between us. If Montana finds out, I'm screwed. Got it?"

CHAPTER 6

MAGDALENA

Back at Horseshoe Cove, fog horns droned a mournful rhythm while a vast river of racing tidal current swept out through the nearby Golden Gate. Although protected by its narrow mouth, the waters of Horseshoe Cove reverberated with the power of the passing torrent, causing the boats in the little marina—including seventy-foot Dream Voyager—to gyrate on their moorings, with lines slapping masts, and water gurgling among the hulls. Overhead, an ocean of airborne moisture—a deluge of pea soup fog—blasted in through the gate and tumbled down from the Marin headlands, cutting visibility to maybe fifty feet.

Adam called his lawyer, Marshall Johnson, who was also a real estate broker, to start the process of cashing in his assets to raise money for the ransom.

This done, he fired up the Yanmar engine, stowed his lines, and soon had Dream Voyager gliding toward the mouth of the cove. As he left the little harbor and accelerated into the tidal current, the boat listed and spun to starboard, then leveled out. Turning to port, he followed along the Marin shoreline, keeping it just barely in view through the mist, but far enough away to avoid rocks. Adam's mouth was dry and his throat constricted as he agonized over what might be happening at that very moment to Peace—and Tripnee!

At one point along the Marin shoreline—in what local sailors called Hurricane Gulch—fierce winds blasted down off the headlands and howled through his rigging, but, with no sails up, Dream Voyager held steady. Soon, he emerged from the fog into the sheltered waters of Richardson Bay. To port, restaurants dotted the Sausalito shoreline, while a mile to starboard, some of the most expensive homes in the world gripped the steep slopes of the Belvedere peninsula.

Adam swung to starboard, heading into the realm of the uber-wealthy. Right on the water near the southern end of Belvedere, the end enjoying the best views, and no doubt considered the most exclusive and desirable—and easily the most pricey—his destination beckoned: the home of Magdalena Alvarado, whose email had warned of Peace's peril.

The structure rose from its own private beach to climb multiple floors up the cliff face. Adam, two hundred yards out, headed into the wind and dropped anchor. Locking the windlass, he backed away downwind to set the hook.

He unlashed his standup paddle board from its mounts amidship on the cabin roof and carried it aft, where steps molded into the sugar-scoop stern took him down to water level. He pulled a long paddle from a lazerette—why on sailboats were these called lazerettes and not lockers? To keep his shoes dry, he slung them with laces tied together over one shoulder. With a soft gaze on the middle-distance horizon, he stepped barefoot onto the standup paddle board. His knees slightly bent and his feet shoulder-width apart, he took several strokes on one side to point the board toward his destination. Drawing stability from having his blade in the water, he settled into an easy rhythm of powerful strokes. Soon the board glided onto Magdalena's immaculate private beach, which was protected on one side by a projecting wing of her home, and on the other by a rocky point.

High above, a woman appeared on an upper balcony, flashed a gleaming smile, called out, "Buenos dias," and waved him toward the beach-level entrance. Adam made his way up a series of interior staircases, gaining the top, the main floor.

Soft melodies of Snatum Kaur floated in the air. Monumental-sized art covered the interior walls. Floor-to-ceiling glass walls and doors looked out on a stunning panorama. To the north was the Bay Area's feminine mountain, the sleeping maiden of Mount Tamalpais. Directly opposite, Sausalito sloped down to Richardson Bay; while out across the central Bay to the south, the San Francisco skyline, flanked by the towers of the Golden Gate and Bay bridges, poked up through billowing fog. In the foreground, on a terrace on the other side of inch-thick glass, stood a leggy, dark-haired woman with a regal air.

As Adam pushed open a glass door and stepped onto the terrace, the woman's face lit up as she slowly looked him up and down. "Dios mio," she said, "Peace did not tell me you were so guapo, so handsome."

Smiling, Adam returned the admiring look, and parried, "No doubt that's because it's you who is beautiful, Magdalena."

"Magda. Call me Magda, por favor," she said as she waved him into a chair at a finely-crafted wood-and-metal table overlooking the Bay. Earlier he had outlined the situation on the phone to her, so he got straight to the point. "Who kidnapped Peace?"

"Peace is a sweetie," she said. "An inspiration, a spirit warrior, but also a Don Quixote, too fearless for his own good."

Doing his best to ignore a fascinating mole on what he could see of the woman's voluptuous right breast, Adam said, "You've got the Don Quixote part right."

"This time, he's challenged un hombre malo."

Leaning forward, admonishing himself for being so intrigued by the mole, which danced as Magda spoke, Adam asked, "Who?"

"The wrong, wrong guy. Dangerous, powerful, terrible. Always gets his own way." And with a snarl that transformed her lovely features, she growled: "Harry Bellacozy."

Looking at her in open-mouthed surprise, Adam said, "Yeah? What did Peace do?"

"What didn't he do!" she shrugged, showing off toned arms and that lively mole. "Bellacozy made billions fracking in the midwest, and wanted to do the same in California. But California, como se dice, how you say, is a different breed of cat. The clever devil Bellacozy paid off bureaucrats in Sacramento to sneak through regulations to open his properties to fracking. The whole thing had to be done on the down-low, no publicity. Then Peace—a school librarian!—blew the whistle on his blog, to his network, to the world. The Internet, the press, the environmental groups went loco. Bellacozy's bought-and-paid-for officials backed off and dropped their support!"

Adam couldn't help but chuckle, "I'll bet Bellacozy was pissed."

"So much, the whole face was squinched and the eyes shot daggers. But there's more. Harry wanted to build a resort on Brooks Island in the Bay, and Peace got the island made into a park. Also, one of Harry's houses is right here on Belvedere, and Harry, secretly at night, he started filling the Bay to extend his property. How anyone today could think such a thing could happen! Unbelievable! It was skinny little Peace who stood up in front of the Bay Commission and got that shut down. Oh, then Bellacozy had to pay a two million-dollar fine—plus, he had to dredge up and haul all the fill away. And there is much more. Mucho mas!"

"Sounds like Peace all right," said Adam. "Probably driving Bellacozy nuts. But kidnapping the guy? You really think Bellacozy is behind this?"

"When you live on Belvedere," Magdalena spread her hands, "the world can seem like very a small place. So many of the real movers and shakers—people with big power—here they have homes. And funny thing is, we're all jammed together. Like a gossipy small town. We catch one another's secrets on the wind."

Magdalena paused and leaned back against the glass terrace railing. Was this woman aware her tilted hips, long legs and dancing mole were on fine display? She continued, her rich voice trembling, and her face looking squinched: "Your uncle and I, we uncovered a pattern of outlaw motion. It permeates the Bay Area. The police, the courts, the politicians, all are involved—and pulling the big strings is Harry Bellacozy." Her lips curled into another snarl as she again spat out the name.

CHAPTER 7

CHAPTER 7

THE NEIGHBOR

A chime sounded within the house. Frowning, Magdalena pulled out her cell phone. Turning the screen toward Adam, she said, "It is my neighbor, Black Elk." The screen showed a security camera view of a guy in his fifties with an Einstein-like shock of gray hair.

Magda shrugged her shapely shoulders, "This guy is a pompous donkey, but he knows Peace, and you should meet him." Then she added with a slow wink, "But let us keep his visit short."

Adam's eyes followed her swaying hips as she sashayed into her entrance hall, a space big enough to hold Dream Voyager. He watched from the terrace through the glass walls as she opened the monumental front door and rose on tiptoe to kiss their visitor on the cheek. The guy stood about 6 foot 2, had a lean build, and, as they came out to meet him, Adam noticed the man's awkward gait. Then he saw it. Considering the length of his torso, the man's legs were too short. For no reason, at that moment Adam's star-shaped scar, which dated back to the massacre of his parents when he was five, flared as though jabbed by a red-hot poker.

As she and the newcomer joined him at the terrace table, Magdalena made introductions. Adam pulled himself together as Black Elk said, "Very nice to meet you, Adam. People call me Blackie."

Cutting to the chase, Adam summarized the kidnapping.

"Terrible!" boomed Elk. "Peace Weldon's your uncle, is he? A bit of a nut, but he means well. Always fighting to create a better world! He's stubborn, a real pain in the neck, and he's made enemies."

"Yeah? Who?" prompted Adam.

But Black Elk wouldn't be hurried, as he pointed out over the water, "See that catamaran?" Sure enough, a huge catamaran sailboat—probably 120 feet long—floated at anchor, midway between Sausalito and Belvedere.

"And look at that bad boy," said Elk, pointing toward the deep water between Angel Island and Sausalito, where a two-hundred-foot mega-yacht had materialized out of the fog and was just dropping anchor. Its size and sleek lines screamed limitless money, as did two helicopters on fore-and-aft helipads, and a small fleet of support shuttle craft, which already darted in and out of mooring bays inside its hull.

"Those boats have something to do with my uncle?"

"Not long ago," Black Elk continued, "Peace was having trouble with Bellacozy. Those are Bellacozy's boats, and the guy is ruthless."

Elk grew quiet, watching Adam from under lowered lids, and asked, "Have you contacted the police or FBI?"

Adam shook his head, "No."

"Probably wise," said Blackie. "My Wealth Watch staff has gotten wind of other kidnappings, and the word is the police and FBI have messed things up and caused some unfortunate outcomes!" He got to his feet, running a hand through his wild tangle of hair, "Well, I've gotta go. But I came by to invite you, Magdalena—and you too, Adam—to a little gathering at my place. The governor, some movers, shakers, and big thinkers, some police chiefs, mayors, and judges, Bill Maher, Beyonce, Clint Eastwood, they're all coming."

The wild-haired man rattled on about his upcoming party, repeating his invitation, then, checking his watch, said, "Right now I have to get going to give a TED Talk, but let's stay in touch. When you have time, you should watch my talk on YouTube."

"What subject?" asked Magdalena.

"How to live life to the fullest, and really, really enjoy yourself!" said Blackie, "Sorry. Not a subject on your minds right now, but good stuff!"

Magda walked Black Elk to the entrance hall, where they talked in low tones for a while, then Elk moved toward the door and Magda, with a small wave to Adam, headed off toward the kitchen, a corner of which was visible through an interior archway.

Oddly, as soon as Magda was out of sight, Elk retraced his halting steps back to the terrace. Rolling his eyes in the direction Magda had gone, he said, "Careful who you trust, young man." Next, handing Adam a business card, he added, "Call me. I can help." Then he made his way back out the front door.

As Adam watched Elk limp away, he was left with the feeling that there was something familiar—as well as repellent—about the guy. Maybe he'd seen him on TV or something? He rubbed his throbbing scar.

Magda reappeared, "You must eat, Adam. I have delicious turkey stew simmering."

He followed her into a kitchen big enough to moor two Dream Voyagers. As she filled hefty bowls with the stew, Magda said, "Blackie's foundation feeds people without homes, and organizes marches for gun control. His TED Talks are muy,"—she thrust a finger skyward. "Frankly, though, there is something malo about that man. For one, he is obsessed with his Wealth Watch website, which, dios mio, does nothing but research the super-rich."

Magda sat with her back to the water, while Adam gazed out at the spectacular Bay view. The heart-stopping beauty of the setting—and the woman—plus the soulful Snatum Kaur music pulled Adam into the present, and he realized he was starving. He began devouring the stew; it was indeed out-of-this-world delicious.

"You like it, no?"

Magda had been watching him, a smile curving her full lips. "Another thing very odd," she began, "Maybe I should not talk, but Blackie is as bad as Bellacozy with his loco displays of wealth. Both spend money like the water, you say? Catering trucks for their parties clog the roads here todo los dias! Their yachts—that one over there is Blackie's—they spoil the view," she waved languidly toward a just-plain-magnificent 100-foot motor yacht moored a quarter mile to the north.

Studying the boat, Adam pointed with a grin, "You have to admit, that boat having just one helicopter shows modesty, and, considering the neighborhood, maybe downright humility."

"I guess I am pot calling kettle black," she shrugged and gave a small laugh. "Blackie and Bellacozy, they are complex. For one thing, they've got huevos. Balls. Big ones. Huevos grandes!"

Adam asked, "What about you? Something tells me your story is amazing."

With a wave that took in her lovely face, stunning figure, and the undulating mole, Magda said, "Looking this way makes life difficult. Men do not believe I have brains, and women, they have jealousy."

Refilling their wine glasses, she continued, "Mi padre was a bracero, a simple farm laborer. Mi madre, my brothers and sisters, we all worked in the fields. In the evenings I read and read—and drew. How I loved to draw, still do. Later I worked as waitress. Paid my own way through community college, then Berkeley—drove mi padre crazy—but I majored in art!"

"So you're now a rich and famous artist?"

"I wish! No, in my twenties I saved to go to Europe—to see Spain, visit great museums. The money finished in Paris. I got the job selling mutual funds to U.S. servicemen stationed in Europe. My boss—and I—helped the boys invest their money, instead of squandering. But my boss—who became my first husband—did not just charge management fee for the fund, he also charged a hefty fee, called a load, just to buy shares."

"So how did you get here?"

"After that marriage ended, I created one of the first no-load mutual funds. The world—todo el mundo—loved it—and the fund it took off into the billions."

"Good for you!" exclaimed Adam. They paused to sip their wine and look out over the water as darkness descended. He asked, "Can you set up a meeting with Harry Bellacozy?"

Magda leaned forward, grasped Adam's hands, causing the mole to bob and weave, "This hombre malo makes people disappear."

"I'll be careful."

"Are you listening?" Her hands tightened on his, "You are one helluva macho man. I see this, but you are no match for Bellacozy—and his goons."

"I've got to do this, Magda. Besides, with you setting up the meeting, Harry will be on good behavior. There'd be too much heat if I disappear right when people know I'm meeting with him."

An alarm—the sound of klaxon horns—sounded from Adam's cargo pants pocket. He checked his phone, and then dashed out to the terrace railing, where he heard the faint sound of his intruder alarm wafting up from Dream Voyager.

CHAPTER 8

BAY IMMERSION

"Someone's on my boat!" Adam gave Magdalena a quick parting hug and took off down the stairs.

Moments later, when he glided on the paddleboard up to the stern of Dream Voyager, the security alarm was still ringing, but he found all hatches and portholes closed and locked. He turned off the alarm, switched on lights, and began a complete topside search. No sign of anything amiss on deck or on the hull above the water line. To check the rigging, he used the bosun's chair to ascend the hundred-foot mast. Sure enough, up near the top, on its starboard side, he found a device the size and thickness of a deck of cards. Same aluminum exterior as the mast, so small it would have been easy to miss. Secured with some kind of superglue, he supposed. He removed it with care, half-prying, half-sawing with the serrated back edge of his Navy SEAL combat knife. Then he slowly lowered himself to the deck while double-checking for more devices.

Now that was stealth! How the hell had someone stuck that device high up on his mast with him on Magda's terrace not two hundred yards away?

Next, he stripped and put on a thick wetsuit, scuba gear, and weight belt; grabbed a powerful underwater headlamp; and eased off the poop deck into the chill, ink-black Bay. Beginning at the stern, working clockwise, Adam painstakingly examined the rudder, keel and hull below the water line, running his hands over every square inch. Finally, after more than an hour in the water, he felt rather than saw a raised area low on the starboard side of his hull that should not have been there.

Son of a gun! Clever! A device the same dimensions as an iPad. Same white color as the hull. Secured with some kind of underwater glue. He carefully removed it, surfaced, climbed back aboard, and took both devices to his compact yet complete workshop in the engine room.

Careful not to damage or set them off, he examined his two discoveries. The one from the masthead seemed to be some kind of tracking or monitoring device. The other from the hull had to be an explosive. He put both in the sturdiest steel box he had, wrapped the box in special blankets that blocked phone, GPS and WiFi signals, then placed the bundle in the dinghy, which he anchored a hundred yards from Dream Voyager.

After swimming back and climbing aboard his boat, he heaved a deep sigh. What the hell! Who was doing this? Must be the kidnappers, but how did they even know where he was? Adam climbed out of his wet suit, yawned and stretched. It was well past midnight. Exhausted, he reset the alarms, crawled into bed, and fell into a sleep alive with nightmares. In one, he'd been run through and impaled on long swords again and again—all underwater.

Chapter 9
The Road to Prophecy

At first light the surface of Richardson Bay glistened smooth and calm. Riding an incoming tide, wavering ribbons of glassy water meandered across a vast black carpet of tiny waves. Swells from the first San Francisco-bound ferry of the morning gently rocked Dream Voyager. The fog of the day before had disappeared. In the distance, lights of cities encircling the Bay glowed, and cars streamed over the Golden Gate and Bay Bridges. Another day going for the gold.

With a mug of fresh-brewed coffee in hand, Adam warmed the Yanmar diesel, eased into a gentle forward, hoisted anchor, and motored over to the dinghy with its steel box still intact, still wrapped in the signal-blocking blanket. Fitting his coffee mug into a cupholder, he brought up the small boat's anchor, took the dinghy in tow, set a course south out into the central Bay, then activated the autopilot.

Minutes later, leaving the shelter of the Marin headlands, he felt a breeze wafting in through the Gate. After scanning the shipping lanes to make sure he would not be run over by any more big ships traversing the bay at 20 knots, Adam pointed the bow into the wind, unzipped the sail cover, and punched the winch button to send the mainsail racing up the hundred-foot mast. Marveling at the full sensual curving shape of the sail—what could be more beautiful?—he killed the engine, adjusted the main-sheet line, and soon, on a broad reach, leaving

Alcatraz well to port, Dream Voyager galloped across the waves headed for the northern shore of San Francisco. As he neared the shoreline, he felt a deep humming energy reverberate out over the water, like a great hive awakening.

The text from Prophecy, Bellacozy's organization, had been terse. It simply said, "Golden Gate Yacht Club 8 A.M."

Adam was just securing Dream Voyager's mooring lines to the yacht club's guest dock, when a male voice behind him said, "Adam Weldon?"

Turning, Adam saw two men, one white, one black, both trim and athletic, in pilots' uniforms. Their open jackets revealed that both wore double shoulder holsters holding Glock pistols. Four guns in all, and maybe others that he could not see. Perhaps simply out of careful habit, or perhaps as a tool of intimidation to silently say don't mess with us, they not only made it obvious they were armed to the teeth, they also stood well apart, covering him from different angles, making it difficult to take them out together.

"I'm Ben, and this is Jerry. You're coming with us," said the white guy.

It was a judgment call. But something didn't feel right. In such cases, Adam instinctively acted sooner rather than later. He had learned through the years that there was nothing quite like the good old element of surprise.

The man on his right, the white guy, Ben, favored his left hand, indicating he was left-handed. Adam smiled broadly, held his hands up and wide in a gesture of openness, and stepped toward Ben, saying, "Gentlemen, generally I appreciate invitations...," finishing his sentence, "but your delivery needs work," simultaneously seizing Ben's left wrist and twisting it while stepping around behind him. Ben was now between him and Jerry. In the same blurred movement, Adam grabbed Ben's right arm and twisted it around behind his back, bringing it alongside Ben's left arm. Pinning both wrists together with his left hand, Adam reached around with his right hand and grabbed one of Ben's Glocks. Flicking off the safety, he pointed the muzzle at the center of Jerry's chest. Caught off-guard, Jerry had managed only to unholster a Glock and was about to raise it toward Adam. Seeing the situation, Jerry lowered his weapon.

"Ahh, I think we got off on the wrong foot," stammered Jerry. "Look, we work for Harry Bellacozy. And we're here to fly you to his Woodside estate."

Realizing these were probably Bellacozy's errand boys, not his dangerous black ops goons, Adam said, "I appreciate the change in tone, guys." But, prompted by innate caution, he added, "But for formality's sake, Jerry, humor me and slowly, holding only the barrel, set your guns—first one and then the other—on the ground and kick them toward me."

After Jerry complied, Adam removed Ben's other gun, released him, and indicated he should go over and stand by Jerry. Once he had all four weapons, one in each cargo pants pocket, one at the small of his back, and the fourth tucked in his belt in front, Adam said, "OK, let's start over. It's nice to meet you guys—I think. Where's your helicopter?"

Ben said, "Mr. Bellacozy owns the building behind you. The chopper is on the roof."

CHAPTER 10
OVER THE SOUTH BAY

I f you want to know the scuttlebutt about what's going on in an organization, talk to the errand boys. Although outwardly professional and tough, Ben and Jerry were essentially big kids playing with a magnificent toy, Bellacozy's seven-million-dollar Sikorsky White Hawk, the same chopper model used by the president of the United States. Getting these guys to really open up—and reveal the inside information Adam needed—was going to take rapport and strategy—and luck.

They soared over the South Bay down the Peninsula toward the epicenter of Silicon Valley. Bridges looked like necklaces stretched across sparkling water. The towers of San Francisco seemed to vibrate in the clear air. Ben and Jerry sat up front. Adam relaxed in the chopper's plush captain-of-the-universe interior—and, using his smart phone and the chopper's wifi, did some quick research.

Most big corporations, inevitably, had disgruntled employees and customers who aired their grievances—both real and imagined—on websites dedicated to negative gossip about the company. Adam found and carefully read similar juicy stuff on PatheticProphecy.com.

Adam moved into the cockpit and took a seat close to the two pilots.

Jerry glanced at him and said, "I'd like to apologize. We kind of introduced ourselves like tough guys back there."

Adam replied, "No problem. I think I overreacted," and handed back their guns.

Jerry looked at him with obvious gratitude and said, "Can I ask a favor?"

"Sure."

"Mr. Bellacozy expects perfection and he's, well, let's say, unforgiving," said Jerry. "The fact is you caught us sleepwalking, which could get us fired. Would you be OK keeping me and Ben's bad just between us?"

Adam said, "Mum's the word, my friends," and saw Ben and Jerry look at each other with relief. "Can I ask a favor in return?"

"Name it."

"Strictly between us. How are things in the Prophecy universe? What's the inside scoop? And believe me, no one will ever know I heard it from you."

Jerry said, "Well, for a lot of people, working for Harry Bellacozy is no picnic."

"That's putting it mildly!" said Ben.

"How so?" asked Adam.

"Bellacozy may be a genius and the richest man in the world," said Ben, "but working for the man is hell! The guy's an insatiable taskmaster. In Prophecy, he's created a corporate culture where the best and brightest drive themselves to the fucking limit, often until they drop. Everyone's performance is measured continuously. Got to turn up the dial. Got to constantly push to beat the competition, stay ahead of the executioner's blade. Winners accrue fortunes in soaring stock. Losers get culled out—Harry calls it purposeful Darwinism."

"All true," said Jerry. "But you've got to give the man his due. Bellacozy has inspired his teams of coders and hackers to create computing miracles, amazing devices so small and flat, they're right out of the realm of pure fantasy!"

"Yeah," said Ben, "but these guys burn out fast. They got no life outside work. And at work, the criticism, the feedback is brutal. Jerry, think of all the guys we've flown to the estate, grown men covered in sweat going in, crying all the way back."

"Sad—but true," said Jerry, heaving a big breath, "Boy, am I glad me and Ben are mostly outside the brutal Prophecy culture."

"I'm going to level with you," said Ben, "The pain here is getting to me. I've had enough!"

Amazed at Ben's candor, and sensing an opportunity to get inside information, Adam said, "Bellacozy's empire encompasses a lot more than Prophecy. Are there any pain-free divisions?"

"Not really," replied Ben. "There's the energy and fracking division. The electric car company. The island. The yacht club—where we picked you up. The America's Cup team. The real estate team. The resort division. The black ops team. The Human Soft division acquired in a hostile takeover. All are deep in the pain forest."

Concealing his excitement, Adam asked, "The black ops team?"

"Yeah, it's all hush-hush," said Ben, "but we share the same helipads and air hangers. Those guys are always wound tight enough to explode, no doubt because Bellacozy pushes them so fucking hard."

"Just out of curiosity, you guys have any idea what they do?"

Jerry exchanged glances with Ben, and said, "No idea."

Shrugging off Jerry's look, Ben said, "Hell, why not spill a few beans? Corporate espionage. Personal security for Bellacozy. Internal security. Caught a Microsoft mole redhanded last month. Plus a bunch of illegal shit. Payoffs and paybacks. Intimidation. Extortion, too, I'd guess. Holding people against their will, probably. God knows what else. It's what super-rich guys do."

To test their reactions, Adam told them about Peace's kidnapping.

"Peace was kidnapped!" Ben said, "No wonder you were on edge and thought we were bad guys!"

"So you're Peace's nephew?" said Jerry. "I love that guy! Many's the time we've flown him back and forth to the estate—and on trips in the 737 with Mr. Bellacozy."

"What!" exclaimed Adam. "My uncle and Bellacozy are friends?"

"I'd say super-good friends," said Ben, "When Peace is around, Bellacozy is a different man, mellow, considerate. Anyone who can do that has some powerful juju!"

Adam was floored. This was a new side to his head-in-the-clouds uncle!

Could these guys be black ops kidnappers? Probably not. Adam's long experience as a military cop and clandestine operative himself told him they just didn't have the requisite wariness or hardness. But Harry Bellacozy and the rest of his people were another matter.

CHAPTER 11

SILICON VALLEY

The San Francisco peninsula, shaped like a thumb extending south to north, forms the Bay's southwestern shore. The city of San Francisco—referred to by locals as "the City"—at the northern end, is the thumbnail. Bustling suburban cities bordering the South Bay sprawl down the eastern side, while along the west, pristine parks and farms slope down to the Pacific Ocean. In the center, wealthy estates intermingle with redwood forests and a string of reservoirs. Silicon Valley's thrumming force-field envelops the entire Bay Area—while its wild, pounding heart occupies the base of this thumb, spread throughout Palo Alto, Menlo Park, and parts of San Jose.

As they whizzed over the Spanish tile roofs of the Stanford campus, the chopper began its descent. Nestled in the hills west of Stanford lies the town of Woodside, Silicon Valley's inner sanctum sanctorum. Here, the nobility of the tech world reside in homes befitting monarchs. Mansions resplendent with swimming pools, stables, riding tracks, tennis courts, pastures, staff quarters, guest cottages and twenty-car garages. The Sikorsky touched down on a helipad within an estate more opulent than its neighbors by an order of magnitude.

After buttoning their coats, combing their hair, and assuming even more erect postures than before, Ben and Jerry escorted Adam along bougainvillea-covered walkways, past a stable where aristocratic-looking horses watched them over half-doors. The trio skirted a dazzling flower garden, and passed through a security check, where Adam was scanned and patted down by a six-foot, no-nonsense Amazon with steely-blue eyes.

At length, the pilots delivered him into a spacious library. Scanning the floor-to-ceiling rosewood bookshelves lining the room, Adam mused, "Hey, there's hope for the printed book yet."

"You're to wait here for Mr. Bellacozy." said Jerry, with a conspiratorial wink.

Adam liked the two men. Their openness had surprised him—and he wanted to reassure them he'd keep their confidence. As they shook hands, he held the gaze of each man and nodded. Nodding back, they seemed to breathe easier. As they made for the door, Adam could not resist saying, "I suggest you gentlemen go and enjoy some ice cream." The men rolled their eyes, smiled, and left.

Ignoring the probability that he was under camera surveillance, Adam explored the room. The books spanned a seemingly endless array of subjects and authors, both fiction and non-fiction. Thumbing through a few books, he noticed that a copy of Dostoyevsky's *Crime and Punishment* appeared to have been well read, as did Michael Gelb's *How to Think Like Leonardo da Vinci*. Likewise, the pages of Nassim Taleb's *Antifragile* and Steven Pressfield's *Do the Work!* were dog-eared and filled with marginal notes.

Comfortable-looking reading chairs and big sofas formed conversation groupings here and there. Warm, soft light filtered in through tall windows that overlooked a vibrant rose garden. Adam was struck by how much the room reminded him of his uncle's house. No wonder he liked it!

"What's this about Peace being kidnapped?" said a voice behind him.

Turning around, Adam saw a man about 6 feet tall, with a small mustache and goatee, who looked to be a trim, healthy and somewhat weather-beaten sixtyish or so.

"Adam, I'm Harry." As they shook hands, Adam felt the man's extraordinarily strong grip. Surprising for an old billionaire.

Harry continued, "What have you learned so far about Peace's kidnapping?"

The guy came off as smooth, commanding and impatient. Adam outlined the situation, leaving out the part about Harry himself being the likely kidnapper.

Finding out if Harry and his black ops crew were indeed the bad guys in this story was not going to be easy. Sometimes just getting to know someone, drawing them into a rambling conversation, could reveal tells, clues, glimpses into the true state of a man's soul. But Harry didn't seem the chatty sort.

So Adam asked, "You and my uncle are friends?"

"Where have you been?" asked Harry. "Peace inspired the first idea that made me rich."

Hoping to draw the man out, Adam said, "Really?" It soon became obvious that no drawing out was needed, however, as Adam discovered that Bellacozy loved talking about himself.

"We were having one of our wine, poetry and wild-ideas-to-save-the-world symposiums," continued Bellacozy. "Did you know the word *symposium* means 'to drink together?' By the way, have a whiskey?"

Not waiting for a reply, Bellacozy reached for a nearby decanter and poured amber liquid into two glasses. Handing one to Adam, he went on, "Peace suggested an app that would turn a phone into a supportive companion. A constant friend flowing with unconditional love and encouragement, able to listen and offer good advice. I ran with it. Got it translated into 23 languages. Made me my first fifty million!"

"I had no idea," admitted Adam, feeling a twinge of regret for having been so out of touch with his uncle.

"Hell, see this?" Harry flipped a thumb toward a massive stone table that glowed in the soft light filtering in from the garden. "Peace and I are neuro-hackers, explorers of the mind, of flow, of peak performance. This table broadcasts a magnetic field that enhances brain function, creativity. It's cut from boulders found in only one place on earth: a tributary of the Yuba River."

Adam was startled. He knew the Yuba well, but had never heard about this. "Yeah?"

"Me and Peace were flying the chopper home from Burning Man when he told me about huge stones that were sacred to the Miwok Indians. We were passing close by anyway, so we took a look. We used neuro-hacking gear from our Burning Man pavilion—including a portable EEG machine—and wow! The boulders induce a deep alpha state!"

Nodding, but skeptical, Adam put his drink down, flattened his hands on the table's polished blue-black surface and closed his eyes. He noticed inside himself the ever-present background chatter of his mind and, below that, the ever-fluctuating, iridescent, undulating layers of what he called inner dreaming. But there was nothing different.

Or was it? In the elemental onrushing inner river of his consciousness, did he detect an uptick of energy? Ha! He had to laugh. Simply going with this suggestion made it so, while deciding to go against the suggestion rendered it nada, zilch!

The fact was, though, he did feel a heightened self-awareness. Maybe that's what the stone did: Juice up a person's ability to look at his or her own consciousness. Didn't ancient mystics— and certain modern thinkers too—see humankind as a vanguard whose key role is to embody the universe becoming aware of itself?

"Fascinating!" he said. "But getting back to Peace. When is the last time you saw him?" And, feeling the tone of his voice raise, he added, "Do you have any idea who kidnapped him?"

"Peace may be the most inspired guy I've ever met," said Harry. "Firing on all cylinders! Going a mile a minute, yet calm—mostly. But he sure can be a pain in the ass! He's pissed off no end of powerful people."

"Who, for instance?" pressed Adam.

"Me, for one!" said Harry as he massaged the back of his neck. "Peace can be a complete curmudgeon! He got my energy division mostly shut down! Cost me billions!"

"Fracking?" Adam watched the man's color rise.

"We prefer the term 'new energy technologies.' Which include fracking, among others," managed Harry, who now rubbed his temples. "Another time, I was all set to turn Brooks Island in the Bay into a fabulous resort. Would have boosted the whole East Bay economy. And he got it declared a wildlife sanctuary!" Harry's mouth took on an angry twist. "That island cost me twenty seven million. Now it just sits there, home to a few seagulls."

Harry started pacing around the room. "The list goes on," he said. "Peace, bless his egalitarian heart, got the Prophecy bus drivers to organize and strike for double pay! And the most recent thing really galls me: the guy blew the whistle on my Belvedere project. OK, yes, I was pushing the limits, doing some, shall we say, under-the-radar real estate expansion." Harry spread his hands and grinned disarmingly, "But, let's face it, in most things, it's better to forge ahead, do the deed, and ask forgiveness afterward, because you'll never get permission beforehand."

"Magdalena mentioned that. Your trucks were actually dumping fill into the Bay at night?"

"Magdalena! My NIMBY Belvedere neighbor! Sometimes I

think she hates me!" exclaimed Harry, his nostrils flaring. "What's five acres less Bay? Who'd miss it? No impact! But a new high-end deep-water marina, hotel, gardens, tennis courts, spa, the sheer beauty that might have been! "

"But Harry, nobody can fill in the Bay anymore," blurted Adam.

"Good, clean fill. No pollution. Let's face it, for people like me, and you too, Adam," said Harry, pointing a bony finger first at himself and then at Adam, "the normal rules don't apply. Especially here in the Bay Area, if you can imagine it, usually there's a way to make it happen!" He finished his drink and slapped the glass down on an antique Sheraton table.

Adam said, "Some limits need to be pushed, but filling in the Bay is not one of them!"

Harry's pacing picked up speed. He spread his arms in a grand all-inclusive gesture, indicating Adam, the room full of books, the estate, the Bay Area, the world. "The imagination! Adam! Your goofy, ingenious, jerk of an uncle is my pal. But he can be such a fool!"

"How so?"

"Back at Tasajara, when I was barely out of college, Peace woke me up to the unlimited possibilities of human consciousness, of the human spirit! Your uncle taught me that if you can imagine it, you can create it! It's so true!"

"That's Peace, all right," said Adam.

"But Peace is always shaking things up, fighting impossible battles. Even back at Tasajara he was quite the rebel monk. When your folks were murdered and Peace left the monastery to raise you—the head monks were ready to invite him to leave anyway!"

"I didn't know that!"

"If your uncle ever learned to be more strategic, pick his

battles more carefully—and advance his own self-interest a bit more—he'd dwarf me."

Adam said, "Some seemingly impossible battles are worth fighting. Especially when it comes to taking care of the planet. But we've got an immediate problem: Peace is in trouble!"

Nodding, one hand rubbing his neck and the other his temples, Harry stared through the glass floor-to-ceiling French doors, apparently lost in thought.

Studying the man to see his reaction, Adam asked, "So, did you kidnap Peace?"

Harry turned back to Adam, "Believe me, he's given me plenty of reasons. Sometimes I want to strangle the old coot. But in some ways, he's like my conscience sitting on my shoulder, steering me in the right direction."

Adam quietly took this in.

"Fact is," Bellacozy grinned, "I love the guy." Then running his hands over the stone table, he continued, "I owe a lot to Peace. His ideas, his vision inspired what I've done. Without his friendship, I wouldn't have done diddly."

Harry looked away for a moment, then, seeming to blink away tears, said, "We've got to rescue the crazy old beatnik."

Adam wondered if the man was a consummate actor, but his gut said Harry was not the kidnapper.

A knock sounded at an inner door. Harry touched a button on his watch, and a small, round man with busy hands and a military bearing entered the room.

Harry said, "Adam, this is General Eisenhower. General is my head of cyber-security and cyber-research."

CHAPTER 12

GENERAL EISENHOWER

After exchanging greetings, Adam said, "Any relation to the president?"

"Distant cousin," said Eisenhower. "And, General is my name, not my rank. Never been in the military. I used to think my parents really messed up, naming me as they did. But it turns out my name has advantages."

"It's memorable," said Adam.

"It also implies competence and leadership. Probably more than I possess," said General, smiling. "But, hey, it got me this job."

"Ike's modesty belies his talents," said Harry, winking at his advisor. "Ike's the best. So many people feel they have to blow their own horn. Able people, though, tend to be low-key, humble." Then, turning to Ike, Harry said, "What have you got for us?"

Ike replied, "We have new information you haven't seen. You and I need to confer in private." Then turning to Adam, "No offense, Adam. Just standard procedure when it comes to sensitive material generated by our proprietary algorithms."

"No need," said Bellacozy. "Adam is the key to rescuing Peace. I want him to hear everything."

Adam asked, "You have access to the FBI's sources?"

"Better than that," said Eisenhower. "We, meaning Prophecy, built key components of not only the Internet but also the global communications infrastructure, and we have, shall we say, unique access to exclusive data, including all calls, texts, email, short-wave, broadcast, faxes, everything."

Adam said, "Why am I not surprised?"

"We've identified the kidnappers," continued Eisenhower. "It's Gaia and her cult."

"What?!" blurted Harry.

"Not what you want to hear, I know," Ike said to Harry.

"Damn straight!" said Harry, "Gaia's…"

"…a special friend," said Ike.

"She's smart as hell," blurted Harry, "drop-dead gorgeous, and thinks she can take on the whole world—and she's right! What's not to like?"

Ike squared his shoulders, drew his short body up to its full height, and said, "You pay me for my expertise, Mr. Bellacozy, and my considered expert judgment, based on overwhelming evidence, is that Gaia and her group are the kidnappers."

Shaking his head and releasing a huge sigh, Bellacozy said, "Well, give us the full, unvarnished scoop."

"Most of Gaia's followers," replied Ike, "are probably just naïve and gullible, but she has an inner circle of criminal fanatics. From what we gather, they blindly follow her orders, like she's a goddess or something. She herself materialized out of nowhere to somehow become a so-called life coach to a number of Silicon Valley CEOs, very big CEOs…"

"Including me!" interrupted Harry. "But come on. I know her group has a rough element, and she has a mysterious past. So-fucking-what?"

"Our scans of Big Data connect Gaia, Total Embrace, and Peace's kidnapping," said Eisenhower. "And you wouldn't be where you are, Harry, if our algorithms weren't accurate."

Harry's shoulders slumped.

"There's motive," continued Ike, "Peace poses an existential threat to Total Embrace. He got their commune kicked off Albany Bulb, and, in a remarkable display of charisma or whatever, he persuaded thousands of people to quit the cult."

Harry resumed pacing, rubbing the back of his neck. Was this exchange between one of the world's richest men and his right-hand man being staged for Adam's benefit? Maybe. But why? Couldn't be; surely it was way too real.

Ike looked at Harry with an expression of compassion, and said, "Got to face bad news head-on. The woman's an enigma. Beautiful and mesmerizing. But so is a black widow."

"Ike, sometimes you really piss me off," said the multi-billionaire.

Adam was impressed. Even in the midst of the man's anger and disappointment, Harry not only tolerated but seemed to value Ike's unwelcome information. Most people with that much wealth and clout probably demanded more deference, and as a result, lived in a bubble of yes-men, cut off from real human interaction. Was he glimpsing a core strength of the man, and a key reason for his achievements?

Adam said, "I need names, addresses, details."

"That's not the type of data we have," said Eisenhower. "This is confidential information based on our proprietary access to Big Data, big chunks of global networks."

Harry, looking miserable, said, "I hate to say it, but Ike has never been wrong about something like this."

"The thing is, Adam," said Ike, "Gaia and the hard inner core of her followers are organized and ruthless. I've strongly advised Harry to sever all contact with the woman…"

"But I won't," interrupted Harry, "and I'm the boss."

Ike continued, "But I'm responsible for security around here—which includes keeping you alive, Harry—so I may as well tell you now: Yesterday, when we first learned of the kidnapping, on my own authority I sent six of our best black ops people to, shall we say, do whatever it took to rescue Peace—and none returned. Our best team disappeared without a trace!"

"Gaia just wouldn't do that!" said Harry. "I'll never believe Gaia was part of that. There has to be some other explanation."

Ike put a hand on Harry's shoulder to comfort the man who seemed to be very much his friend, as well as his boss. Then Ike said to Adam, "Look, we know your history. You were an incredibly effective Navy SEAL and military investigator. And you took down an entire cartel on the Kern. OK, you're good at this stuff. But Total Embrace is far, far more dangerous than anything we've dealt with before!"

CHAPTER 13

THE SLOT

Back aboard Dream Voyager, Adam pulled on a fleece-lined waterproof jacket, warmed the engine, cast off the lines, and motored from the shelter of the Golden Gate Yacht Club marina out into the howling wind of the Slot. Hoisting sail, he set a course straight downwind for the East Bay. As twilight deepened into night and a full moon rose above the East Bay hills, he flew along wing-on-wing, with main sail to starboard and jib to port. The wind, now at fifteen knots, pressed in through the Golden Gate and thrust Voyager's sleek hull forward through the blackening water.

Off to starboard, Leo Villareal's light sculpture pranced and shimmied upon the Bay Bridge. At the bridge's east end, Adam made out the lights of the plucky town of Emeryville—once an industrial waste site, now a shopping, tech and condo mecca. North of that was the odd-ball capital of the world, the People's Republic of Berkeley, the university town with its own foreign policy.

Just north of Berkeley lay his destination: Albany Bulb, a wild 13-acre lollipop-shaped peninsula jutting into the Bay. Created when filling in chunks of the Bay was still permissible, the Bulb is a warren of hillocks, dense vegetation, meandering trails, and hidden nooks and crannies that had been home to a plywood-hut community of followers of Total Embrace—before Peace got them kicked out. What was it like now?

Because much of the Bay—including the stretch along this shoreline—was less than ten feet deep at low tide, Adam kept an eye on his depth meter. He dropped anchor due east of, and well out from, the Bulb. As well as avoiding going aground, this action had the advantage of concealment. Even with the moon full, and despite Dream Voyager's size, to those on land his boat would be lost in the vast expanse of darkness. Adam toed a deck button to lower the dinghy from the stern davits. Going for stealth, he left the outboard tipped up, got out oars, fitted them to the oarlocks, and began pulling for shore, assisted by the still-powerful incoming tide.

Evidently, online chat rooms had been buzzing about the big Total Embrace event happening here this night. Excellent! A perfect opportunity to infiltrate and learn. Peace was out there somewhere. Did this bizarre cult have him? Adam was god damned well going to find out.

CHAPTER 14
ALBANY BULB

From out on the water, the Bulb appeared as a dark mass, a black hole in the broad Milky-Way array of the East Bay's night lights. Propelled by silent, rhythmic oar strokes and a surging king tide, Adam's skiff glided closer and closer. The sound of drums and tribal hubbub grew ever louder. He saw the flickering glow of campfires and the silhouettes of people bobbing and dancing with arms upraised. Waves slapped the shore. Perhaps it was the moon—or the tribal energy—but his heartbeat quickened and he stirred with anticipation. The tribe had gathered. Some kind of bizarre shamanic magic was no doubt on the agenda.

Rather than row straight into the middle of things, Adam rode the tidal current around to the north side of the peninsula to a quiet beach with no one around. Here he pulled his skiff up above the tideline. Then he picked his way along twisting pathways by the light of the moon. Cresting a low hill, he came upon what must have been thousands of people spread out over undulating terrain. They were divided into small groups gathered around a wild profusion of campfires.

A gigantic moon glowed overhead painting the Bay silver as it stretched out around them. Wild drumming pulsed in long oscillations, building, crescendoing, and subsiding. Each campfire seemed to be its own center of ardent talk. The scene vibrated with caveman energy.

A helicopter—a Sikorsky by the sound of it—passed low overhead to land somewhere close by. In the dark, Adam could just make out two sleek black power boats nose in and extend inflatable gangplanks to the rocky beach. A dozen or so burly men clambered ashore. Amazing! Wasn't that Black Elk among them?! Oddly, Adam's old shoulder scar flared up at that moment.

Still rubbing the site of his childhood wound, Adam went down and wandered among the campfires. The atmosphere felt fired up but friendly. He sidled up to a campfire where a spirited debate was underway.

A bearded walrus of a man was saying, "In the desert, there are powerful swirling earth energies that can uplift or cast down your spirit. They can bring on shifts and sadness. Not all of the shifts are good. Some are downright evil."

A young woman, whose long blonde hair glistened in the firelight, said, "Give me a break. Can you hit it with a hammer? No such thing!"

Rolling his eyes, the bearded man said, "OK, OK, truth is multifaceted. But I'm telling you, in cities there are so many forces that the earth vortex energies get lost and are indistinguishable. But here out in the Bay on the Bulb, the earth's vibrations assert themselves."

"Give me a break! " repeated the blond woman, laughing. "Nothing real here. These are not the drones you're looking for. Best to move along."

Adam grinned. This was not what he expected. His first impression was that this was not the groupthink of a cult. These people seemed to be freely expressing themselves, disagreeing at will—and having fun.

"You're both right—and wrong, " said a man in a well-tailored overcoat. "We're earth people. Human consciousness and the human imagination evolved with and into this planet.

Co-mingled. At one with. There is no separation between us and this place. Whatever we imagine takes on its own reality. Envision it deeply, and it manifests as real. Think it, and it is so."

The blond woman, her blue eyes dancing, turned to Adam, "I see you nodding. What do you think?"

Oops, there went his low profile. Everyone looked at him, seeming to be curious and friendly.

Thinking "what the heck," he said, "Well, I see multiple sides to most issues. My first impression is, you guys as a group seem to do the same. I like it."

Adam's listeners laughed.

"I guess that's why they call this whole thing Total Embrace," said the blonde, "And why we call our little group right here the Hodgepodge Family. We disagree with each other—and enjoy—and, yeah, doubt—every minute of it."

The guy in the suit, his polished shoes reflecting the flames, said, "You must be new. Welcome! One of Gaia's favorite stories is the metaphor of the elephant: We're all blind men feeling our part of the elephant. One is holding the trunk, another the leg, an other an ear, the side, the tail. The guy holding the tail says, 'This animal is long and skinny, like a snake.' The man holding the ear says, 'No way! It's broad and flat, like a big sheet of paper.' And so on. Each speaks his honest truth—and they are all right."

"I hate that story," interjected the blonde.

"The bigger truth," continued the sharply dressed man, smiling, "is multifaceted, layered, contradictory. Even directly opposite, mutually canceling points of view can be true, when seen from a more complete perspective."

"That's so unsatisfying!" blurted the blonde. "Deep down, I want certainty!"

"Black and white."

"Us versus them!"

"Now you're talking."

"All true!"

They all laughed.

"Hello and welcome!" purred a resonant, somehow familiar, amplified voice. "Embrace that moon! Drink in that shimmering Bay!" The drumming subsided. "Fill your lungs! Feast your senses, minds, and hearts." Then with special emphasis, pausing after each word: "Take - in - this - place! We - are - here! We - are - Total - Embrace!" The whole place exploded in a crescendo of beating drums, sustained applause, and wild-man yells.

Craning his neck to see over the sea of heads, Adam located the speaker, a woman in a white, flowing, hooded robe, who—like the resplendent Bay behind her—glowed in the moonlight. Arms and legs spread wide in a powerful stance, her face in shadow under the hood, she stood on an actual, literal house of cards—an otherworldly, Alice-in-Wonderland structure of huge playing cards—a queen of hearts and an ace of spades, among others—each card at least 10 feet by 6 feet.

This must be Gaia! At her signal, a group of well-amplified musicians—playing tabla, sitar, cello, harmonium, and guitar—filled the salt air with rich rhythmic harmonies—as she led the group in a series of call-and-repeat chants. As the beat and the group energy throbbed, somehow the moon seemed to brighten, lighting up the whole place. Adam could see that the crowd included people of all races, adorned in every imaginable form of dress. If there was a trend, it was a strong sprinkling of new age costumes—lots of flowing white robes, long hair, and thin vegetarian bodies with straight spines. But all body types were well-represented. There were about two women to every man. Enraptured, swaying in unison, the crowd bellowed Gaia's chants, and seemed to vibrate with delight, completely enthralled.

Holding up her palms for silence, Gaia said, "Radiant Health. Meaning. Compassion. These are our subjects on this full moon night. In keeping with our Total Embrace tradition of welcoming inspirational thinkers and spirit guides—and just plain interesting people—to our midst to share their ideas—I would like to welcome a well-known Bay Area inspiration, a man whose leadership at the Wing Foundation contributes to the vibrant spiritual awakening we feel around us here in the Bay Area! Please give a warm welcome to Black Elk." Oddly, Adam's scar burned like a road flare.

To vigorous applause, Elk moved in his rolling, short-legged gait to the microphone, his atomic mushroom cloud of gray hair luminescent in the moonlight. "Wow! I feel your Total Embrace!" intoned Elk in his rich, mellifluous voice. "Thank you for this privilege and honor."

"I'll be brief. The results of hundreds of studies involving millions of people can be boiled down to six key tips for radiant health: First, be conscientious. Second, be adaptable. Third, sleep seven to eight hours per night. Fourth, figure out your life purpose and work hard fulfilling it. Fifth, cultivate healthy relationships and sexual balance. And sixth, exercise, do yoga, tai chi chih, chi gong. ...." Elk elaborated on each point and then, with a simple namaste, left the stage to loud applause.

Hmm. Evidence-based. Not that preachy. Seemed like solid advice. Maybe it was the heightened excitement of the moment, or maybe simply because the message was less crazy than he expected, but Adam was surprised. Would he need to revise his estimation of Black Elk, Gaia, and Total Embrace?

"Good advice, but don't be fooled," said the blonde. "The guy's a total creep."

Gaia ushered out a second speaker—holy mackerel!—Magdalena!

As a scatter of dutiful applause subsided, Magda extended her hands toward Gaia, then swept them wide to indicate everyone present, and said, "Dios mio! What a pleasure! To be with Gaia—and all of you! Allow me to say something muy importante—of overarching importance—to each of us as individuals and to our planet as a whole."

Drawing out each word for emphasis, she said, "Meaning. Life purpose. Dharma."

"Figure out what you care about. Apply the full force of your soul in that direction. Keep trying new ideas, new solutions. Sure, we fall, we fail, but we keep getting back up, we keep trying. We're anti-fragile. Challenge and struggle actually make us stronger.

"Let go of dualism: let go of the idea that spirit and matter are separate. They are one! Profit and spiritual growth go together. Both individuals and companies are spiritual entities; both, to be sustainable, must balance efficiency and resilience. Sustainability is key. It's up to us—you and me—to save our planet…"

As Magdalena went on in this vein, the crowd seemed to gradually warm to her message, erupting in occasional applause. By the time she concluded, the gathering was won over enough to explode into enthusiastic cheers. As Magda left the house-of-cards stage, her gaze lingered on Black Elk. Was there something between the two?

"Another hypocrite," said the blonde.

Just then Gaia's hood slipped back, revealing her face for the first time—it was Tripnee!

CHAPTER 15

TRIPNEE

The crowd settled down; then Tripnee spoke. Here was someone who really knew how to use a microphone. Instead of projecting or yelling, she held the mic close and spoke in a soulful whisper.

"Compassion. Kindness. Caring. On the one hand, we are amazing beings with infinite potential on a magically beautiful planet, and, on the other hand, at the very same time, our world is filled with sadness, pain, and fear."

Adam instantly recognized one of Tripnee's favorite insights—something she called the Really Big Picture. Even though he'd heard it before, his pulse quickened and he savored her words. This was his Tripnee!

"Any adventure in nature shared with caring companions gives us a glimpse of our planet's magical loveliness and our own vast inner potential. And, on the other hand, any newspaper, any newscast confirms that ours is a world in which people do unthinkably hurtful things to one another. Part of the dilemma is that the pain, suffering, and fear can feel so pervasive, so global, that they can make the earth's magical beauty and our infinite potential seem empty and hollow."

Go, Tripnee! Adam marveled at how completely she threw herself into this Gaia persona. She was acting—but in the process she was drawing on something real, or at least it seemed so to him. Her words made deep sense. He was transfixed, and, apparently, so was everyone else.

"Unfortunately," she continued, "I don't have a solution for this Really Big Picture. But I do have a suggestion: Cultivate compassion. Treat others and yourself with kindness and appreciation. In an atmosphere of support and acceptance, we can relax, stop defending ourselves, open up, blossom and grow. And in so doing we come alive—really alive—to ourselves, to others and to our planet!"

In the moonglow, with the ever-churning Bay waters ebbing and flowing behind her, Tripnee as Gaia extolled the natural wonder that is San Francisco Bay, its magic, its energy. Adam's rational mind settled back, disengaged. He, and apparently everyone around him, seemed to open as in a dream to this druid woman. Her words, and something of her essence, coursed through him like a tidal current, lapping his body and mind, propelling him into some kind of altered state of consciousness.

She concluded, not with a rise in volume, but with an amplification of some deep soul connection, a way she had of implanting her words directly into the minds of her listeners, "What does it take to move your life forward? Ask this of yourself, of your dreams. Know that you are one with everything."

When Tripnee concluded her Gaia performance, the vast crowd sat transfixed, mute in a reverential stillness. Then, as one great beast, they leapt up, cheered and beat their hands together in a surging ovation that boomed far across the Bay. When the applause died down, people started hugging one another, eyes moist, faces grinning. Everyone, even the skeptics around Adam, seemed exultant, and repeatedly exclaimed, "Wow!" "The most amazing experience I've ever had!" "I love it!"

As if waking from a dream, Adam flexed his muscles and

shook his head, wondering: Did that really happen? It didn't fully compute or make sense. Yet, look at the effect it had on all these people! He decided to file it under: Tripnee is amazing!

Regaining his grip on reality, Adam made his way through the pandemonium, moving closer, but not too close, to the house-of-cards dais. Rough-looking cohorts held back the crowd. Distinct contingents of security people formed around Black Elk and Tripnee. The men looked serious, tough, and capable. Elk's group had a certain military discipline—and looked willing and able to carry out Blackie's faintest whim.

The people around Tripnee looked like a blend of bikers and rough new age types. As Adam drew a little closer to Tripnee's security detail, he picked up a malevolent, ruthless vibe. What was that about, he wondered? Some of their gazes lingered in his direction. These guys looked alert and formidable—but also cunning and vicious. One guy in particular—clearly, their leader, given the deferential body language of the others—exuded a polished but lethal aura: his hard gaze ever roaming, missing nothing; his short gorilla body tensed for action—a dangerous man if there ever was one. Lucifer leading an army of wily devils.

There was something very wrong with this picture, a real disconnect between Tripnee and her rough escort. If ever anyone did *not* need protection from a crowd, it was this woman. The jubilant gathering adored her. Perhaps some protection from overzealous worshipers was a good idea. But this tough inner core of Total Embrace gave Adam the impression that their focus was less on protecting Tripnee and more on…what? Intimidating people? Controlling her? Was she their captive?! He sensed Tripnee was in deep muck—perhaps way over her head—and one false move could blow up everything. As much as his heart ached to do so, this was no time to make contact with her.

To deepen his feel for Total Embrace, Adam mingled at various campfires.

"As always, that was totally worth the $500!" said a hollow-cheeked woman bundled up in a worn wool coat.

"$500?" said Adam.

"Yeah. The $500 'Enlightenment Fee' to get in here." Then, seeming to sense that he was a sailor, she asked, "Don't tell me! You snuck in by boat!"

Adam gave a noncommittal smile.

She said, "Hey, I don't blame you. These full-moon gatherings are damned pricey. But worth it. Still, hey, can I sneak in with you next time?"

At another campfire Adam overheard a man saying, "We used to control this whole place. Some of us lived here full-time in great little plywood houses. For some, this was their only home. Most of us, of course, have actual houses. In Orinda, Marin, all around the Bay. But when the Bulb was ours, we grooved together 24/7. We were tight, a real community! The music we made! Maybe it was the Bulb energy vortex! A bunch of people got pit bulls so we could keep the place to ourselves, keep strangers away. Then Peace Weldon got us kicked out. Said this whole place should be a park open to the public. He's right, of course. But now, dammit, we have to get a special use permit just to have these full-moon gatherings."

The entire Bulb was alive with subgroups of all sorts. As he wandered among the campfires, Adam eavesdropped on dozens of conversations, some of them full of ranting, some intimate and soul-revealing.

Back at the Hodgepodge campfire, he found the group enjoying a heated debate. During a lull, he asked, "You all seem to constantly disagree with each other. What holds you together?"

The blonde, whose name was Linda, sidled up beside him

and said, "I guess we're inspired by Gaia. 'Human differences—she says—of race, religion, politics, appearance and so on—are the spice of life.'"

The guy in the suit inserted himself on the other side of Linda. "Everyone, when you get right down to it, is a unique individual, a group of one. You want to connect? You want community? You gotta love the endless variety!"

The big walrus of a man stepped into the center of the circle and said, "One of Gaia's few 'don'ts' is: Don't impose your views on others. We get it. We're sharing, revealing ourselves. Celebrating our differences. Gotta love it!"

When it was time to head back to Dream Voyager, Adam retraced his steps to search for his dinghy in the dark. And there it was, right where he had left it. There was no need now to be quiet, so he considered using the motor. But the lapping waves, the moon glittering on the water—the whole setting—had hooked him and reeled him in. The tide having turned, he left the motor untouched, got out the oars, pushed off, and settled into rhythmic rowing. The salt spray, the low bellow of distant foghorns, the night hum of the surrounding megalopolis and perhaps some tentacles of earth energy flowed through him as he rode the outrushing tide back to Dream Voyager.

Why would Magdalena and Black Elk associate themselves with Total Embrace? Beneath its benignly oddball public image, some very weird and sinister shit was going on. Vast shapes moved below the surface. How could he see them?

What an incredible soul Tripnee was! As dark waves slapped his little hull, Adam shook his head in wonder, marveling how, on that house-of-cards dais, she held so many in thrall. God! How he wanted to take her in his arms, look upon her, touch her, feel her touch and make sure she was safe. His whole being overflowed with yearning for his extraordinary sweetheart.

The danger she was in tore at his guts like the jagged teeth of a great white shark. He folded in the oars, and let the skiff ride the current. Pulling out his cell phone, he quick-dialed Tripnee's number. He had been trying to call her for months without success, but maybe this time he'd get through. Damn! Once again, just endless ringing, no voice mail, nothing. Was she being so closely watched that she dare not answer? Was she OK?

Tripnee was pulling off an extraordinary role as only she could—under deep cover, surrounded by extremely dangerous people. His passion and worry for her welled up like a tsunami, tumbling him in its deep belly. The Bay brooded, black and empty. Distant lights encircling the vast watery blackness punctured the night like distant, pin-prick moons. The ebb tide swept him in silent agony away from land, out into a dark void.

There was Dream Voyager. Wait a minute; something was wrong! The interior cabin lights were on. He had intruders!

CHAPTER 16

ABOARD DREAM VOYAGER

How could anyone have found his boat? How'd they get aboard without tripping the alarm linked to his cell phone? Was this some kind of omniscient enemy? A foe far more sophisticated than he imagined? Did he have to rethink his whole strategy?

Thank God, his approach had been silent, potentially giving him the element of surprise. Like an ancient hunter stalking a sabertoothed tiger, even as his veins coursed with adrenaline, he stilled his mind and sharpened his senses.

To suss out the situation and determine how many interlopers were on board and where they were located, he quietly circled Dream Voyager at a distance. A single aluminum skiff bobbed at the stern. No one was visible on deck or through the portholes. Moving in, he felt the skiff's outboard motor. Hot to the touch. Whoever they were, they hadn't been there long.

Without a sound, he secured his dinghy to a stern cleat, eased off his shoes, and ever so slowly, careful to cause no movement of the bigger boat, eased his weight aboard. Guided by feel, his fingers found, activated the combo, and opened a hidden lazaret in the sugar scoop stern. He reached in, selected a Sig Sauer pistol, and closed the small hatch.

He ascended the stairs until his head was just at deck level. Light streamed from the companionway. Still no one visible on deck. He crept forward, his Sig Sauer at the ready, safety off. As he moved forward along the starboard rail, he crossed the poop deck and then moved alongside the midship cockpit. He hunkered down to peer right and left through, first, one porthole, and then another, but saw no one.

In the cockpit, his back to the cabin bulkhead next to the companionway, he listened. What was going on down in the cabin? Silence. Nothing. It was time to make a move and, hopefully, take whoever it was by surprise.

Suddenly, singing poured up out of the salon. It was a rich, melodious, female voice! "One of these mornings, you're going to rise up singing. Then you'll spread your wings and you'll take to the sky…" Holy shit! It was Tripnee!

Of course! Who else knew the alarm code? Who else could even locate the boat? She must've used Find My Mac—after all, her iPad was on board.

Adam leapt down into the cabin, and was greeted by that radiant 5,000-watt smile. Raven-haired, big blue eyes glowing, with the unconscious physical grace of a panther, Tripnee swaying in front of his laptop computer, dripping wet, wrapped in a towel.

"Hey stranger," she beamed.

"If it isn't my earth goddess Gaia!" His heart pounded.

"If it isn't my Garden of Eden Adam!"

She rose and came to him. They embraced with a playful flourish, then plunged into a long kiss that left them both breathless—and aroused. Her towel fell away. Their bodies thrilled with pleasure and excitement at the feel, the smell, the reality of being together. She made quick work of removing his clothes, and…

Klunk! Kerplunk! What!? People were climbing aboard at the stern. Adam emitted a strangled, 'Aaaaaaahhhhh!' Yanked out of this wonderful real-life dream come true, Adam and Tripnee clung to each other for a moment, then separated, and pulled on their clothes. Adam tucked his Sig Sauer into his belt at the small of his back, flicked on the deck lights—and together, he and Tripnee climbed up to the cockpit.

CHAPTER 17

PIRATES

"Well, well, well! Lookee here," said a short, square, goateed man as he aimed a 38 special revolver at the center of Adam's chest. "Two beautiful people on their yacht. Awww, did we interrupt something? Too fucking bad! Put those hands nice and high!"

The guy stood on the stern deck between a burly, puffy-faced black man and a tall, sinewy, hard-eyed Asian woman. All three had the black teeth and jittery look of meth tweakers. Only one guy had a gun, but the other two held nasty-looking knives. The black guy's knife had a curved, foot-long serrated blade, while the woman's knife was straight, long, and narrow—essentially, a small sword.

As Adam and Tripnee raised their hands, Adam inched his right foot over the port winch deck button.

"This be my kinda boat," said the black guy. "It's got style. And I'll bet there's plenty of booze, brew, food and cash. And look at this, one bodacious babe."

"Hell, now we got it made!" said the guy with the gun. "This ship can go for weeks, months. Maybe head down to Mexico. Score some really good shit. But make no fucking mistake, Bo, you took the last beer, so the babe is mine first."

"Fuck that shit!" said Bo. "Seth, you yelling at me for having the last beer is totally unfair, 'cause I didn't have any of the speed." Then Bo advanced toward Tripnee, his knife blade glinting in the glare of the deck lights. "Now you say the babe be yours first. That messed up!"

"I'm telling you, Bo," said Seth. "Stay away from her, or I'll do you right now while I do the guy."

Bo, looking back at Seth, backed off Tripnee a step, his knife still out.

"Shut up, you assholes," said the woman. "We're keeping them both alive, for now." Approaching Adam, she pointed her blade into his right eye, and said, "What's your name, sweetie?"

With Bo and the woman blocking his line of fire, Seth yelled, "Shit, Frederika,..."

Adam toed the deck button. The sudden grinding of the winch caused Frederika to glance to her left. That moment was all Adam needed.

He seized Frederika's knife wrist and twisted her arm, spinning the woman, all the while using her body to shield himself from the gun. With one hand he jammed the woman's arm high up her back, and with the other hand he grabbed her stiletto and launched it straight at Seth. At the same time, Tripnee kicked Bo's knife hand, sending the blade skittering overboard, then kneed him hard in the groin. As he doubled over, screaming, she hunkered down to keep his bulk between her and Seth's weapon.

The knife caught Seth in the bicep of his gun arm, penetrating deep. Shrieking, he dropped the revolver. As Adam brought his Sig Sauer around from the small of his back, Seth took one look at it, ran to the starboard rail, and threw himself into the black waters of the Bay.

Tripnee covered Bo and Frederika with the Sig Sauer, while Adam turned on a powerful spotlight to search for Seth, but the creep was nowhere to be found. Bo blubbered for mercy, and Frederika offered to do anything, anything at all, if they would cut her some slack.

Interrogated separately, both at first claimed they had simply been out for a full-moon pleasure cruise. But when confronted by the duffle bags from their 20-foot Zodiac that were bursting with electronics, jewelry, and other valuables, first Bo, then Frederika admitted they had pulled a home invasion robbery in Marin, and had stumbled upon Dream Voyager by chance on the way back to their base, which was some kind of floating hulk far up the Oakland estuary. Questioned about their meth source and fence for stolen goods, they clammed up tight. When Tripnee asked if they knew anything about El Dragón or El Patrón, their eyes grew wide, their bodies actually convulsed, and they refused to say another word. Adam and Tripnee gagged and hogtied the the two, belly down in their separate forward cabins, making sure they were completely immobile and plenty uncomfortable.

CHAPTER 18

THE BAY AT NIGHT

Falling easily into the smooth teamwork they had developed on their long sailing voyages, Adam and Tripnee made hot drinks, fired up the engine, secured Dream Voyager's dinghy up in davits, hoisted anchor, and, towing Tripnee's skiff and the pirates' Zodiac, set off through the night for Richmond's Marina Bay.

As they snuggled together under fleece blankets on the cockpit bench, Adam asked, "Are you OK, baby? These creeps remind me of some of the goons surrounding the podium at Total Embrace. Dangerous people."

"Tell me about it," she said. "These three are benign compared to the bastards behind Total Embrace!"

"Yeah?" said Adam.

"Yeah!" said Tripnee. "They're the meanest bunch I've ever encountered. All the more reason to bust every last one of 'em!"

"Fill me in."

"Total Embrace is a sideshow, a diversion. Behind it is La Casa."

"La Casa?" blurted Adam, flummoxed. "The same cartel we took down on the Kern?"

"One and the same."

"Damn!! Won't this thing ever die?!" said Adam. "At least Reamer Rook and Toro Canino are dead and gone, the monsters!"

"Tell me about it." said Tripnee, "But La Casa's back stronger than ever. Enough of their people must have survived in Mexico to expand into El Salvador, Guatemala, and Columbia. Now they've refined their methods and have a stranglehold on the Bay Area. Drugs. Human trafficking. Shakedowns. Kidnapping. Prostitution. Blackmail. Identity theft. Home invasions. Plus a long list of legitimate businesses and foundations to launder money."

Adam snuggled her close, listening.

"Oro o agua," Tripnee continued. "Gold or water. That's the choice El Dragón—or just plain Dragón—their enforcer—gives judges, politicians, cops. If they choose gold, they receive regular payments that make them rich—and the cartel owns them forever. If they choose water, they get the Bay Way, meaning they're dropped naked in front of a speeding container ship, run over, and chopped into fish food, leaving no trace."

"Reminds me of 'No Muss, No Fuss,' on the Kern," said Adam.

"Yeah, same thing. Disappear people without leaving corpses behind. The cartel figured out that slaughtering whole families—and leaving the bodies—like they do south of the border, brings down too much media attention, too much law-enforcement heat. So they've mastered subtler, leave-no-trace—but equally effective—techniques that keep them below the radar."

With the boat on autopilot, Adam poured mugs of hot café au lait from a thermos and gave one to Tripnee. "The worst of Mexico coming to the Bay Area."

"It's gotten so bad in some areas of Mexico," continued Tripnee, "that teachers, businesses, anyone with a steady income has to pay protection money to the cartel in order not to get whacked. It's a horrible contagion—eats away at the heart and soul of a culture—all the more so, because it's silent. Police chiefs, district attorneys, judges never let on they're on the take. But once they're corrupted, they only pretend to enforce the law. They make a show of being tough on crime, but in reality they only prosecute small fry and enemies of the cartel. They never go after the real bad guys, Patrón and other cartel honchos."

"Who are these honchos?" asked Adam. "Who's Dragón? And Patrón?"

"I'm close—so close—to finding out," she said, holding her right thumb and index finger an inch apart.

Adam asked, "Why's the cartel mixed up with Total Embrace? What's in it for them? Seems bizarre."

"Damn right it does," replied Tripnee. "It's complex. A mystery wrapped in an enigma. Partly, it's a recruiting tool. Total Embrace attracts all sorts of people, some very strange and lost. A guy named Proudfoot—a snake of a man who would give even you the chills—pulls the ruffians, potential prostitutes, and other 'useful' people into a sort of sub-cult for cartel recruits. Partly, it's a good cover: a cloak of new-age oddness, even altruism. Something to distract the media and the world while the cartel sucks the lifeblood out of the Bay Area. Partly, of course, it's a moneymaker. But mostly, I think it has to do with Patrón. Whoever that is, he or she has some kind of flip-side obsession with spiritual awakening."

Adam tapped a button on the autopilot to alter their course a few points to port. He said, "I was surprised. Tonight on the Bulb was actually uplifting. You were the star, but Magdalena and Black Elk also did a good job. How did they get on the program? What's their connection with Total Embrace?"

"I approached them," said Tripnee. "They're part of what you might call the leadership council. Both are on my short list as possibles for Patrón."

"Makes sense," said Adam. "But Patrón or not, why

wouldn't people of their stature keep their distance from a crazy cult?"

"Like I said, Total Embrace is a huge, motley group, almost a movement. And in the Bay Area there's less stratification. Rich and poor, black, white, brown, and yellow, hip and not-so-hip, spiritual and depraved, there's tremendous intermingling. Whether it's naïveté or insanity or open-mindedness, or all of the above, the Bay flows with tolerance and acceptance. Besides, both Magda and Blackie are, well, out there. You saw that tonight."

"On that house-of-cards stage, you did more than just put on a show," said Adam. "You tapped into something. Logically, it makes no sense, but I was transported."

Tripnee grinned. "I'm really getting into the Gaia role. The cartel likes cheery spiritual awakening as an opiate for the masses—and as a sort of fig leaf to cover their naked barbarism. But they miss the big paradox."

"The big paradox?" asked Adam.

"The universe, reality, is rich, deep, complicated, and contradictory. A thing can be two—or more—apparently opposite things at the same time," said Tripnee. "Gaia is a sham, but also, at the very same time, she's genuine."

"How's that again?" asked Adam.

"Good question!" laughed Tripnee.

"One thing for sure," said Adam, "Something happened back there on the Bulb. We all felt it."

"Gaia would say, 'Spirit is real,'" said Tripnee. "'Real seeds are taking root. A lush garden is blooming right under the cartel's nose!'"

"Whatever you're doing, it's amazing!" said Adam. "How in hell did you manage to become the cult's star guru so fast?"

"Total Embrace, like Silicon Valley, the whole Bay Area, and, come to think of it, the cartel itself, admires and rewards ability and initiative. When I returned six months ago, I used my contacts to slip back into my old role as life coach to some prominent but shady Bay Area characters. One was Harry Bellacozy. Soon I was invited to a party where I met Blackie and others. Then, out of the blue, I was asked to be on a panel attended by thousands of cult members. In the process, I discovered the group's connection to the cartel. Pretty soon I was speaking to huge Total Embrace gatherings, mostly in the East Bay, but also in Marin, down the Peninsula, in Big Sur and up in Mount Shasta.

"Being Gaia seems to be working. I'm close to learning the inner relationships, who really calls the shots. But somehow, right now, I've hit a snag. These guys are super-cautious and paranoid. Did you see Proudfoot and his so-called bodyguards? The guy has a certain surface cool, but he makes my skin crawl. Tonight, after the event, something happened, and they all headed off to deal with it. So I slipped away, borrowed the skiff at the Berkeley marina, and motored out to the boat. The fact that they cut me loose when something big happened shows I have a ways to go to gain their trust. But I'm on the verge. I'm close. I'll crack this nut!"

"I don't like it," said Adam. "These people are using you to rake in money and grow their cult, but I don't see them letting you into their inner circle. And if they ever get an inkling you're FBI…"

Tripnee's eyes flashed, "I know what I'm doing! Yes, I'm putting a good face on their cult. And yes, the cat is playing with its food—and I'm the food. But I'm getting damned close to identifying the key players. Dragón. Patrón."

Despite his concern and frustration, at that moment Adam felt his heart dance.

"This thing has got to be stopped!" she continued. "If we don't nip it in the bud here, it'll spread. Very likely throughout the United States and beyond. It'll totally corrupt our legal system. It'll end the rule of law! Look at these three meth idiots tonight. You saw how they clammed up when I asked about Dragón and Patrón. They're way, way down the food chain, but they're cartel-connected, alright. They're part of a horrific, toxic, spreading cancer. Can you imagine what the world would be like if we don't stop this here? It'll metastasize everywhere!"

She gripped his arm with so much strength, it was all he could do not to drop his coffee. "Yes there's risk, but I've got to do it," Tripnee said with conviction. "Besides, we've got to find Peace before it's too late. His abduction has the cartel's fingerprints all over it. Kidnapping for retribution and ransom is what they do."

Adam was not going to win this argument; nonetheless, he persisted, "I still don't like it. It's just too dangerous. You said so yourself: They make people disappear without a trace. OK, they have to be stopped. But there're other ways to do it. Stay with me. Together we'll figure this out. Getting you killed is just not something I'm willing to let happen."

Tripnee set her jaw, arched her back, and said through gritted teeth, "Typical man. I've gotten this far, and I'm seeing it through. This is me! This is what I do! So back the fuck off."

Then, catching herself and then, realizing he was expressing concern for her, not macho domination, her face softened, "I'll be super careful, and I'll stay more in touch," she said.

Still frowning, Adam cocked a questioning eyebrow.

"The cartel's electronics are better than the FBI's," she said, "so we have to assume our phones are bugged. But I can communicate through a friend in the cult. Her name is Linda and she's completely trustworthy. She can pass messages between us."

"Blond, about five ten, slim hips and big chest? Part of the group that disagrees with everything?" asked Adam.

"That's her," said Tripnee, her eyes narrowing, apparently not entirely pleased that Adam already knew the woman.

Then they looked at each other, and laughed. When they snuggled together, the world, including the Bay enshrouded in darkness, felt warm and uplifting—and its challenges seemed manageable.

Guided by his iPad GPS navigation app and his own intuitive Bay map, developed through years sailing these waters, Adam rounded the Richmond breakwater and swung the boat to starboard. As the old seamen's motto, "Red to the right when returning," crept unbidden into his mind, he headed east up Potrero Reach toward Marina Bay, keeping the red buoy lights to starboard.

Tripnee explained the cartel's ingenious entrepreneurial structure, which was flat, with few employees. A vast number of "entrepreneurs" did the actual drug and human trafficking, kidnapping, extortion, robberies, identity theft, you-name-it, and paid 20% of their gross to the cartel. In return, they got free money laundering and fencing, and the protection afforded by the cartel's vast network of corrupt cops, judges, border and customs agents, prosecutors, lawyers, and politicians. Often, as long as they cleared their operations in advance with El Patrón, they were granted exclusive franchises and territories—which limited competition. Seed money to finance operations was available at 30% interest per week. These loans, plus interest, became due and payable, regardless of whether a particular operation succeeded or not. Because the cartel had encryption far superior to anything the feds or anyone else could break, almost all communications and payments were handled over the Internet—making it very difficult to identify Patrón or any of the other key players. Everyone was so terrified of Dragón and the Bay Way, few ever stepped out of line or failed to make payments when they were due. But when they did fall behind, the terrible penalty redoubled everyone's abject obedience to El Patrón.

"Whew!" breathed Adam. "The guy's a diabolical genius!"

CHAPTER 19

MARINA BAY

As the first morning light rose over the East Bay hills, Adam and Tripnee tied up to the tee end of a dock on the eastern shore of Marina Bay.

"We've got a problem," said Adam. "If the pirates Seth, Bo or Frederika ever figure out who you are and get word to the cartel that they saw us together, the consequences…"

"I thought of that," said Tripnee. "There's nothing we can do about Seth, if he's even alive. With Bo and Frederika, we can't turn them over to the local cops, but the FBI can hold'em until the operation is complete."

Adam frowned. "I don't like it. We'd be betting your life there're no leaks in the FBI. And if Seth survived…"

"I'm already betting my life there are no leaks in the FBI," said Tripnee, knitting her brow and flattening the curves of her irresistible lower lip. "Besides, we've already had this discussion. I've got to do this. Case closed."

They walked along the dock, passing a few early birds preparing their sailboats and fishing boats for a day on the Bay, and climbed the hinged shore ramp, which sloped up steeply, due to a minus tide. Crossing the shoreline path at the top of the ramp, ahead of them were a vehicle turnaround, two parking lots, and the Tradewinds Sailing School clubhouse, which overlooked the marina.

In the Tradewinds lobby, Tripnee used a land line to check in with the FBI and summon a team to take custody of their prisoners Bo and Frederika. Meanwhile, after making a few calls of his own, Adam left Tripnee deep in a hushed, earnest conversation with her FBI cohorts, and headed back to the boat.

Onboard, Adam entered the cabin where Bo lay hog tied. He removed the man's gag, but left him tightly trussed, belly down. "I'll get straight to the point, Bo. If you cooperate, I'll make sure no one knows the information came from you. You have my word on that. But, unless you tell me right now everything you know about Dragón, Patrón and La Casa, I'll put word out all over Oakland that you, Seth and Frederika are singing to the FBI."

"Man, you know what they do to snitches? That's a fucking death sentence!" pleaded Bo.

"You got that right," said Adam. "And one more thing, if I find out that you lied to me—and if you do lie, I *will* find out—the news you're singing gets broadcast from the rooftops, in the media, everywhere. But if you talk right now, and tell the truth, I'll keep it just between you and me."

"No way, man. They find out, they'll kill me!" said Bo, shaken and sweating. "You're a heartless motherfucking sonabitch!"

"Have it your way," said Adam, "the word goes out." Adam got up, opened the cabin door, and was just stepping through it when Bo sobbed, "Okay, okay."

Bo sang, and sang true. He, Seth, and Frederika were on the periphery of the cartel world. Their connection was someone called El Matador, who operated out of a warehouse on the Oakland waterfront. El Matador supplied them with meth, fenced their stolen goods, and collected the cartel's 20% piso or tax on all their transactions, which were clearly small potatoes in the realm of La Casa.

After finishing with Bo, Adam came on deck to find Tripnee

bristling from her phone call with Judd Wagstaff. He and an FBI team were on their way there, and she had to be gone before they arrived. When Adam asked why, she said it had to do with FBI bullshit that she would explain later. He didn't really buy this explanation, but knew it was all he was going to get for now. They embraced and kissed. "Love you," he whispered. "Please be careful."

Tripnee jumped into her skiff, cranked up the outboard, untied her bow line, backed into the marina fairway, and headed out toward the main harbor basin and the open Bay beyond. With her raven hair trailing in the wind, she looked back and waved, flashing him a gorgeous smile. Then she turned to face the sparkling water ahead, the line of her back and shoulders just plain elegant, looking every bit the earth goddess Gaia.

If indeed she needed to avoid Judd Wagstaff, she had departed none too soon. Minutes later, an out-of-breath Wagstaff showed up, with three other FBI agents.

"Adam!" he huffed, "Where's Tripnee?"

"Just missed her."

"Dammit! I told her to stay put," Wagstaff said. "We need to debrief. She's been out of touch for months. Finally she checks in, and now she's disappeared already!"

Adam told the men where to find the meth pirates and their stolen loot, and Wagstaff sent his three companions below to collect them.

With just the two of them in the cockpit, Adam said, "Bo and Frederika have to be held completely incommunicado; otherwise, Tripnee's cover could be blown and she'll wind up dead."

"Right, right. But I'll have to clear it with a judge, get a court order," said Wagstaff. "Like everyone else, they have a right to talk to their lawyer."

Holding the man's gaze, Adam emphasized, "Tripnee's life is at stake."

"If she had stayed here like I ordered, she wouldn't be in danger," Judd said, releasing a big breath. "She's put herself in this position."

Adam stepped close, "You'll get it done?"

"Of course, I'll get it done," said Wagstaff, shrinking back. "We can't let these lowlifes jeopardize Tripnee's safety."

After the FBI departed with the prisoners, carried away their stolen loot and loaded up their skiff, Adam cast off the mooring lines and motored back up Potrero Reach out onto the Bay. After clearing the Richmond breakwater, he hoisted the mainsail, unfurled the genoa, and killed the engine. As a gentle morning breeze filled the sails, Adam looked for but couldn't find that old uplift that billowing sails usually gave him—that upwelling aliveness, that sense that things were OK. Instead, he glided south over the rippling blue water awash in apprehension—for Tripnee, for Peace and for the Bay.

GOLD BAY: AN ADAM WELDON THRILLER

CHAPTER 20

BILLY CALHOUN DAVIS

Dream Voyager skimmed south through sky-blue water. Off to port, Brook's Island swarmed with cormorants while, further to port, Albany Bulb still smoldered from the campfires of the night before. On a course parallel to and well out from the East Bay shoreline, Adam noticed on this fine morning that all traffic on the shoreline freeway Highway 80 had ground to a dead stop in both directions. What a world, when a sailboat is faster than a ten-lane highway!

As he cleared Berkeley's derelict municipal pier, Adam heard a cacophony of gunfire. A little later, as he slowed in the wind shadow of Treasure and Yerba Islands, Adam looked over to see the reason for the traffic jam and the source of the gunshot sounds. A dozen police crouching behind their cop cars were blasting away at a lone black sedan that had stopped, with flattened tires, in the middle of the westbound lanes of I-80. What the hell?

Adam floated on, passing within a few yards of the elegant but vulnerable-looking single tower of the Bay Bridge's eastern span. Taking advantage of the island's wind shadow, he did a controlled jibe, setting the main for a run up the Oakland estuary. As he glided past dystopian Star-Wars cranes furiously unloading container ships, Adam rigged mooring lines and fenders along his starboard side. At Jack London Square, he started the engine, dropped sail, centered and secured the boom, then motored into the public dock at the foot of Broadway. Parking a car around here cost a fortune, but docking a luxury yacht was free! After securing bow and stern lines, Adam was just tying a diagonal spring line when he heard a booming voice.

"Sweet docking, captain, as they say in Jokeland, you soft in the pants NOT!"

Twenty yards away across the marina fairway, lounging on the poop deck of a classic wooden Chinese junk with the name Big Zen on its stern, was Adam and Peace's longtime friend, Billy Calhoun Davis. Tall, muscular and black, Davis wore faded jeans, a blue polo shirt and a huge grin.

"BC, you young rascal!" called Adam, "I love your boat!"

After locking Dream Voyager's hatches and activating the alarms, Adam made his way along the floating piers to the junk. BC greeted him with a bear hug that might have broken the ribs of a less robust man, and ushered him into a comfy deck chair on his elevated poop deck.

"What's it been, eighteen years?" said BC. "It seems like yesterday that you, me and Peace sailed Lake Merritt."

"Those were good times!" said Adam. "The Kids and Cops program. I'll never forget you winning the big race going wing on wing, stealing our wind, and passing us like we were standing still."

"Without that program and Peace, I never would've become a sailor—or a cop," said BC, flashing a big smile.

Turning serious, Adam filled his old friend in on the kidnapping, and asked if BC had heard of El Matador or El Patrón.

"Those guys are legends," said BC. "Big, really big, cartel honchos. We've been trying to track'em down for years, but they always seemed to be several steps ahead of us."

"Because of informers inside the Oakland Police?" asked Adam.

BC frowned, looked around, and in a low, tense voice said, "Just between you and me, oh, yeah."

Either the kidnapping or the mention of the cartel kingpins—or both—troubled BC. The tall, powerfully built cop hunched forward, wrung his hands and cast his eyes from side to side. Even though the morning was cool, he poured sweat. The man's initial calm had disappeared, revealing a soul-wrenching stress. Sensing his old friend needed to talk, and guessing BC's stress and Peace's dilemma were connected, Adam invited BC to open up and pour forth. Employing the same words they had used to get one another to talk as kids, Adam said, "Talk, man, talk."

"A lot has gone down in the eighteen years since you were here," said BC, who paused to slowly let out a long breath while running his big, shaking hands over his bald head. "Burglaries, robberies, murders all doubled, and arrests have been cut in half. We got a crime wave! Dead bodies on the streets are the new everyday normal."

"How much is tied to cartels?" asked Adam.

"Most of it is cartel turf wars," said BC. "The worst thing is, they use kids, 'cause the penalties for kids in the juvenile system tend to be gentle, even for murder. Kids admire thugs. And these days, kids are damn good shots because of all these first-person-shooter video games."

"Wasn't Peace working with these kids?" asked Adam.

"Yeah! Peace figured out how to get kids to leave their gangs!" said BC. "Peace talks to kids in the hospital right after they're shot. Bullets hurt like hell! If he talks to them within 36 hours of getting shot, when the pain is fresh, Peace can persuade them to leave their gangs. Then these same kids talk other kids into leaving their gangs. Peace has been saving a lot of kids from a brutal, short life!"

"Enough kids to slow the crime wave?" Asked Adam.

"Not yet. But eventually, yeah!" said BC. "Peace pioneered a program in Richmond, and then brought it to Oakland. They sit down with guys who gonna most likely get shot. Peace and a bunch of his converts—who've became social workers, community organizers, parole officers, cops, and re-entry counselors—are hella' good at getting people to turn away from a life guaranteed to get them maimed, killed or thrown in jail."

The talking—and Adam's listening—seemed to help BC. Apparently calmer, BC looked out over the channel between Oakland and Alameda. But the stress and shakes returned as BC pointed a wobbly hand toward a boxy, sixty-foot power boat heading toward the main bay. "They call it a love boat. There's a whole fleet of boats that go out to foreign ships anchored in the bay waiting for dock space. Sailors like'em because the sea can be lonely. The problem is, most of the girls are trafficked in from Asia and south of the border by cartels. Exploited sex slaves. But getting them to testify is impossible."

"But here, too," continued BC, "Our man Peace—and his friend Magdalena—are making changes. They've got women's shelters—safe houses—where the women can go. Lots of the women help with Magdalena's urban gardens, find jobs, and get their lives together. Get on a completely different track. And lots of these women continue working with Peace and Magdalena, helping them rescue other women from the love boats and cartel street pimps."

BC grew calmer and his eyes steadied. His voice, his whole body began to vibrate with positive excitement: "Peace is huge. He's moved away from the old top-down way of doing things! He doesn't talk down from above, he gets the community, the people themselves involved in creative collaboration. He flows with compassion, man, and he brings out the best in people. These are people who have been there, who were on drugs, in gangs, in that life. They're the very best people to reach out and help others get themselves together, and escape that life."

BC paused, studied Adam, then leaned forward with even more intensity, "What's really wild—I can hardly believe it myself, Adam—Peace is changing the mindset of the Oakland police! He's doing ride-alongs, taking part in squad room meetings and narc squad busts. The guy's amazing, who he is, his presence, his compassion. Instead of the old us-versus-them mindset, Peace is helping us see it's all us! Like a Vulcan mind meld, inside the department we're getting it together, and also with the community. We're connecting. We're seeing things from the other guy's point of view."

This all sounded far-fetched. After all, they were talking about his goofy Zen Buddhist flower-child uncle Peace! But BC definitely had Adam's attention.

"I'm talking evolved cops!" BC went on. "Cops with heart—and communication skills, who listen and connect. We absolutely arrest the bad behavior, but even then, we see the perps as human beings. We have compassion, they're human souls—souls, man—and at the same time we insist that they not break the law."

"Hey, it's not easy with some of these bad guys! But it's a revolution, man. It's big. It's amazing. We're on the road now, baby! This is happening! We're going to save this whole place. You can feel it. You can see it in the street murals—art covering three- and four-story buildings. Just walk along Webster Street. You can feel it in the restaurants. You can feel it around Lake Merritt. There's a vibe of community, of connection, of oneness, of appreciation for diverse individuals. I never thought I'd talk like this or see things this way, but here I am. It's real and it's happening, baby!"

As much as Adam liked the sound of this and wished it was real—a wild, wonderful fantasy come true—he just didn't fully buy it. BC had always seemed like a level-headed guy, but apparently he had a screw loose! Still, just talking about Peace seemed to do wonders for him.

"These changes are big!" BC exulted. "They definitely threaten the cartels and the gangs they control. Change is coming, and the bad guys don't like it. I think they know Peace is quarterbacking the change. He doesn't lead in the old top-down way. He plants the seed. I am not be surprised they would go after him—in fact, I figured they would—so we got to help him!"

Despite Adam's doubts, BC was opening his eyes to seeing Peace in new ways. But Adam recalled that, ever since Peace had taught BC to sail, all those years ago, it was a bit weird how the young black man had worshipped Adam's uncle. Very likely, this was more of that blind adoration. Before the three of them had met, BC's older brother had killed a cop—and was serving a life sentence. BC's parents, who were now dead, had been into drugs. For BC, meeting Peace had been like finding the Messiah, so, very likely, this was coloring BC's perception of events. Still, clearly, Peace had done more than enough to get targeted by the cartels.

BC grew quiet, looked out at a yawl cruising down the estuary, lifted his gaze to the blue sky, closed his eyes and seemed to drink in the sunshine lighting up his ebony face. Then he looked Adam straight in the eyes and said, "I've been waiting a long time. I've been having to satisfy myself with little, tiny steps toward healing this place, but now these new developments inspired by Peace, they inspire me. We, this town, and really our world, have hope. But, Adam, I've got to prepare you—the cartel gangsters are brutal, deadly thugs, the worst sonofabitch villains you can imagine! I've been biding my time for years, waiting for a chance to take these guys down and clean up this town. We're going to really come up against them, and I want you to know I'm with you a thousand percent. I'm talkin' danger. We could die!"

An involuntary spasm suddenly shook BC's body, scrunching his face with pain. Adam leapt forward. Grabbing the man's shoulders to keep him from pitching over, he asked, "BC, are you OK?"

Almost as quickly as it had begun, the seizure subsided. BC's muscles stopped quivering and he said, "What'd you grab me for? I'm fine."

"BC, you almost fell over."

"Just a micro blackout."

"Micro my ass," said Adam with concern. "We've got to get you checked out."

"Later," said BC, "Right now, we've got a bigger emergency—and an opportunity. I'm with you on this. I'm committed. I've been waiting for this. This is where I choose to be. My soul, my whole self is all about this."

Extending broad, trembling hands toward Adam, BC continued, "Whatever you need from me, you let me know. With you on board, we got the best chance we've ever had! These guys have gone too far, and now they've taken Peace! We're going to rescue him. You just let me know what you need from me. I'm with you all the way. Count on me. I'm in!"

CHAPTER 21

EL MATADOR'S WAREHOUSE

Adam walked along the floating piers to Dream Voyager and returned with the two devices that had been attached to his boat off Belvedere. "You still the tech wizard?"

BC smiled, "A lot of people see this Chinese junk and don't think much of it. Which suits me fine. But I've got a complete electronics lab aboard, and I'll check 'em out."

*   *   *

Next, Adam packed a bag with some gear that might come in handy, and borrowed BC's car to go see what he could learn about El Matador. Bo the pirate had revealed the existence of the waterfront warehouse, its location, and its function as a key cartel fencing operation. The thing was that, as a low-level character on the fringes of the organization, Bo knew little. But at least Adam had some sort of lead. Who knew what agonies Peace was undergoing even now? Adam was determined to tear the cartel apart chunk by chunk until Peace was free.

BC's dark blue Tesla Model 3—the guy really did worship Peace, right down to driving the same make of car—surged forward like a spaceship. Interestingly, it blended right in in the Bay Area, where every other vehicle was either a hybrid or all-electric.

The warehouse was a rusty, corrugated metal building in a grimy part of the Oakland waterfront. A half-block away, Adam parked on a busted-up, litter-filled patch of pavement where he could surveil the scene without being noticed. El Matador's neighbor on one side was a bustling recycling center, where an ongoing hubbub of forlorn-looking homeless people poured in from all directions, pushing shopping carts laden with cans, bottles and junk.

On the other side, a vast rambling structure with a fenced yard housed an artists' collective called NIMBY. Here two dozen or so people, spanning all ages, races and genders, were building a fifty-foot-tall wooden horse! The NIMBY artists seemed to move with upbeat energy and focus. Excellent neighbors on both sides for a fencing operation, where a trickle of people showing up with miscellaneous items would hardly stand out.

Keys to successful surveillance include patience and staying awake, so Adam had come well-armed with a hearty farm-to-table sandwich from Jack London Square and a big cup of coffee. Wide-awake, chewing and swallowing, he studied the scene. You never know what detail—however small—might be significant. The neighboring sites buzzed with activity, while the cartel building stood silent with only a few people leaving, and no one entering. The rest of the street? Nothing, that Adam could see.

After a while, it was time to take a closer look. Adam opened the bag on the seat beside him, pulled out his laptop and compact quadra-copter drone. Unfolding the latter into flying mode, he touched the Tesla's control screen to open the sun roof and reached up to place the tiny device on the car's roof. Using the computer's keys and touchpad, he got the four propellers whirling, flew the drone straight up a couple hundred feet, then piloted it forward. Matador's warehouse came into view crystalclear on the laptop's screen. What a gadget! This was going to make surveillance a piece of cake!

That thought no sooner crossed his mind, than the laptop image shook and went dead. Try as he might, he couldn't get the picture back—and soon the drone itself no longer responded to his commands. Looking up, he saw the drone wobble and then drop into the cartel compound. No doubt operating with an unlimited budget, the cartel probably had the latest anti-drone technology to detect, commandeer and capture spy drones!

Very likely, this had alerted Matador's crew to his presence, but Peace was in trouble, time was of the essence, and Adam wasn't about to give up. He waited awhile, watching for any response. Seeing none, he climbed out of the Tesla. As he walked toward the NIMBY yard, BC's computer-on-wheels car sucked in its handles and locked its doors, windows and two trunks. Inside the yard, he approached a clean-cut young man— who looked like a poorly disguised undercover cop.

"That's some horse!"

"It's for Burning Man."

"Mind if I take a look?" asked Adam.

"You've come at a good time. We're just applying the finishing touches, numbering each part, getting ready to take the whole thing apart to bring it to Nevada's Black Rock Desert, where we'll reassemble it. Eventually, it'll go up in flames as a big part of the closing rituals."

"You're building this beautiful fifty-foot-tall horse just to burn it?"

"Yup. It's a full-scale Trojan Horse. Paid for by the Burning Man organization. In fact, they're paying me quite well to be the lead artist and chief docent."

They shook hands and Adam learned the young man's name was Chris.

"By the way, do you know anything about what goes on next door, over that fence?" Adam indicated the fence separating the NIMBY compound from El Matador's place.

"Can't say I do. Running this motley crew of volunteers, racing to finish by deadline, has me swamped right here," said Chris. "Speaking of which, I've got to get back to work. Make yourself at home and explore the horse. You'll see where there'll be a full bar and a pulsating light show inside the belly. And you can climb clear up into the head and look out through the eyes."

Adam took Chris up on the invitation, and climbed up a hollow leg into the horse's belly. From there, he found his way to the neck and climbed up into the head where, looking out through the great horse's eyes, he could look down into the cartel compound. Except for two boats pulling away from the dock at the back, there was no one to be seen.

As he climbed down out of the horse, Adam kept an eye out for—and eventually found—a tool box. He waited until no one was in view, and, hoping the rattle of tools would not draw attention, dug through the box. At last, at the bottom, he found what he needed: a pair of bolt cutters. Checking to see that no one was watching, he hid the cutters under his jacket.

Back on the ground, while pretending to admire the monumental horse from various angles, he scoped out the yard and found the place he was looking for. There was a narrow space hidden behind empty packing crates where he could go to work on the cyclone fence between NIMBY and the cartel compound.

Adam cut through the fence, slipped through the hole and moved nimbly among shipping containers and fifty-five-gallon fuel drums—all empty. Still no one was around. Once he was near the building, he pressed his face against a dirty window, but could see nothing. Making his way to a rear door, he tried the doorknob. The door was unlocked; something wasn't right, for sure. Backing away from the door, he climbed onto a dumpster, then scaled a downspout to the roof. He broke a glass panel in a skylight, cranked it open, and stuck his head down to study the interior. No one around that he could see. Except for an assortment of apparently empty crates and drums, the building looked empty.

As he dropped to the floor, a crash shattered the silence. He instinctively tucked and rolled in behind the nearest cover—a stack of empty crates. For a long moment he peered into the gloom, holding his breath—what the hell made that sound? Suddenly there was a scrambling sound that echoed through the empty space—he grinned as a gigantic rat skittered off into a dark corner. Rising to his feet, he moved silently to the unlocked back door—where, sure enough, he found a booby trap—a trip wire connected to a Claymore mine. If he or anyone else had opened that door, they would have been blown to pieces. He had to admire the handiwork as he disarmed the device.

Adam searched the building, but the place had been stripped clean. The only thing of interest: on a table in a far dim corner was a Droneshield control system set to automatically detect, commandeer and fry the circuitry of approaching spy drones. Clearly the work of pros. Pros who were many steps ahead of him.

CHAPTER 22

RASHEED

Strolling with deliberate nonchalance back to the Tesla, Adam caught glimpses of a little head poking above the roof line of a three-story brick building a half-block beyond the car. Just a few brief sightings—but they were enough. The tallest building in the neighborhood. The perfect vantage point for a cartel lookout.

Turning around, Adam casually walked away in the other direction. Reaching a corner, he turned right. Hidden from view, Adam raced to the next street, where he turned right again to circle back to the far side of the tall building.

He climbed an exterior fire escape to the roof. Through a maze of rooftop cooling towers, at the far edge of the roof he saw the back of a small black boy. As the boy scanned the street below him, Adam saw that his little hands held an AR-15 automatic rifle, the muzzle tracking the kid's roving gaze. The boy turned, and at the same instant Adam ducked behind a cooling tower. Gripped by an icy calm, not sure if he had been seen or not, Adam wondered if bullets were about to blast through the thin sheet metal of the tower to rip him to shreds. He took a slow breath. Then another, waiting for it....

Nothing happened. After a few minutes, Adam decided to hazard a look. The kid—apparently a child not much older than twelve—was again looking the other way, studying the street below.

Creeping forward, Adam did his best to make no sound and to take advantage of every scrap of cover. When he was about ten feet away, the boy, sensing something, spun around. With lightening-fast reflexes that had kept him alive in many a war-zone encounter, Adam leapt forward and seized the boy's AR-15, a split-second before it could zero in on his chest. Adam held the surprisingly tiny lad in a gentle but firm grip, and said, "It's OK. I won't hurt you. Just want to talk."

The boy struggled, his eyes bulging with fear. Then, finding escape impossible, he grew still.

"My name's Adam. What's yours?"

"Rasheed."

Racking his brain for a way to convey that he meant the boy no harm—and to win the boy's trust—Adam decided to simply speak the truth. "I'll level with you. La Casa kidnapped my uncle. All I'm looking for is a way to get him back."

The young boy narrowed his eyes with suspicion, his mouth clamped shut.

"They threw him into a black armored van near the Golden Gate Bridge. I chased them, but they ended up getting away on a boat on the Bay—and disappeared into the fog. I'm really worried about what they might be doing right now to my uncle Peace…"

"Peace? I know Peace!" Rasheed blurted out, suddenly animated.

"Yeah?" Adam was incredulous. "You know my uncle Peace?"

"Sure do! Me and Vocab got shot bad, see?" Rasheed pulled up his hoodie sweatshirt to reveal a scar bulging from his little stomach. "Peace found us in the hospital. The pain was so bad, sooo bad!"

"Vocab? You and Vocab work for La Casa?"

"We did. But not now. Peace helped us see! If we stayed

working for La Casa, we were on a fast road to more and more pain and prison and death."

"You're not up here working as a lookout for La Casa?"

"No. No. No. El Matador—El Dragón—La Casa—put out a contract on me and Vocab."

"So you're up here why?" asked Adam.

"Vocab don't know I'm here. But La Casa don't let nobody quit. They trying to hunt us down and kill us." The boy's eyes filled with tears. "They never gonna let us alone. We'll never be safe and free—unless I kill 'em!"

Adam remembered reading about Vocab, the notorious child sicario—hitman—whose uncanny accuracy with an AR-15 assault rifle was legendary. So this was Vocab's buddy!

No doubt Vocab and Rasheed had a long history of performing cold-blooded murders and other tasks for La Casa. Had Peace really been able to persuade two infamous young killers to renounce violence? Didn't seem likely. But beneath the boy's bravado, Adam glimpsed a scared child. No doubt, to survive in his world, the boy had to be a superb little actor—so who knew the truth? Was the boy genuinely opening up? Or cleverly saying whatever would manipulate Adam into going easy on him?

Apparently showing a maturity beyond his years, Rasheed said, "So Peace is in trouble. I've got to take you to Vocab. He'll know what to do. Thing is, he'll be pissed I was here, but that can't be helped. We've got to save Peace."

CHAPTER 23

VOCAB

Cartel sicarios—especially the older, hardened ones— were not people you would ever want to meet. They no doubt thought nothing of offing strangers who came nosing around. For professional killers, this would be a basic precaution, a necessary survival tactic. Even with Rasheed accompanying him, what were Adam's chances of survival sauntering into Vocab's hideout? But this juvenile hitman might be the key to finding Peace.

With Rasheed scrunched down on the floor, forward of the front passenger seat, they drove south into East Oakland. Adam hoped he had been right to return the AR-15, which the boy clutched to his chest like a security blanket.

In most parts of the world, the neighborhood where Vocab was hiding out would qualify as upscale. Yes, there was litter here and there, and a group of sullen-looking African American young men and boys hanging out across from a school two blocks from Vocab's address. But the streets were wide and orderly. The homes were mostly single-family bungalows, each sitting on its own fenced lot. The lawns were reasonably, if not fastidiously tended. Cars new and not-so-new occupied most driveways and lined the streets. This was the famous Oak Town ghetto?

Rasheed had Adam park in the narrow alley behind Vocab's house, and they entered through a weathered back door, opening, and then relocking behind them, four deadbolts. Rasheed sang out a slow, melodious, "Hepwaaa Baaabbaa." Syllables that apparently signaled everything was OK.

Despite the password, when they made their way along a short hallway and entered a large room in the front of the house, they were greeted by the business end of Vocab's AR-15.

Rasheed, entering first, said, "This is Peace's nephew, Adam."

Vocab studied Adam for a moment, then said, "Peace talked about you!" and stepped forward to shake hands.

Rasheed told Vocab about Peace's kidnapping—leaving out the part about his lying in wait to kill El Matador and El Dragón. Vocab, when he heard where they had met, gave Rasheed a look that left little doubt that he knew what his friend had been up to.

Unlike its battered exterior, the home's interior was, if not exactly neat, at least reasonably well-kept—except for piles of newspapers, books and assorted junk piled against the walls facing the street. The two boys worked together to remove a stack of computer hardware from an overstuffed chair, offered the seat to Adam, then took up positions on a tattered but comfy-looking couch. Adam marveled that Vocab was fifteen and Rasheed only twelve. As they talked, Vocab's fingers continuously tapped the keys of a much-used Mac Book Pro laptop, and the eyes of both boys moved back and forth between Adam and the computer screen.

Adam didn't know what surprised him most: their youth, their friendliness, or the fact they—especially Vocab—talked more like graduate students than street thugs. Figuring it might be best to just make small talk while they got to know each other, Adam asked how Vocab got his name.

"Short for vocabulary," said Rasheed. "He's got game—word game—going on!"

"Yeah?" said Adam.

"My grandfather used to read bedtime stories to me," said Vocab. "By the time I was six, I was reading stories to him. When I was seven he gave me a Roget's Thesaurus. My favorite book ever—right up there with this Mac Book Pro!" he said with a wink.

They talked about Peace.

"An extraordinary man!" said Vocab.

"That's putting it mildly," said Rasheed.

The two boys, who clearly were deeply attuned to one another, despite their age difference, explained how they had dropped out of school and served together as lookouts and hit men for La Casa. Both had been shot—Vocab in both legs and Rasheed, as Adam knew, in the stomach. Peace had visited them in the hospital and, with the pain of their bullet wounds still fresh and excruciating, had persuaded them to leave La Casa. The penalty for quitting the cartel was death, and there had already been two drive-by shooting attempts on their lives. They had changed hideouts; and fortunately, within the last month, there had been no further attempts to impose this punishment on two of the cartel's most lethal killers. Three Oakland police officers—all friends of Peace—had let it be known that if any harm came to the boys, there would be hell to pay. Tragically, two of those cops had been found dead in their squad car just two weeks before.

The bottom line was, the boys were in terrible danger and anything could happen at any moment. For the foreseeable future they needed to disappear—and so, they were holed up temporarily in Rasheed's Uncle Mamood's flat. Mammood held two minimum-wage jobs. Hoping to one day launch his own restaurant, he worked the day shift in a hospital kitchen on Oakland's Pill Hill, and evenings he flipped burgers at In-N-Out in Pinole.

Adam felt the horror of their situation. Here were two young boys grappling with life in a deadly war zone, right in the middle of the Bay Area. They were accomplished killers, but at the same time—in essence—they were just two frightened kids. As they told their story, Rasheed's eyes welled with tears and Vocab's body shook, which was a positive sign. Instead of being withdrawn and shut down, as one might expect, the boys could be tender, vulnerable, and could express a full range of emotions. Maybe because each was an extraordinary companion for the other—or perhaps because of someone else? Perhaps, Peace?

"How are you boys holding up?" Adam asked. "Are you okay?"

"Yeah, we're good," said little Rasheed, who seemed small for his age. "I have nightmares and wake up in cold sweats, but Vocab talks me down and gets me back to being able to maintain."

"I have nightmares too, and wake up trembling," said Vocab. "And Rasheed, he helps bring me back."

"What's the solution? How about I get you boys out of here and take you someplace safer?" asked Adam.

"Thanks," said Vocab. "But the cartel has eyes everywhere. And I mean everywhere! We have other places where we can stay, and we even thought of hiding out at Peace's house. But right here, this is off La Casa's radar. Anyplace else we could go would be even more dangerous."

Was it possible? Fear had made these kids age far beyond their years. Adam guessed that being a child hitman would do that. They were sometimes jittery, but overall carried themselves with solemnity, even gravitas. Amazingly, they still occasionally bubbled over with spunk and innocence.

"I can see the strain you're under," said Adam. "But I have

to tell you, I like that you show calm under pressure—and that you can still smile!"

"We have Peace to thank for that," said Vocab, "both for getting us out of that life, and for helping us so much since!"

"That's the truth!" said Rasheed. "You should see the videos!"

"The videos?" asked Adam.

"Yeah, me and Vocab have our own YouTube channel," said Rasheed. "We used to just do street dancing and sideshows. And some went viral!"

"You know," inserted Vocab. "Sideshows, those car rallies on the streets of Oakland."

"With me and Vocab having to lay low," said Rasheed, "We switched to making Peace videos. And they're going viral even bigger!"

"Peace videos!?" asked Adam.

"Watch this," said Vocab as he tapped a few keys and turned his laptop screen toward Adam.

On the screen, the title "Peace Video #21" broke into a pixelated swirl which re-formed to spell "A Vocab & Rasheed Video." This credit in turn swirled away to reveal Vocab and Rasheed sitting on their couch.

Looking directly into the camera, Rasheed said, "Everyone has imposter syndrome."

"We see ourselves from the inside—our fears, worries, imperfections," said Vocab, also looking straight into the camera. "But we see other people from the outside. We see the face they put on. They hide their fears, their doubts."

"They're faking it till they make it," said Rasheed.

"But inside they're afraid," said Vocab.

"We're all afraid!" blurted Rasheed.

"There's physical fear," said Vocab. "Am I going to get hurt?"

"Maybe die?" said Rasheed.

"And social fear," said Vocab. "Am I going to get rejected?"

"Or disrespected?" said Rasheed.

"And deepest of all," said Vocab, "Everyone—all of us—are secretly wondering: Am I OK? Can I do what I gotta do?"

"Yeah," chimed in Rasheed, "Am I OK? Can I do what I gotta do?"

"Don't matter if you're rich, poor, black, white," said Vocab.

"Or whatever," said Rasheed. "Everyone is faking it."

"Putting on the brave face," said Vocab. "The thing is, it's best not to come out and tell people you see they're afraid."

"That would just scare them," said Rasheed.

"And make them feel threatened," said Vocab. "It's better to assuage their fears. The best, the biggest thing is to not act tough. Instead, smile, be friendly."

"Yeah, smile, be friendly," repeated little Rasheed.

"This lets them know you're not going to do them any harm," said Vocab. "Hey, it's compassion! Put yourself in their shoes!"

"Pretend you're them," said Rasheed, smiling big.

"This helps them be less afraid," said Vocab, also smiling. "And helps us be less afraid."

"Yeah. It helps everybody be less afraid," said Rasheed, still grinning. "It works!"

The video ended with an invitation to subscribe to Vocab and Rasheed's YouTube channel.

Impressed, Adam said, "You sound more like river guides than sicarios. Do I detect Peace's influence?"

"Oh, yeah!"

Without warning, a cacophony of automatic weapons fire

erupted outside. The big window facing the street shattered in a hail of bullets. Adam and the boys dove to the floor, and Adam saw the logic of lining the outer walls with newspapers and books, which transformed the room into a bunker impervious to gunfire. As long as they stayed low, they should be safe. The volume of incoming gunfire doubled and then doubled again, then plateaued in a sustained ongoing hell of flying lead. It was as intense as any firefight Adam had undergone anywhere.

Adam pulled out his Glock. Vocab and Rasheed brought up their AR-15 assault rifles. Keeping low, moving with practiced ease, the boys took up positions on either side of the big, blown-out window. Instead of spraying bullets wildly and indiscriminately like their attackers had done, they bided their time, and released short, carefully aimed bursts. After each burst, there was a reduction of the incoming gunfire.

Crash!! The sound of a door splintering came from the back of the house. Then something came flying in, skittered across the floor, and came to rest against Adam's right leg: it was a live grenade, its pin pulled! His instincts kicked in. People unfamiliar with grenades don't take into account the delay between the pull of the pin and detonation, and so they throw it too soon. Hoping to God this was the case—and, what choice did he have, what with the thing wedged against his leg?—he seized the explosive and hurled it back through the rear doorway from which it had come. Rasheed and Vocab watched this and gave Adam a thumbs-up as an explosion and then a bloodcurdling scream reverberated from the back of the house.

A second grenade came flying in the front window and came to rest two feet from Vocab. With the speed and grace of a pro ballplayer, Vocab hurled it straight back where it had come from with uncanny accuracy, very likely bouncing it by the feet of whoever had thrown it, where it went off amid more screaming. As suddenly as it had all began, the barrage stopped.

Outside there was the sound of running feet, some scraping and moaning as wounded attackers were dragged into vehicles, then the roar of engines racing away.

"Time to find you boys a better hideout!" said Adam.

"No way!" said Vocab. "Rasheed is right. They'll never leave us alone. We gotta kill'em."

CHAPTER 24

KINGS RIVER

"Look," said Adam, "I see you're more skilled than the La Casa guys, but the cartel is a vast organization with huge resources. Even if you kill twenty or a hundred of them, there'll still be more coming for you."

"Don't matter," said Vocab. "We'll take 'em all down!"

"Defending yourselves just now was essential," replied Adam, "and, I have to admit, very well done." At this, the boys noticeably stuck out their small chests, stood a little straighter—and gripped their weapons more tightly.

"But have you forgotten," asked Adam, "what Peace taught you?"

The boys looked at each other.

"You have your whole lives ahead of you," continued Adam. "You're kids. If you continue down this path, you're going to wind up in prison or dead. Even if you won't do it for yourself, at least think about each other."

This touched a chord. Rasheed's eyes welled up. Vocab nodded thoughtfully.

Once he had their agreement—before the boys changed their minds—they had to get moving.

Adam gave Vocab and Rasheed a moment to grab a few possessions, allowing them one duffle bag each. Making sure the coast was clear, they all hustled out the back door into the alley, and clambered into the Tesla. Adam headed east on 580 toward the central valley of California. En route he left the highway several times and looped around on surface streets to make sure they were not being followed.

As they sped out of the Bay Area, Adam asked, "Who do you think kidnapped Peace?"

From the back seat, Rasheed, his small voice sounding amazingly adult-like, immediately said, "La Casa! Peace got so many people to quit! He put a target on his own back big-time."

Vocab, also seeming to channel his inner adult, said, "It has to be La Casa. Peace definitely pissed them off, and the cartel loves to do kidnappings—but usually they go for huge ransoms—way more than Peace could muster."

Adam let that go, and asked, "Do you boys have any idea where they might be holding Peace...?"

"Could be anywhere," said Vocab.

"...or which cartel crew actually did the kidnapping?"

"Same answer," said Vocab. "Could be anyone. In La Casa, information about specific kidnappings and hits is closely guarded, shared only on a need-to-know basis."

Adam asked, "What do you know about El Patrón and El Dragón?"

The boys froze. "Haven't met them," said Vocab in a trembling voice, "and I hope we never do! Those are truly evil dudes!"

"How so?" asked Adam.

"You don't want to know," blurted Rasheed.

"I need to know," said Adam.

"Well, OK, then," said Vocab. "Nobody knows what they look like—but they're the big, big cartel bosses. Anybody and everybody who crosses them gets the Bay Way. They take you out at night, strip you naked, and throw you in the Bay in front of a humungous fast ship. The prop chops you to smithereens and the sharks eat your tidbits."

Nightmarishly gruesome all right, thought Adam. These guys definitely knew how to keep both the cartel's workers and its enemies in line.

After crossing over the Altamont Pass, Adam headed south on Highway 5, east on 152, and then south on 99. In Fresno they stopped to recharge the car's battery at a Tesla supercharger in front of a Whole Foods. It was free. Amazing! After hooking up the charger, Adam ushered the boys into a café down the block, where they ate dinner in a back booth out of sight from passersby.

Adam, who sat facing the entrance as they ate, noticed a thickly muscled man in sunglasses push through the front door of the café and scan the place. The guy abruptly turned around and left. Something felt very wrong.

On an instinct, Adam told the boys to grab their food and hustled them out the back, through the kitchen. They had just stepped into the alley when the café exploded behind them. Judging from the force of the blast, it might've been a grenade or a shoulder fired-rocket. Moving as fast as deer, Adam and the boys ran along the alley and entered the Whole Foods market through the rear loading dock. They paused in an alcove behind pallets of organic produce.

"Son of a bitch!" said Rasheed. "That was close. If we'd gotten out of there two seconds later, we'd be fucking dead right now!"

"How did you know to get the hell out of there?" asked Vocab.

Adam shrugged, "Some kind of sixth sense I developed as a Navy SEAL."

"Must be what they call survival radar," said Vocab. "Gotta have it to stay alive. Thanks, man. We'll stick with you."

Figuring whoever fired the rocket would have disappeared, Adam poked his head out the front of the store. Half a block away, a fire truck had pulled up diagonally in front of the cafe, with one tire on the sidewalk. Its crew was already attacking the fire. Sirens in the distance signaled that more help was on the way. Adam unplugged the Tesla, and he and the boys got in and sped away.

"What do you think?" asked Adam. "Was that a cartel hit? Do they operate way out here?"

"Oh yeah," said Rasheed. "They're out here."

"Out here, and spreading everywhere," said Vocab.

Adam pulled into a truck stop, and parked in a secluded back corner, hidden in a clump of 18-wheel semi-trucks and trailers. He and the boys searched every inch of the Tesla from end to end, top to bottom. Sure enough, they found not one but two magnetic tracking devices, each the size of a silver dollar. Adam stuck them onto an 18-wheeler that was being refueled for a long haul to some distant destination. To shake any tails that might have been following them, Adam drove in meandering circles along backroads.

Adam then headed east, up into the Sierra foothills on Trimmer Springs Road toward Kings Canyon. As day turned to night, they penetrated deeper and deeper into the mountains, and eventually found themselves following the meandering shoreline of Pine Flat Reservoir, which shimmered and danced in the moonlight.

Fears of being followed and attacked gradually subsided. As they covered the miles, the boys relaxed, opened up, and talked. About anything and everything. The more they shared, the lighter the mood in the car became, and a kind of catharsis stole over them.

Adam learned that neither boy had ever known his father. Vocab's mom, raising six kids, had fought an ongoing battle with depression and alcoholism. His three older brothers, one by one, joined a neighborhood gang that worked for La Casa; they had become lookouts, relishing the money and newfound status. Vocab resolved to go a different way, and threw himself into his studies at a free charter school called the Life Academy, a few blocks from the family's East Oakland apartment. Things began really looking up when the Prophecy Corporation gave free laptops to every kid in his school.

Then tragedy struck. When he was 10 years old, a carload of sicarios from a rival cartel gunned down Vocab's three older brothers in the street, right in front of the family's apartment. The next day, the killers returned to riddle the entire fourplex apartment building with bullets, this time killing Vocab's mom and two younger sisters, plus four neighbors. For some godawful reason, they had targeted ten-year-old Vocab for assassination. To survive—and to avenge his family—he went to work for La Casa. After proving himself as a lookout and a drug mule, he seized an opportunity to become a sicario, performing his first murder. Thereafter, with single-minded focus, he dedicated himself to honing his skills and learned to execute La Casa's enemies with uncanny efficiency and accuracy. Gradually, word about him spread. Vocab became one of the most feared, and respected, sicarios in the Bay Area—by age 14.

During this time, he met Rasheed. Also an intrepid sicario, Rasheed was an orphan who had joined the cartel both as a way to survive and because he was desperate for companionship. The boys—two lost souls adrift in an urban war zone—developed a deep bond. Rasheed insisted on helping Vocab do whatever he needed to do—including avenging his mom, two sisters, and three brothers.

The two of them hunted down and put to death the entire hit squad that had murdered Vocab's family. It was at the conclusion of doing this—when they were putting three AR-15 rounds into the forehead of the last member of the hit squad—that they both got shot. Instead of the satisfaction of consummated revenge, Vocab writhed in pain—and grief. Jagged bullet holes savaged his flesh while searing remorse for his own deadly deeds cut even deeper. His hits—both for the cartel and for revenge—replayed over and over in his mind, plunging him into crying jags, forcing him into the fetal position, wracking his small body with convulsions. It was then—when he was at the edge and even beyond—that Peace had come to the hospital.

Strong and direct, yet gentle and soft-spoken, the old guy seemed to be the wise, caring father the two boys had always yearned for but had never known. The timing was right. They were torn up about what they had done, and were relieved at the prospect of never again inflicting, or enduring, such unbearable physical pain. Also, it seemed to Adam, the two boys had learned that exacting revenge seldom achieved satisfaction. They both yearned for a positive way forward, for what Peace might call soul-level healing and wholeness.

In the boys' eyes, Peace embodied an empathy and humility that broke with the street norm of putting on a cool, tough exterior, of macho hassling and hazing, of bragging and put-downs. Instead, simply and forthrightly and "on-the-nose," he appreciated people, he saw and brought out the tenderness, the vulnerability, the openness in others. He must have seen the boys as kindred spirits, wounded, each one bravely fighting his own inner battles. Something in them was ready to hear this message. The very qualities that had propelled them to become top sicarios—their intelligence, drive, alertness, ingenuity, and what one might call their powerful chi, or life energy—responded to Peace's philosophy. It was almost as though, on some subterranean level, they had been preparing, waiting, searching for this very thing. Life on the streets and in the cartel was all about being tough. But Peace had tapped into a tenderness below that hard surface, a simple powerful human compassion that welled up and burst out from within.

Despite everything that he had been learning about his uncle, Adam was floored. Peace had seemed tone-deaf to Adam's own strangled youthful screams for understanding. And these boy sicarios had killed more people than he had in three tours as a Navy SEAL. Yet somehow, Peace had nudged Vocab and Rasheed toward a healing path. Their transition, of course, was not instantaneous—or even guaranteed. It was an ongoing struggle with an uncertain outcome. Yet there Adam was, driving deep into the California back country with two boys who ricocheted back and forth between thuggish toughness and displays of tenderness, humility and empathy that were a delight.

As they continued to wend their way along the meandering shoreline of Pine Flat Reservoir, going deeper and deeper into Kings Canyon, the boys grew quiet.

Vocab abruptly said, "Peace's in trouble and we're running away! We've got to find him!"

Rasheed agreed, "Yeah! We've got to help him."

"You both came within a hair's breadth of getting killed not once but twice today, and you're still more worried about Peace than your own safety. You're good men," said Adam. "The thing is, getting you killed won't help Peace. The priority right now is to get you boys someplace safe."

"Someplace safe?" questioned Vocab, "Where the hell are you taking us?"

Rasheed, looking at his phone, said, "I'm not getting any signal at all. There's nothing out here, man, no phone, no text, no Internet!"

"That's part of the idea," said Adam. "You boys need to

disappear, and to do that you've got to drop off the grid. No phone calls. No texting. No going online. Up ahead is one of the most isolated places in California. It's not that far mile-wise, but it's hidden in one of the deepest river canyons in North America. There's no phone signals or Internet—unless you've got a satellite phone."

"That sucks," said Rasheed.

"So that's part of the idea," said Vocab. "What's the rest?"

"Well, this whole place will do you good," said Adam. "There's nothing like spending time in nature to de-stress and heal the soul. You boys ever been whitewater rafting?"

"No way!" said Vocab. "I hate snakes! Besides, we got to go back and rescue Peace!"

"I need you to trust me on this," said Adam. "The search for Peace will go better if you boys are somewhere safe, out of the line of fire."

The boys didn't look happy.

"The Kings River," continued Adam, "is the safest place I can think of for you boys. Think of it, this'll be your first immersion in nature."

"Immersion?" questioned Vocab. "We don't even swim!"

"Trust me," said Adam, "Your fears are completely normal. Everyone is afraid at first. Look, Peace pointed you boys in a positive direction—I can tell you that the world of the river is an excellent next step."

The boys rode in silence.

Eventually, Rasheed said, "Well, Peace did talk about unplugging from the infinity machine, the Internet. Taking time to reflect, absorb, think about things."

"*Way to go, Rasheed!*" thought Adam.

After a seeming eternity—which was, in fact, about an hour—they pulled into the parking area of the Fulfillment Voyages Kings River base camp and climbed out of the Tesla into the warm, fragrant night. Towering canyon walls rose around them, lit by a swath of brilliant stars. A low rumbling sound filled the air.

"So many stars!" exclaimed Rasheed. "Where'd they all come from?"

"They're there all the time," said Adam. "In the Bay Area, city lights and air pollution hide them. It's only out here in the mountains that they become visible. Amazing, yeah?"

"Yeah!!"

"What's that sound?" asked Vocab.

"The Kings River, biggest river in the Sierra. Follow me." Adam turned on a flashlight and led the boys downhill onto a broad, sandy river beach. "I want to introduce you now to some wonderful river guides."

*   *   *

An hour or so later, chomping at the bit to get back to the search for Peace, and having placed the boys in good hands, Adam was saying his goodbyes when Vocab took him aside and said, "I've been thinking—something you should know: There's a rumor La Casa put out a hit on a blond follower of Total Embrace, a teacher named Linda. Word is, the contract is still out on her."

"Thanks, Vocab. It's important you told me!" Adam was reeling with the news. It had to be the same Linda who was Tripnee's Gaia confidante! Did this mean the cartel also knew that Gaia was Tripnee?

CHAPTER 25

EL SOBRANTE

W ith his teeth grinding, Adam let loose the Tesla's power and flew through the night. When he was far enough out of the mountains to be back in cell phone range, he speed-dialed Tripnee's Gaia number, but got no answer.

Then he called Linda and, even though it was 2 a.m., she answered on the first ring. He told her about the death contract. "You and Gaia are both in danger."

"I'll tell her," Linda's voice trembled ever so slightly. Tough cookie!

"Leave your home and don't go to work. You need to totally vary your routine."

"Got it."

"Can't say more on the phone. Let's meet."

They agreed to meet first thing the next morning in El Sobrante, the town where she—and Peace—lived. Adam had just ended the call when his cell phone rang.

"Adam, it's BC. Those devices! One's an IED explosive, which I disabled. The other monitors all—I mean all—communication generated nearby. Super-sophisticated. Way better than anything the Oakland police have. And both send out a GPS tracking signal."

Adam asked, "Can you hack into them to locate whoever is controlling them?"

"I'm working on it," said BC. "I'm also hacking in to root them."

"Root them?"

"Take 'em over, so it'll be us controlling them, rather than the other way around."

"I like it!" said Adam. "So it would be us monitoring their communications?"

"Not just that, but we could turn on and record the mics and cameras on their phones and computers!"

"That's possible?" breathed Adam.

"Ever since the Snowden dump, NSA spy craft software has been floating around the internet," said BC. "Golden Eagle. Screaming Wind. They allow you to remotely turn on the microphones and cameras of TVs, computers and even phones. Top cartel coders can do it. And, given enough time, so can I."

*   *   *

Adam raced through the night back to the Bay. He feared for Tripnee, for Peace, for Linda, for all the cartel's victims, including its own child soldiers. His mouth was dry, his pulse pounded, and his thoughts took strange turns. He worried that while the Bay Area and Silicon Valley were outwardly the seemingly unstoppable engine driving much of the world economy, beneath the surface a virulent cancer was devouring its vital organs. Suddenly the unbidden thought exploded into his mind: *If you only knew!*

Struggling to ground himself, to sort fact from fantasy, he focused on his immediate destination—El Sobrante—the town where he had lived with his Uncle Peace from ages 5 to 18. Nestled in the East Bay hills in a grass-sloped valley between Richmond and Orinda, the low-key town of El Sobrante, which means "the leftover" in Spanish, was—or used to be—insulated from the frenzied tech boom zeitgeist that permeated the rest of the Bay Area. Perhaps because property values, and, hence, rents and mortgage payments, were lower here than elsewhere around the Bay, people felt less driven—more relaxed.

Adam pondered how the town's relative calm, combined with its being surrounded by the vibrant culture of the Bay Area, made El Sobrante a natural sanctuary for writers, thinkers, teachers and a variety of souls plying roads less traveled. Unlike many parts of the Bay Area, in El Sobrante it was still self-evident that the latest hot new restaurant, or the next big new thing, was less important than one's own inner life. Here, there was less craziness, more time to cultivate relationships, and space to carve out a life in touch with one's own heart, one's own soul. Here, people could actually hear one another talk in restaurants. Suddenly, from nowhere, came this thought: *Not much longer.*

Adam came out of his tormented reverie as the Tesla surged up the steep driveway of the Lakeridge Athletic Club. Carved into a steep hillside at the southeastern end of El Sobrante Valley, the place had changed. When he used to come here as a boy with Peace, the club had been surrounded by a fragrant forest of Monterey pines. Now the trees had been sawn off at ground level, and in their place, filling the sky overhead were towering solar panels—or maybe it was a giant spaceport for UFOs. Adam found a parking spot and headed into the club.

An hour early for his meeting with Linda, and bone-weary from driving all night, he changed into swim trunks in the men's locker room and went out to relax in the sauna. Stepping into the small, darkish room, he practiced good sauna etiquette—taught to him by Peace—by quickly closing the sauna door behind him to conserve heat. The place was packed with sweating, half-naked men and women seated on the floor and on two redwood benches, one low and one high. As people shifted to make room for him, Adam squeezed into a space between two men on the top, the hottest bench.

A man's voice asked, "Aren't you Adam, Peace's nephew?"

As Adam's eyes adjusted to the dim light, he recognized his uncle's songwriting crony and exclaimed, "Randy Mayer, it's good to see you! How's the music going?"

Randy smiled, "Good to see you. The videos are going viral! Remarkable!"

Looking around, Adam recognized many of Peace's friends and grinned. "It's the gymnosophists!"

"That's us, the naked philosophers," said Scott, who, Adam recalled, was a professor of creative writing.

"Where's Peace?" asked a female voice. It was Zuzanna, Peace's swimming buddy, a scientist at Berkeley National Lab.

Adam told them about the kidnapping.

Zuzanna exclaimed, "My God!"

"Oh, no!"

"That's terrible!"

William, a former prison guard and one of Peace's closest friends, said, "I'm not surprised."

"Yeah?"

William slowly shook his head, "The guy doesn't know when to lay low. When to play it safe."

"Peace is a love," said Zuzanna. "Always shows respect."

"But he constantly confronts the demons," said Randy. "Astonishing!"

"Real, actual, monsters that can kill you," said Scott. "The guy never backs down."

"That's Peace, alright," said Adam. "Do you know who he's tangled with recently?"

In a lowered voice, Randy said, "Peace has not been himself lately. Something huge's been weighing on him. I begged him to talk. Hell, we share everything from breakdowns to breakups to mountaintop epiphanies."

"And what did he say?" asked Adam.

"He said he didn't want to put anyone else in danger," said Randy. "I guess what I can tell you is: Peace was worried and afraid. Which is amazing! Anything that would make Peace afraid, would flat-out terrify me."

Several friends asked, "How we can help?"

Adam thanked them and said he'd let them know.

They exchanged contact info and continued talking for a long time, and then gradually, made their way to other parts of the club.

One of the last to depart was a svelte bodybuilder named Michelle, who said to Adam, "Peace is our center, our heartbeat. Let me—let any of us—know how we can help."

Although the gymnosophists had not provided much in the way of leads to pursue, they had shed light on Peace's state of mind. It was the hope of just this sort of meeting that had inspired Adam to suggest the Lakeridge Club as the meeting place for him and Linda.

Adam moved from the sauna to the club's huge hot tub. Before long, Linda emerged from the women's locker room, looking very fit in a string bikini. She slipped into the bubbling water beside him.

Adam said in a quiet voice, "You seem amazingly relaxed for someone targeted for a cartel hit."

"It's a bluff, believe me," she said, looking around to make sure they were not being overheard. "I'm scared as hell, but why broadcast it?"

Impressed, Adam said, "Why would the cartel want you dead? Could it have anything to do with your friendship with Gaia?"

Linda brushed her hair out of her eyes, leaned close and whispered, "The teachers at my school are scared shitless. If we don't pay La Casa 20% of our salaries, they'll kill us." Looking around again, she hissed through gritted teeth, "Just talking with you could get me—and you—killed!"

They climbed the steps out of the spa, went outside, and walked around to the far end of a spacious pool. With no one else around or even visible, they sat in side-by-side patio chairs, hardly noticing the aquamarine water sparkling in the warm morning sunlight.

Linda, her hands clenched into fists, said, "I think it's a trial run, a pilot program they're trying out on teachers here in the East Bay. Three teachers are already dead and two others are missing—and now, Peace!"

"You know Peace?" asked Adam.

"He's our school librarian—well, actually more like everyone's life coach, father and best friend rolled into one. He's our rock, for sure. I think the cartel's testing to see just how vulnerable a group of meek sitting ducks we teachers are. So Peace, who has more spine than the rest of us put together, has to be on their list."

Suddenly gripping his arm with a furious strength, she cried softly, "They said if we told anyone, they'd kill us and anyone we told!" Then, in a strangled whisper, "And talking to the police will get us tortured and killed. Henry Sandpiper, one of our best teachers, said he was going to the police anyway, and we haven't seen him since. That was a week ago." Linda's eyes filled with tears again and her shoulders shook. "I'm scared for Peace, Henry—all of us. What are we going to do?"

"That's easy, we put the bastards in jail—or kill 'em if we have to. We brought their California operation down before, we'll do it again," said Adam, as he thought, *Yeah right! How the hell are we gonna do that? La Casa's grown into a hydra-headed monster—a beast infinitely more advanced and sophisticated!*

Adam asked, "How does the cartel communicate? Can you describe any of their people?"

"They email and text. You never see them—except when they kill you, but probably not even then," she said, valiantly trying to control her quivering lips.

He asked, "What's your take on the connection between Total Embrace and the cartel?"

"I've asked myself that very thing," said Linda. "I'm pretty sure Total Embrace has a rotten element."

"Yes?" said Adam.

"I love Gaia," said Linda, "She's new, and not part of the underworld element. Some of those people, Proudfoot and his cohorts, give me a really bad vibe."

"How so?"

"One thing that really chaps my ass is the $500 so-called donation for every blasted event! Gaia battled the powers that be to create sliding-scale scholarships for some of us, but for everyone else it's $500 a pop, over and over! Crazy!" She paused, shaking her head. "For some people I guess it's no big deal, but for most, it's insane. How's that fundamentally spiritual? Yeah, right! They say by giving generously, you receive generously. But, frankly, the organizers of Total Embrace are more about money than spiritual growth!"

"What if I told you," asked Adam, "that the cartel is almost certainly behind Total Embrace?"

Linda weighed this for a moment, then nodded, "That would make sense!" Then, wiping her eyes, straightening her back, and seeming to steel herself, she said, "That's terrifying—and it really pisses me off!"

"Two nights ago on Albany Bulb, you said Black Elk was a creep and a phony. What do you know about him?"

"Well, when I first arrived in San Francisco a few years ago, I was between jobs, and felt lost. I went to one of his talks at his Wing Foundation, in a huge old church in downtown San Francisco. The guy came on to me. Then he tried to hand me over to his pimps. I met other girls who had the same thing happen. Black Elk hides it and keeps it in the background, but the Wing Foundation definitely has a sideline of enticing girls into prostitution. Blackie is a blackguard! He likes to be seen as a spiritual guru, but don't believe the hype. The guy is a real, genuine, hundred-percent creep!"

As Linda fell silent, Adam thought, 'Hmmm, El Patrón, Black Elk, and half the population of the Bay Area want to be seen as spiritual gurus!'

Linda looked around. Her fists eased open and her shoulders lowered. "You're right. We've got to stop them," she breathed. "I'll help any way I can." Then, smiling weakly, she said, "You know something I love about Peace? When he faces big problems, he gives them his full attention for as long as needed, then he gets quiet and relaxed, totally lets it go, and focuses on other things. I think it keeps him from getting swallowed up by the darkness."

CHAPTER 26

THE PINEAPPLE

A dam maneuvered the Tesla from El Sobrante to Oakland through morning traffic on the I-80 freeway, notorious for being one of the most congested stretches of road in the world. Thanks to the Tesla's zero-emissions stickers, he got to use the faster carpool lane. Looking past drivers gnashing their teeth in the slower lanes to his right, Adam surveyed the Golden Gate, the islands of the Bay and the vast mud flats exposed by an ebbing tide. The Bay was being drained not just of water, by the pull of both moon and sun, but of its very vitality, by diabolical forces. Kidnapping. Transforming children into killers. Shaking down teachers. Home invasions. Rockets into restaurants. This spectacular Bay view had always fired his imagination, but now it felt empty, joyless. The place was going down. We're all in trouble, we got problems.

Adam parked and plugged in the Tesla in BC's Jack London Square garage. Seeing Dream Voyager gently swaying at the public dock provided muted relief. And there, closeby across the marina, was BC's funky 60-foot Chinese junk Big Zen. Adam walked along the floating piers and knocked on the junk's forward starboard porthole. No answer. He knocked again, more loudly. Still no response. Was BC okay?

BC's bald head came poking up out of the companionway, followed by his big shoulders and tall straight spine. His broken boxer's nose came into view as his large brown eyes turned toward Adam. There was a look of grim satisfaction on BC's face. Adam tossed over the Tesla key fob.

"Progress!" said BC. "That surveillance gadget was locked down like crazy—potted electronics, eFuses, lots of encryption—but I finally got in!"

"Way to go!" exclaimed Adam, grateful for any tidbit of good news.

BC went on, "I was able to root it and break into the command and control server, so now we just might be able to spy on the people trying to spy on us. With some tinkering, I got GPS coordinates on Google Maps!"

"Somewhere in Oakland?"

"You won't believe it: Magdalena's place in Belvedere!"

No! Adam didn't believe it. Magda was Peace's friend!

He and BC went below, into Big Zen's compact but impressive electronics lab. "When I reverse-engineered the device, I used some WiFi Mac address geolocation databases, and triangulated the controller's physical location," BC explained as his fingers tapped a keyboard, pulling up a Google Map satellite view of the whole Bay Area. BC hit more keys to magnify the view, which zeroed in first on Belvedere, then on the island's southwest shore, then on Magdalena's house, and finally came to rest at maximum magnification on the roof of a small outbuilding at the edge of Magda's property.

Adam recoiled, but as this information sank in he had to admit that it might explain several things: The devices had been stuck on his boat when he was anchored a hundred yards off Magda's beach. The woman played some kind of key role in Total Embrace—which was connected to La Casa. Her network of urban farms might well be just an altruistic, do-good cover—and her ex-con farmworkers might, in fact, be cartel soldiers.

Assuming Harry Bellacozy was innocent, had Magdalena's

suspicion of the tech billionaire been an honest mistake? Or had the voluptuous woman implicated Bellacozy to deliberately send Adam off in the wrong direction?

Adam felt sickened by a sense of profound betrayal. Was Magdalena's entire friendship with his gullible uncle Peace just a ploy to keep track of a known whistleblower and troublemaker?

"If Magdalena is part of the cartel," said Adam, "I can't just show up and openly poke around without alerting her."

"And getting killed," BC said. "But if we can plant this device inside that control station, from here I can monitor and record their phone, web, email, text, Bluetooth, all wireless communications and more."

An idea forming in his mind, Adam said, "Hmmm...tonight is the night of Black Elk's party and he lives right next door."

"Yeah?" said BC.

"I could attend the party and then slip away to check out Magdalena's electronic spy base—and plant our reverse-engineered transceiver."

"I dunno," said BC. "Magdalena's spy base is gonna be heavily guarded. And from what you've told me, there's more to this Black Elk than meets the eye—and his people are going to be combing the grounds also."

Adam said, "I'll just have to be careful."

"Super-careful," said BC quietly.

CHAPTER 27

BLACK ELK'S PARTY

Late that afternoon, after a much-needed nap, Adam motored Dream Voyager on an outgoing tide, directly upwind along the Oakland estuary toward the central Bay. Once out on open water, he power-hoisted his main sail and unfurled the jib. Close-hauled, he first tacked southwest to clear Yerba Buena Island, then headed northwest on a bearing that took him under the western half of the Bay Bridge and then out across the Slot, where twenty-knot winds—winds that would have challenged other boats—merely caused Dream Voyager to list a few degrees as it flew across the whitecaps. Not long after Alcatraz flashed by to port and Angel Island glided by to Starboard, he glided into the calm and warmth of sheltered Richardson Bay. As seals bobbed nearby, he dropped anchor just off the southwestern shore of Belvedere. A hundred yards away, vast expanses of glass—no doubt all bullet-proof—belonging to Magdalena and Black Elk reflected the golden glow of the setting sun.

Adam went below to shower and change into clean dark slacks and a dark dress shirt. With BC's electronic tracer and pineapple in his pockets, he lowered the dinghy, fired up its outboard and skimmed over to Black Elk's private beach.

As he dragged his skiff from the water, a Latino security guard with protruding lips and a receding chin emerged from an outbuilding and walked down to the water's edge. The guy was fully decked out in law-enforcement gear, including an ear piece, a gun, handcuffs, a taser, pepper spray, a body camera no doubt hooked into a property-wide surveillance network, and a tight black uniform stretched over bullet-stopping body armor. As the man—who was a foot shorter than Adam but built like a gorilla—drew near, he cracked a big-toothed smile, although his narrow eyes looked lifeless, "Adam Weldon?"

"That's me."

"Welcome. Mr. Elk is expecting you. You'll find him on the top terrace. Elevator is through there." The security man jerked a thumb toward a beach-level entrance to the multi-story edifice towering behind him.

Adam said, "Thanks, but I'll walk up," and started toward a trail that snaked up around the left side of the building.

The guard, with deep-set eye sockets set close together like the muzzle of a double-barrel shotgun, moved to block his path and gestured again toward the door leading to the elevator, saying, "Mr. Elk prefers guests to use the elevator."

Adam stepped around the man, passing within an inch or two, close enough to smell the man's rotten-egg odor, saying, "Good to know," and kept walking up the path. As he followed the steep switchbacks, the dead-eyed guard fell in behind him, staying about twenty feet back. Adam looked around with wide-eyed, innocent curiosity, while in fact he paid particular attention to where Elk's property bordered Magdalena's—committing to memory, for later use, the layout of outbuildings, drop-offs, boulders, and breaks in the dense ornamental vegetation.

As he walked, Adam noticed many more guards—all outfitted like the man dogging his steps—positioned around the perimeter of the estate. How much security did a party at a private home need, anyway? Well, Adam reflected, given the state of the world, maybe this small army made sense for a gathering of billionaires, A-list celebrities, and big-time movers and shakers. Thing was, these swarming guards, and especially this guy hot on his tail, weren't going to make it easy for him to slip undetected over onto Magda's property next door.

Interesting. He recognized many of the same bodyguards that had attended Black Elk at the Total Embrace gathering on Albany Bulb two nights earlier. At one point, feeling eyes boring into his back, he turned to see the coiled, tense leader of Blackie's Albany Bulb security team. There was something strangely familiar about him. Oddly, soon after Adam met the man's gaze, the guy abruptly turned away and disappeared into a side building.

Continuing up around to the uphill side of the estate, Adam found himself wandering through a garden with its own pump-driven stream, which poured over a low waterfall into a lagoon-swimming pool. Along the way, through the trees, he glimpsed a parking area packed with stretch limos and a helipad crowded with choppers. Guest cottages were sprinkled here and there in the foliage. Whenever he looked back, there was Dead-Eye watching him.

Adam passed through sliding glass walls that rolled aside to merge the outside with the inside—to find a marble-floored, art-filled, ballroom-sized space. At its far side, through still more sliding glass walls, was a broad terrace of similar size. The entire place, of course, overlooked one of the most spectacular views in the world—San Francisco Bay—from Mt. Tam in the north around to San Francisco and the Bay Bridge in the south—with the Golden Gate Bridge dead center, directly opposite, basking in all its splendor, lights just winking on in the twilight.

Both the ballroom and the terrace teemed with mingling, chatting people. The women were slim, gorgeous and dressed to the nines, while the men were mostly wearing casual shirts and slacks. Adam noticed a number of TV and movie stars and famous tech entrepreneurs, many surrounded by acolytes. The richer, more powerful the man, the more he seemed to dress down, while the hangers-on wore blazers and even the occasional tux. It was definitely a diverse Bay Area crowd, with Asian, black, white, Latino and every skin tone in-between on display. As waiters circulated with trays laden with drinks and hors d'oeuvres, there was an "us" feeling. Something about the setting and the people, something in the very air, screamed this was a gathering of insiders, of the well-known privileged "one percent."

To blend in and escape his tail, Adam moved deeper into the crowd and plucked a glass of champagne from a passing tray. Moving in deeper still, he noticed a circle of people, drinks in hand, out on the broad terrace. Their relaxed, I-own-this-place manner communicated that they were the coolest of the cool. Oddly, at that moment he felt a sharp, painful awakening of his childhood star-shaped wound. Was it all these celebrities and billionaires that set it off?

Black Elk's voice called out, "Welcome, Adam!"

As he drew near, Adam saw Black Elk standing with tech billionaire Harry Bellacozy, FBI honcho Mercedes Montana, his wealthy neighbor and Adam's person-of-interest Magdalena, plus a few other unknowns.

Harry Bellacozy shook Adam's hand, saying, "Good to see you, Adam. How's the search for Peace going?"

Adam turned to Montana, "Yes, how's the search going?"

"Can't comment on an ongoing investigation," said Montana, rather automatically. Then, softening, perhaps in deference to the wealth and power of her present company, she said in a low, conspiratorial voice, "Suffice it to say, we're on top of the situation...."

Her meaning was clear: The subject was off-limits, and this

suited Adam just fine. The last thing he wanted was to reveal the status of his own investigation and why he was, in fact, there tonight.

The mention of Peace had put a damper on the party mood. No shit, Peace was in serious trouble and might even be dead. Black Elk, no doubt the concerned host trying to salvage his party, said, "I'm sure the fabulous FBI is doing everything possible to rescue Peace."

Mercedes, no doubt also eager to shift the conversation in a more positive direction, said, "Thanks Mr. Elk. Something I can comment on is a joint project of the FBI, the Oakland police, and your Wing Foundation: the Sniffer Program."

Harry tossed out, "Good for you, Elk. Your Wing Foundation's finally doing some good?"

Elk looked nonplussed, but Mercedes stepped in, "A grant from the Wing Foundation is allowing us to use atmospheric sniffer triangulation to locate and bust meth labs. It's one of the most successful programs the Oakland Police have ever implemented!"

Elk chimed in, "The sniffers have even located gang locations where no meth was cooked!"

Magdalena, looking skeptical, said, "Interesting. In Mexico, the big drug cartels finance sniffer programs to help the police eliminate their competition, the smaller cartels."

Adam thought—how interesting that Magda knows the inner workings of Mexico's cartels. But why would a cartel don broadcast her knowledge?

Eager to get on with his mission, Adam realized he needed to create some sort of mild diversion that would allow him to slip away unnoticed. Nothing so big that it would put Blackie's army of guards on high alert. Just something that would draw people's attention.

Adam noticed that even in this crowd of luminaries, Harry

Bellacozy's mere presence—as one of the world's richest and most creative men—drew all eyes, and his every utterance created a stir. If he could get the billionaire to hold forth on some hot topic, the gathering would be transfixed and Adam could fade away unobserved. Adam caught Harry's eye and, winging it, asked, "How are things in the tech world?"

Harry had had a few drinks and did not disappoint, waxing eloquent with, "If you're a worker just putting in hours, you're hamburger. If you're a worker with talent, you're good. Then again, if you're an entrepreneur with drive, luck, and a good idea, or an inspired friend with a bunch of good ideas," Harry continued, smiling, "the world is golden."

Noticing Magdalena wince at Harry's statement, Adam said, "Some say the tech world is brutal."

"People who are motivated and able to succeed on their own terms can lead lives of incredible meaning," said Harry. "Their work impacts millions, and their products change the world! But the creative potential is there because it's a meritocracy. Inevitably, there is a tremendous, ongoing selection process, and the mediocre get weeded out."

"If it's a true meritocracy, why are there so few women in tech?" asked Adam, feeling only mildly guilty for baiting the group so easily.

"To make it in tech," boomed Bellacozy, obviously hooked, "you've got to be hard-driving and give it your all. You've got to live and breathe tech 24/7. Let's face this fact: men are better at all-out concentration than women. That's why more men get to the top."

"That's bullshit, and you know it!" Magdalena shouted from across the circle.

"The real problem," exploded Mercedes Montana, "is that your tech bro culture systematically marginalizes women!"

Harry flashed a wicked grin, "Yeah? The real problem is

weakling, slacker, mediocre complainers—soft women and men. Great achievement takes total commitment—including a willingness to ignore complainers. Did you know that Columbus' crews almost mutinied? Did you know that Washington's army complained bitterly and almost collapsed again and again? Do you think Steve Jobs or Jeff Bezos or I would have achieved what we did if we'd listened to the complainers?"

Harry was on a roll. Blackie's guests—and even his guards and waiters—gathered around, riveted. Dead-Eye was nowhere to be seen. Adam moved unnoticed to the back of the crowd and faded away. He was finally free to do a little research next door.

CHAPTER 28

THE SURVEILLANCE STATION

Sneaking undetected around Elk's and Magdalena's properties was not going to be easy. Guards, motion sensors, laser traps and hidden cameras had to be everywhere. Skills Adam had honed in countless Navy SEAL night raids, plus his black balaclava and dark clothing would help, but they wouldn't be enough. Fortunately, he also had BC's ingeniously modified Motorola droid tracer. The size of a cell phone, the device could not only point the way to the surveillance station, it could also detect movement sensors, infrared laser traps and even hidden cameras. With it, he began moving through the luxuriant foliage of Black Elk's Belvedere estate.

Many of Elk's guards seemed to be posted on the perimeter facing outward, focused on stopping intruders. But just as many or more guards patrolled the grounds inside. On his reconnoitering trip coming up the switch-back path from the beach, Adam had noticed that guards and surveillance devices were mainly concentrated closer to the water, but were more spread out, the further you moved uphill away from water's edge.

So he worked his way uphill and inland, staying off the lit pathways to avoid patrols, and kept to the darkness, the trees and bushes. Adam moved carefully, often changing course to avoid sensors and cameras. Several times he fell onto the ground and crawled on his belly to squeeze under and through dense clumps of vegetation. One patrol passed within arm's length as he scrunched his tall frame into a tight ball under rhododendron bushes.

The actual property-line wall turned out to be a ten-foot-tall, three-foot-thick barrier of sheer brick, with jagged glass shards projecting vertically along its top. Adam climbed an oak tree, hand-over-handed his way along a sturdy branch and dropped down on the far side of the wall, onto Magdalena's property. He then crept out onto a rock outcropping, a vantage point from which he could study his surroundings.

Sitting on a stone shelf, he slowed his breathing and heart rate, and tuned in to an ancient sapien awareness—the same honing of the senses that enabled our cave-dwelling ancestors to detect, outwit and evade faster, larger, stronger foes equipped with deadly talons and razor-sharp teeth. Hyper-alert for any sound, vibration, smell, or motion, Adam searched sensed into the surrounding night for anything at all, whether tiny or big: a dog, a raccoon or a cartel sentry clicking off the safety on his AR-15 prior to unleashing a torrent of lead. Ahhh, OK! Mingled with a low, discordant hubbub coming from Elk's compound and the sound of waves lapping at the shore down the hill, he heard mice near the base of the wall off to his left, a couple of rats scurrying through leaves some distance to his right, and a raccoon dragging something, probably a fish, up from the beach—but nothing sinister.

On Magdalena's side of the wall, all was quiet. He found himself savoring the night panorama—an almost magically beautiful scene extending from the kinetic light sculpture dancing across the cables of the Bay Bridge to the lights of San Francisco and the Golden Gate Bridge to the dark outline of the Marin skyline silhouetted against the starlit night sky.

Moving deeper onto Magdalena's property, he was surprised

to find no guards or other security. He checked BC's Motorola droid tracer. Oddly, it indicated the cartel's command-and-control center was back in the direction of Elk's property! How could that be? To leave no stone unturned, he searched Magda's entire property, including her elegant main house, and a guest suite over her 5-stall garage. A state-of-the-art security system with cameras and motion detectors was completely turned off. He checked every room, every closet and found no hidden rooms, no secret basements or caverns, nothing. Once again, he took out BC's device, It still pointed back toward Elk's place.

Hmmm. OK. OK. On some intuitive level this started to make sense. Sometimes we have to spend a lot of time gathering evidence, simply to convince our logical minds of what we knew in our gut all along. Adam remembered his initial intuitive trust in Magdalena, and his instinctive wariness of Elk. So, he's got to go back to Elk's. Easier said than done. From a cedar chest in the guest house, Adam pulled out two dark, heavy, wool blankets, and from a lumber pile suspended on rafters under the main house, he grabbed a twelve-foot-long 2 x 6, and made his way back to the uphill, less-heavily-guarded corner of Elk's compound.

Selecting a secluded spot, he made a ramp by tilting the 2 x 6 against the brick wall. Walking up this ramp got him within grabbing range of the top of the wall. He tossed the blankets up to cover the upright glass shards, then hoisted himself up—and over the wall.

He dropped to the ground. Something was wrong. The hairs on the back of his neck stood up, vibrating. Had he tripped a motion sensor? For a few moments, all seemed quiet, but soon he heard someone approaching, getting closer. With dogs, who seemed to be trained not to bark—after all, this was a Belvedere estate with genteel pretensions. Even so, the dogs' whimpers and low yelps, plus the coaxing and urging of their handler, were mere yards away and approaching fast. They'd be on him in seconds.

What to do? Wait, what was that gurgling? Twenty feet away, Elk's artificial river surged up from below-ground pumps. Adam dashed to the wellspring pool and, in the nick of time, slid below the surface. Peering up through the roiling water, he could see a powerful flashlight beam light up the pool surface and surrounding bushes. Three big Dobermans straining at their leashes emitted angry yowls and sniffed the pool with jaws snapping. In the darkness, through the distortions of a foot of water, he could see and feel the dangerous pent-up energy of their handler—the fierce, coiled dragon of a man he'd glimpsed earlier. The cool water around him felt hot compared to the soul-freezing chill spilling from that muscular brute.

Blasting up from the pumps below, the ongoing belching, bubbling torrent thrust him upward toward the surface, straight toward the gnashing teeth of the Dobermans. Desperate for air, Adam longed to surface, but knew that if he did, he'd be done for. Fighting to keep his torso, arms and legs down in the dark depths of the pool, he shifted over to a shadowy alcove and brought his nose and mouth to the surface under a low, overhanging tree limb that was enmeshed in vines. Oooh! The air was so delicious!

After churning around in the upwelling pool, the water tumbled off and away, down Elk's man-made stream bed. Adam stayed deep and let himself go with the flow, sliding along, only occasionally getting clobbered by a midstream rock or gnarly outjutting of riverbank. Fortunately, his phone and BC's tracer transceiver and the pineapple were waterproof. He occasionally surfaced to take a breath, each time listening to determine if the dogs were still on his trail. And yes, they seemed to be tracking him, somehow following his scent.

Chilled though he was, his best option was to stay submerged in Elk's phony river. Sliding and bouncing along, the artificial stream carried him away from the perimeter, where the guards and dogs were most concentrated. For one short stretch, the waterway flowed by a bunch of armed guards, parking valets and limo drivers who were eating food from catering trucks— the help, scarfing up some of the gourmet goodies. Adam stayed submerged and glided on by.

Finally, far from the perimeter and, apparently, far from dogs and sentries, he crawled out of the stream just above the final waterfall above the swimming lagoon. He was close enough to the ballroom and terrace to hear the peal of loud voices— jeering, yelling, laughing. Sounded like the evening was well on the way to become another of Black Elk's notorious raucous bacchanals.

Adam pulled out BC's tracer, which pointed toward Magda's property, but he now knew it was zeroing in on something on Elk's side of the line. Sopping wet, covered in mud, he worked his way through the foliage, this time frequently checking the tracer's scanning. Twice he had to duck behind bushes and press himself flat into the dirt to evade patrolling sentries, but the tracer soon guided him to a low concrete outbuilding about ten feet by ten feet.

Looking around, he saw no one. Searching up close in the dark, he found a door with not one, but two locks. One was a key lock that he could pick with no problem; but the other, a biometric scanner, required the living palm print of an authorized user. Thwarted! He hunkered down, pondering what to do. It all made sense now: this had to be the cartel surveillance station. But he had to get the pineapple device inside in order to monitor and outwit these bastards. Peace's life, and a whole lot more, hung in the balance!

He circled the square structure, searching for any other way in. Nothing. Just solid concrete walls. Hunkering down in the dark, still sopping wet, he wracked his brain for an idea. There had to be some way he could get in.

Wait! He heard voices and sensed movement—as though far off—or, maybe, close-by but muffled by the thick walls. The door's locks were being opened from the inside! He jumped back into the shadows, glad he was covered with mud, hoping he blended into the darkness. The heavy door swung open and three guys in Reconquista t-shirts emerged.

"Hook, I'm scared shitless!" said a skinny guy.

"I'm telling you, Marvel, El Patrón'll never know!"

"But all of us? At least one of us should stay!" pleaded Marvel.

"No way," said Hook. "Got to be all of us. So we're all in? No one can squeal on the others."

"I don't like it," said Marvel. "What about El Dragón? Man, I'm telling you, El Dragón'll kill us! The Bay Way!"

"Hay huevos?" said a third voice, "Grow a pair! It's party after party around here, and we're stuck underground, glued to flat screens!"

"Yeah, it's about time we got a little something good," said Hook. "Besides, we'll be right back."

The heavy door clicked shut as the three guys walked off into the night in the direction of the catering trucks.

OK, the place—at least for now—was apparently unoccupied. But Adam checked the door and it was locked tight. So, how to get in? He hunkered in the bushes. Wracking his brain. Waiting. Watching. Hadn't he always found a way forward? If you knock, a door will open, right? Seek and ye shall find. But no solutions came. He waited, and wracked his brain, and waited some more. Nothing. As more and more time passed, his inner doubting critic amped up.

Of course he was thwarted! This was a monolithic super-cartel. Did he think he could just waltz in and plant spyware in their com center? Think again! Better to slink away and come up with a real plan, a well-thought-out adult plan. But instead of fading away, he stayed on, took long, slow breaths, and waited, and thought.

Footsteps. Through the foliage, he saw skinny Marvel, alone. The guy pressed his palm against the biometric reader and the big door swung open. Desperate, Adam crept forward. If Marvel turned suddenly, the gig would be up. But the wiry cartel geek did not look around. Instead, shoulders hunched, he trudged straight into the building. Darting forward, Adam caught the door just before it closed, holding his breath as he slipped inside. Marvel, still not looking around, shuffled across a small room and down a flight of metal stairs. Adam let the door click shut behind him—only to realize instantly that opening the door to leave would require an authorized palm to activate the biometric lock. Well, he'd deal with that challenge later.

Peering down the stairwell, he heard the hum of computers and the sound of Marvel moving around. After a while, Marvel seemed silent.

Adam glided far enough down the steps to look out on a huge subterranean bunker filled with electronics, computers, and dozens of flat screens. He couldn't see Marvel, and hoped Marvel couldn't see him. Praying that his wet, muddy footprints would not betray his presence, Adam descended the stairs and crouched behind a row of floor-to-ceiling computer racks.

As he checked the tracer, he found it pulsating—this was ground zero. This room had to be not only the command-and-control hub of the cartel's surveillance operation, but also the key nerve center for all of La Casa communications. Just like rooms full of electronics anywhere, under just about every desk and counter were surge protectors, and tangles of cords and adaptors plugged into power strips. Adam crawled to one such wire mess under a nondescript desk. Carefully, he plugged in

BC's pineapple device, which (he hoped) looked enough like the power adaptors around it to blend in.

Time to get the hell out of there. His and BC's plan would work only if no alarms were raised and the pineapple device went undiscovered. Adam knew that if he was caught in that bunker, the cartel would search the place and find the device; then he'd get the Bay Way, and Peace and the world would be toast. Definitely can't let any of that scenario happen!

Marvel still seemed lost in the forest of tech gear. Adam moved silently to the stairs and was climbing them three at a time when suddenly, he heard voices through the door. He immediately reversed direction, and silently hid behind some boxes in a shadowy alcove behind the metal staircase. Two sets of heavy footsteps banged down the stairs.

"What the fuck? Hook? Toosk? Marvel?" It was Dead-Eye.

"Back here!" came Marvel's voice.

"Where's everyone else?"

"Sheeet! Fuck!" roared the second man, whose bulging arm and neck muscles, seen from behind, revealed him to be the coiled man-dragon, the guy with the Dobermans. Was this El Dragón?

As the two men fanned out to search the room, Adam crawled under a desk. Thick black shoes passed within inches of him, but kept moving. A man roared. It was Dead Eye: "Gobbling at the catering truck!"

"Loose! Those assholes are fucking loose!" exploded the man-dragon. "Got to tighten up. Set an example." Slamming his fist down on the nearest computer table, the guy screamed, "Heads gonna roll. Whip these fools back in line. Bay Way the motherfuckers!"

Trapped, Adam prepared to fight his way out. If the men continued their search, they'd find him in a heartbeat.

Instead, brimming with rage, the pair turned and rushed back up the stairs. Whewwww! But Adam still wasn't out of the woods. The fact that they had left the bunker was good. But if they closed the door at the top of the stairs, Adam would be locked inside. Making as little noise as possible, and hoping to God Marvel was cowering off somewhere with his head down, Adam speed-climbed the stairs, racing after the men, and just managed to catch the heavy door before it locked him in. He held the door slightly ajar for a moment to give the men time to move off into the darkness. Then he walked out of the building and headed down towards the beach. Got to stop doing lame-brained stuff like this! Was he lucky to still be alive, or what!?

He had to drop flat and kiss the sand on the beach twice to avoid detection as he crept to his skiff. But within minutes he was back aboard Dream Voyager, raising anchor and heading out to some safer anchorage, swallowed up by the night.

CHAPTER 29

PINEAPPLE JUICE

"**B**rilliant! Data has been pouring in ever since you powered up the pineapple last night," said BC, his eyes glowing. "You pulled off a miracle there, bro! Don't know anyone else who could'a done that!"

Last night, Adam slept on his boat in Ayala Cove on Angel Island and sailed back to BC's Jack London Square marina at first light. The two big men sat in the belly of BC's Chinese junk, facing an array of computer screens right out of the Matrix.

"What's amazing," replied Adam, grinning, "is that crazy little pineapple device. How's it work?"

BC grinned back, "Not to get too technical, it's a superbug that can listen in on radio waves. I upgraded it with leaked NSA software and a technique called Tempest Attack to spy on nearby computers, phones, anything. The info is flowing like a river. You must'a got it right inside their com center!"

Adam asked, "Don't they have firewalls?"

BC said, "Sure. But we see their passwords as they type 'em in. Nothin' like passwords to get you past firewalls."

"Cool. But isn't their stuff encrypted?"

"Oh, yeah," replied BC, "but our Metasploit software opens just about anything encrypted. It's kind of like a skeleton key. If there is any vulnerability, any hole at all, Metasploit finds it and goes through the hole."

"These cartel techies are damned clever," continued BC. "Sometimes they use an encryption app called Signal. So bulletproof, it's even approved by Edward Snowden. CEOs use it to share passwords. But Signal only protects stuff while it's in transit. When the data's at rest on their turned-on phone or computer, that's when we can see it. It's only encrypted when the devices are off. They have to have it decrypted to see it themselves. And by data, I mean emails, texts, photos, videos, voice mail, Excel spreadsheets, everything."

"That's incredible. You're incredible!" Adam flashed a wide smile at BC. "But if they're so clever, I'm surprised the cartel techies don't take countermeasures to keep from being spied on."

"Oh they do, big-time," chuckled BC, "but we use a method called steganography, so our VPN connections are hidden. Mixes our activity in with normal data. Makes it look like something else, something their sensors expect to see."

BC's electronics lab was surprisingly spacious, considering it was deep in the bottom of a sailboat, but the ceiling was low. BC's size and ramrod posture meant that his bald head frequently grazed, and occasionally collided with, the beams supporting the deck overhead.

Adam asked, "So we're getting data. What have we learned so far?"

"La Casa is a Pandora's Box of evil," said BC. "Spewing all kinda shit into the world!"

"Show me!"

BC pointed at a computer screen that was streaming text and numbers. "Ever drink from a venom-filled firehose? It's mostly random bits and pieces of information. Gonna need sleuthing to put it all together."

Adam asked, "It's all odd pieces?"

"Every so often, we get a beautiful big chunk," said BC,

releasing an appreciative sigh, "One chunk was a list of passwords, syncing a password manager database unencrypted over what they thought was a private network. A treasure trove!"

"So, things are fitting together?"

"We're a long way from seeing the whole picture, but already the data shows they're deep into drugs, kidnapping, robbery, human trafficking, and extortion."

"Yeah?" said Adam, leaning forward.

"Well, for example, Elk's whole WealthWatch thing, his TED Talks, and the fancy Wing Foundation fundraisers, are fronts for gathering inside information on the super-rich. Mostly to find targets for blackmail and kidnapping.

"The Sniffer Program right here in Oakland!" groaned the tech-savvy cop. "Man, I worked it myself. The whole thing is funded by Elk's very own Wing Foundation." BC gripped, almost mangling, his computer counter. "I can't believe I didn't see what it was!" Fortunately, the counter was built solidly into the ship's hull and looked beefy enough to be one of Peace's creations.

"I pieced it together," BC continued, "La Casa cooks its own meth in industrial-scale facilities south of the border, so the program does them no harm—but it slaughters their competition—the other cartels and small-fry tweakers who cook meth locally. I should have figured that one out!"

BC fell silent for a moment, then remarked, a tremor in his voice, "These bastards are even shaking down teachers and librarians, including Peace! La Casa wants twenty per cent of everyone's pay! What kind of world are we lookin' at?"

"Is there anything about Peace? Or Tripnee?" asked Adam. "Are they OK? Where are they?"

"Nothing so far," said BC, "but more details are pouring in every minute. It's gotta be only a matter of time before we find them."

Praying for some tidbit that would lead them to Peace and Tripnee, Adam searched several computer screens.

"These guys are entrenched, dug in, confident," continued BC. "They're on a roll. They're not gonna be easy to stop. But we got to! We gotta stop the bastards!"

As the two friends studied the river of data pouring in from the pineapple, they were both fascinated and appalled. The number of people involved, the torrential flow of money, the sheer volume of kidnappings, coercion and violence! It was an avalanche—a staggering, cataclysmic avalanche. Felt like having front-row seats to the Apocalypse, like pulling back the curtain on an ongoing hell that was unfolding around them.

Interestingly, except for drive-by shootings, the cartel kept most of its mayhem out of the media. How much could any society stand—even one as vibrant and resilient as the Bay Area—before La Casa broke into the open and the whole region came apart at the seams?

Not everything was smooth sailing for the cartel. Although overall, it seemed to be an unbelievably efficient, well-oiled machine, here and there, Adam and BC noticed signs of trouble. For example, a number of messages indicated that the kingpin El Dragón was not answering urgent requests. In fact, he might have gone missing that very morning. Also, some of the cartel's boats were unaccounted for and unresponsive to calls.

As Adam and BC combed through the avalanche of data, a tiny bit of info—a tidbit exposed, perhaps left unencrypted ever so briefly due to some momentary error—caught Adam's eye: an odd, extremely long line of apparently random symbols, letters and numbers. They'd seen hundreds of similar strings that proved to be useless, but somehow this one was different. Could it be an ultra-secret password? It failed to open twenty-three firewalls, but then—Aha! Yes!—on the twenty-fourth try—which involved some kind of super-protected section of the cartel network—it proved to be exactly the correct password! There, in plain view on the big flat screens were some very juicy facts about El Dragón—information so locked down, it was accessible to only one person in the entire cartel—and that person was not El Dragón himself. This info, accessible only to El Patrón, provided a way to track the man! It was just like the paranoid jefe of a drug cartel to have a secret way to track everyone—including his second-in-command. BC got on it, and suddenly there was the info on the Google map, on the big screen right before them: El Dragón's current location—the old whaling station on Point Molate in Richmond. Adam's gut told him this was significant. This, somehow, involved Peace or Tripnee—perhaps both!

CHAPTER 30

THE WHALING STATION

It was time to check out Point Molate. After leaving BC to monitor the flow of information coming from the pineapple—trusting that he would for sure relay important updates—Adam walked back along the floating piers in the late afternoon to reboard Dream Voyager. Easing away from the public dock at the foot of Broadway, he motored west along the Oakland estuary directly into the setting sun. Out on the wide Bay, he hoisted sail and, in the gathering darkness, glided under the signature tower of the Bay Bridge and then fairly flew across the Slot northward. Skirting the Richmond coastline, he passed under the Richmond-San Rafael Bridge and around the Brothers Islands with their ancient lighthouse, now an upscale bed-and-breakfast. In deep darkness, guided by his iPad GPS, he dropped anchor in a sheltered cove up-current from the long-defunct whaling station on Point Molate.

The last whaling station on the west coast, the place had been the subject of many a tale told by old-timers when Adam was a boy growing up in Richmond. The stories teemed with blood-soaked men wielding saws, knives and axes—some longer than the men themselves—chopping up whale carcasses forty, fifty, sixty, eighty feet long, then shipping them off as blubber, oil, meat and bone. As far as Adam knew, the place was now an empty, decrepit structure, probably half-rotten, with busted windows and doors falling off their hinges.

Eager as he was, Adam took a minute to dial Tripnee's number for the umpteenth time. Again, no answer. The woman was headstrong to the point of driving him nuts. Why the hell was she staying totally out of touch? Had she been found out by the cartel? Was she in trouble, maybe being tortured even now? This old whaling station was just the sort of place El Dragón would use as a torture chamber.

Time to go in. He pulled on a wet suit, strapped a combat knife to his right leg, and buckled on a large waterproof fanny pack containing his Sig Sauer pistol, extra ammo and a collection of grenades. Easing off the sugar scoop stern into the cold black waves, he let the tidal current sweep him toward the whaling station. The salt water, the Bay at night, this was his element. Beware, dragon man, just what in hell are you up to?

Adam swam among the pilings under the dilapidated building, listening, sensing into the darkness around and above him. All seemed quiet. He eased out of the water onto the bottom rung of a rickety ladder. Taking out his Sig Sauer pistol, he scaled the ladder, doing his best not to put weight where the rotten boards were weakest, ready to break through. At building level, he paused, listening. Still no sounds. No sign of any cartel sentries.

Wait. Faintly at first, then louder, he heard footsteps, voices. A door opened and closed. Then, from somewhere inside the building came a primordial roar followed by a prolonged battering and banging. The animal energy of it made the hairs on Adam's neck vibrate. More silence. Then another chilling scream, again followed by cacophonous thrashing.

Hunkered on a walkway running along the bay side of the building, Adam took long, slow breaths, slowing his pulse, girding himself for action. His awareness heightened. His senses went on full alert. A split-second hesitation, a millisecond of slowness could spell the difference between life and death.

He pulled a stun grenade from his fanny pack. Non-lethal, but able to temporarily blind, deafen and disorient anyone within forty feet, the flash bang grenade could make that crucial difference when entering an unfriendly room.

Crouched low, pistol and grenade ready, he crept forward below a window toward a ramshackle door. His plan was simple: kick in the door, toss in the stun grenade, dive to cover his own eyes and ears from the flash bang, then go in fast, ready to subdue anyone still able to pose a threat. He was about to make his move when his old star wound sent searing pain through his body—but in two seconds he was back, focused, and ready to act....

Suddenly the window above him banged open and he felt an icy steel gun barrel jam into the nape of his neck.

"Freeze, asshole! Very, very slowly open your hand and drop the gun."

"Tripnee?"

"Adam?"

They grabbed each other and hugged, looked each other over and hugged again.

"Oh, baby, it's you!"

"Are you OK?"

"I'm good, especially now. And you? Are you OK?"

Adam went in through the door, and Tripnee led him into an inner room with soft light, and a laptop open and glowing. Aha! The laptop displayed split-screen night vision scenes of all approaches to the whaling station. Clever Tripnee! No wonder she had gotten the drop on him. From deeper in the building came another howl of primal rage.

"What's going on?"

"Don't mind him," said Tripnee. "It's El Dragón."

"You've got that animal chained up?" asked Adam.

"We've been gradually softening him up. He's now bouncing around between rage and sobbing and talking…"

"We?"

"Me and Linda," said Tripnee, "She's playing dominatrix bad cop, and I'm playing sympathetic good cop. It's working."

"Tell me."

They held each other.

"How'd you nab him?" Adam asked.

"Lion tranquilizer darts. Linda got them from Wild Safari, where she volunteers. I was afraid we'd kill him if we used too much, so we used a lighter dose. Wasn't enough, and he nearly overpowered us. Thank God we had tasers. Zapped him long and good! Even so, we barely subdued the brute. Now we've got him in triple wrist and ankle manacles secured to a steel frame, and boy, is he pissed!"

"Thank God you're OK, but this is something we should have done together."

"Look, I'm outside the law on this," explained Tripnee. "This is an abduction. Illegal as hell. I don't want you implicated…"

A blood-curdling scream mingled with the stench of death and intangible sadness permeating the place.

"We're not leaving any marks, but we are torturing the guy. The information Linda and I extract will not be admissible. That's why we've got to keep you out of it. You've got to stay uncompromised, so you can corroborate what we learn, and present clean untainted evidence in court."

Without pausing, all the while keeping an eye on her laptop screen, she turned to give him another hug, "Besides, honey, sometimes you're so bound by your idealistic rules of fair play, I wasn't sure you'd go along with my plan."

"You've got a point there. In this case, though, it's damned tempting," said Adam. "But, thank God you grabbed him when you did. BC and I broke into their computer network, and they have contracts out on you and Linda!"

"I knew it!" exclaimed Tripnee.

"With Dragón coming for you, how'd you get the drop on him?"

"The guy's a macho narcissist. Too self-absorbed to realize I never bought his act of being my head bodyguard, Gaia's protector. He didn't suspect that mere women could outsmart him."

"You're actually getting him to talk?"

"He acts tough—but he's the type who breaks first. Like they say, the flexible bend, the hard and rigid break. We grabbed him early this morning. Started with a triple whammy," said Tripnee, cracking a wry grin with those irresistible lopsided lips. "We shot him up with sodium pentathol—the truth drug. Chained him up naked—nothing like taking away a tough guy's clothes to make him feel vulnerable. And used a variation on the old good cop/bad cop routine."

Just then from the next room there was the crack of a whip, followed by retching and sobbing.

"Linda is so great," continued Tripnee. "She can be a worrywart, but she's really playing her role well. We experimented at first, and found that the skimpier her leather strap dominatrix outfit, the more El Dragón went into meltdown. There's something about Linda! She's an incredible natural dominatrix. Every time she waves her bare tits, shakes her naked bottom and cracks her whip inches from his eyeballs, Dragón goes into a conniption fit. Sometimes he howls with rage until he passes out. Other times he poops and pisses and retches all over himself. Humiliates the shit out of the murderous son of a bitch. Then I come in and listen, and a very tiny scared person in there somewhere starts talking…"

"That really works?"

"Even all that wasn't enough at first. What finally worked—the chink in his armor—his secret weakness—is that he hates El Patrón. For over twenty years he thinks he's the one who's done the real work of building La Casa. Murdering their rivals. Putting down mutinies. Executing countless terrified people often with the Bay Way. Totally throwing himself into it, while El Patrón preens and prances, throws parties, poses as a spiritual guru and presents himself as the top guy. But in Dragón's eyes, it's he himself who's been the driving force, the real Patrón."

"Fascinating."

"They're both American Indians," said Tripnee, who is a full-blooded Choinumni Indian herself. "But Patrón is lighter-skinned and Dragón darker. Dragón resents the hell out of this! Poking and prodding and pouring salt into this wound really gets him talking."

"We've gotten a lot out of him. He's confirmed what we already knew about sex trafficking, teacher extortion and serial murder. They love the Bay Way for the terror factor, and because it leaves no bodies behind. Minimal media coverage keeps 'em below the radar."

Adam felt deep appreciation for these warrior women. He marveled that Tripnee, who held thousands in thrall as Gaia, and Linda, the schoolteacher, the skeptical spiritual seeker, were busting the chops of El Dragón! In this old whaling station, where countless great innocent beings had been slaughtered, a vast evil empire was finally being brought down.

Tripnee, who had been keeping one eye on her computer screen, suddenly whirled, ran to an inner door, and yelled, "Linda, gotta go! Gotta go!"

On the laptop's screen, Adam saw that four black SUVs had pulled up on the inland side of the whaling station; and a swarm of armed men were pouring out of the SUVs. Then it struck him! Of course, if he could track El Dragón, so could the cartel!

Tripnee barked, "No time! Dive into the Bay."

The two women tore out the door and threw themselves over the railing. Adam hung behind just long enough to leave welcoming gifts for the cartel goons in the form of well-placed stun grenades on time-delay fuses. Then he too dove into the swirling black water.

Fortunately, their swim to Dream Voyager was aided by a counter-tidal eddy current and by tide-borne warmer water from the delta. Still, Linda became hypothermic and too weak to swim, so Adam and Tripnee pulled her to the boat, bundled her aboard and warmed her up with hot soup, blankets and the ship's heaters.

CHAPTER 31

THE TAKE-DOWN

E arly the next morning, with Dream Voyager again moored at the public dock in Jack London Square, Adam, Tripnee, BC and Linda, together with FBI agent Judd Wagstaff, sat around the big table in the main salon.

Adam and Tripnee had doubts about the local FBI special agent in charge, Mercedes Montana, who seemed to be way too cozy with Black Elk. Judd Wagstaff was an odd fellow but had shown himself to be a clean, straight shooter—and they had to trust someone.

"Torture? What in hell were you thinking?" Judd Wagstaff glared at Tripnee, sucking on his big teeth and shaking his head. Then, looking around and taking a breath, he seemed to soften and said, "Still, I think we've got enough to prosecute. With the pineapple treasure trove, which keeps growing, and everything else we've put together, we've finally got enough to bring La Casa down for good."

"Black Elk is the prince of fucking darkness," said Tripnee. "These guys have the best lawyers in the world. They're slippery as hell. Yes, we have a lot of evidence, but to seal the case we need even more. We need Elk himself on video, talking—in detail—boasting, in fact—about the cartel's crimes."

"I can do that," said Adam. "The cartel has no idea I was at the whaling station—and knows nothing about the pineapple— so they won't be on their guard. Elk actually gave me his card and invited me to call, implying he could help rescue Peace. Ironic when you think about it. The gall of the man!"

BC said, "We can set you up with micro cameras—super high-tech—the latest."

Wagstaff, warming to the idea, said, "You get Elk talking and boasting. We'll be listening. We'll have the cavalry—including Tripnee and me—close by, ready to swoop in at a moment's notice."

Putting a hand on Adam's arm, Tripnee said, "I don't like sending you in alone. Too dangerous."

Linda nodded agreement.

Wagstaff turned to Tripnee. "You and I would be close, moments away. If you went in with Adam, and Dragón was there, you'd have an instant fire fight."

"What about Dragón?" asked Linda with a shudder.

"I don't have to tell you he's a wild card. A fierce animal," said Wagstaff. "We'll track him, just like BC and Adam did. We'll put two teams on him, and bring him in the same time we bust Elk. If we grab one and not both, the other will spook, disappear, wreak havoc."

With a sweeping gesture that took in his four companions, Wagstaff continued, "I'm glad you came to me, and not Montana. To be blunt, I think she's in bed with Black Elk. So we'll keep her completely out of the loop. We'll use teams of FBI, and local and state police who are solid and carefully screened. At the same moment we take down Elk and Dragón, we'll roll up dozens of cartel cells. And one of those cells will have Peace, I'm sure. I've been laying the groundwork to bring down this cartel for years, and now finally, thanks to all of you, we're ready to get'er done!"

BC, his eyes wet with emotion, said, "Amen to that!"

CHAPTER 32

INTO THE LION'S DEN

"**E**verything's in place. Land-, helicopter- and boat-based teams have Black Elk's compound surrounded. They're hovering out of sight, ready to pounce at my signal," said Wagstaff to Adam over the phone. "Other teams are in position to seize cartel assets all around the Bay."

Having completed his final check-in with Wagstaff, Adam asked his Uber driver, a friendly, cute redhead in her sixties, to pull out of the Blackie's Pasture parking lot and drive the final mile to Elk's property. As she threaded her way through a labyrinth of twisting Belvedere roads, most little more than driveway width, Adam mentally inventoried his equipment. No gun, no knife, no weapons at all. Instead, he had an FBI micro spy camera, with a concealed mic, in his bolo tie clasp, and a second camera in the zipper pull of his black Baubax bomber jacket. In addition, from his own gear stash, Adam had a high-tech nano camera, with mic threaded into his thick hair: an ingeniously tiny device on a soft wire, with two bulbous ends the size of match heads.

Twenty-foot stone columns flanked Elk's fortress-like front gate. No gatekeepers were visible, but when Adam got out to engage the intercom, Dead-Eye, from the night of the party, plus three other frowning, heavily armed guards materialized out of a side door. The mere sight of the place and guards caused the Uber driver's face to go ashen. With pursed lips and white knuckles, she jammed her red Honda Accord through a three-point turn and sped away.

After a thorough pat-down, Adam was invited to ride a posh chauffeured electric cart down a steep driveway that snaked through dense ornamental greenery. As the stretch-limo-style golf cart pulled up by Elk's swimming lagoon and palatial main entrance, Adam's old shoulder wound flared, making him almost pass out. Stunned, he plunged back, back, back to the moment when he was a five-year-old, and his mom and dad imploded before him in a hail of bullets, just as they were tucking him into bed. The pain, though, was something he knew how to handle, and Adam soon willed himself to come back into the present.

Black Elk came rushing as fast as his odd short legs would carry him, his amorphous mass of gray hair blowing in the Bay breeze. "Absolutely great to see you, Adam!" The guy seemed downright joyous. Weird, thought Adam. Oddly, a deja vu feeling nibbled at the back of his mind. Did he know Elk from somewhere long ago?

The older man radiated energy, as though lit by an inner fire. How the hell did despicable people live with themselves? If there was any justice, evil-doers should suffer and get dragged down. But this villain bubbled and waved expansively, as if he was on top of the world.

Well, so be it, thought Adam. *Expand, get loose, gush, flow. Let your guard down and let it all hang out. The better to catch you out and capture your true nature on video.* Cameras are rolling, and we're streaming everything.

"What a world! What a life! So wonderful to have some private time, just you and me, my boy!" said Elk as he ushered Adam through the grand entrance and then into a spacious office with a desk, couches, walls of books and that billion-dollar view of the Bay and Golden Gate.

Amid the avalanche of feelings Black Elk evoked in Adam, there was some kind of weird bond, a twisted recognition, a thread of rapport, even empathy. *Real or not, this was good,* Adam thought. To get this guy to open up, he would have to: first, lay on the flattery—narcissists eat that up. Second, play to Elk's sense of victimhood—almost everyone these days—especially the guilty—feels like a victim. Third, and perhaps most important, Adam would have to plunge deep into his own dark side to find common ground, a palpable connection.

Finally Adam said, "I was at Albany Bulb four nights ago, and it was painful to see Gaia steal the spotlight."

Black Elk looked at him keenly. "The crowd adores her."

Adam continued, "Anyone with a brain could see you were letting the crowd think *she* was the guru. It's obvious you're the real deal. *You* deserve the adulation."

Black Elk seemed to drink this in, and mused, "Yeah?"

Adam continued, "For you to play second fiddle to Gaia has gotta suck!"

Elk blurted, "You're damned perceptive, Adam. Yes, it galls me—GALLS ME!—to have to stay in the shadows while the Gaia woman takes the spotlight!"

"Can I level with you?" asked Adam.

"Absolutely!"

"You, Elk, are an extraordinary man."

"Well, I admit I've done extraordinary things," beamed Elk. "Did you see me in the media? Me partying with the president! Who would'a thought! Me! Is this a great country, or what!"

"It's obvious," said Adam, "you're the creative impulse behind not just the Wing Foundation, but also Total Embrace, and a whole lot more."

"Such sweet music, especially from you," said Elk, smiling

broadly, spreading his arms wide. "OK, OK, you got me. I'm a genius, a phenomenal genius."

Elk regarded Adam with a level of attention the younger man found hard to read: a blend of amusement, condescension, pride, excitement and paternal affection. And damned if Elk wasn't bubbling with joy! Adam, forgetting himself, almost regretted for a moment the grief he was about to bring down on Blackie.

Adam responded, "It's great to really get to know you. How do you do it?"

"Adam, you're amazing yourself. Two great spirits together can travel where neither could alone," said Elk. "I really see you, Adam. I know what you've done. What you're capable of."

Yikes, thought Adam, *how much did Elk know? Who was playing whom?*

Elk continued, "Adam, you and I are imagination workers. We imagine things into being. Once we perform the miracle of imagining, of creating the vision, then the specific concrete steps to manifest the vision become obvious, and can be done by other, lesser people.

"Interestingly, I have an associate who—though effective on his level, a lower level—is blind to the hierarchy of things. He can't understand that the vision, the imagining of the thing, is the genius. Doing specific steps to bring the vision into being is important. But that's like falling off a log compared to the godlike task of creating the vision out of nothing. Creating things out of chaos." Elk grabbed Adam by the shoulders, "Chaos, Adam, that's the enemy. Order, that's the goal!"

Adam said. "So you create order?"

"Order! I could tell you about order!" said Elk, drawing himself up, thrusting out his chest, "Without me, there'd be utter chaos."

While the two talked, the deja vu feeling gnawing at the back of Adam's mind grew stronger. Studying the guy in close proximity, it dawned on Adam that under his mushroom cloud of wild grey hair, Elk's head—from what he could tell—was as round as a bowling ball. A thought struck him, but no, it couldn't be. That guy was long dead. And much taller. But so similar!

Adam asked, "Have we met before?"

Elk replied, "I was wondering when you'd catch on. You're no fool."

Adam blurted, "Reamer Rook?!!"

"That's me. Your other dear uncle."

"Impossible! He's dead! Died in the Kern flume penstock generator."

"No Muss No Fuss."

Adam stood there open-mouthed.

"Hey," said Rook. "I invented No Muss No Fuss. Naturally I left myself an escape hatch."

This was astonishing—and courtroom gold!

"You're really Reamer Rook!! You had a secret way to escape the Kern penstock?"

"Of course. This isn't some novel or movie. This is real! What idiot wouldn't set up an emergency escape hatch? A last flume hatchway no one knows about. Except a power company guy who mysteriously disappeared."

Adam had a flash of insight: "You and Toro Canino. Proudfoot—El Dragón—is Toro Canino!"

"Bright boy."

Adam frowned, and exclaimed, "Impossible. Reamer Rook was six foot six."

"You never heard of people getting their legs shortened in Sweden? They took two inches out of my upper and lower legs, and, voila, I went from six foot six to six two. Also, they did some cosmetic and vocal cord surgery. Changed my face and voice. The ultimate disguise. Except to someone like you."

Adam said, "So Peace's kidnapping is about revenge."

Rook said, "And getting back Indian Rock Resort—or at least the value of it!"

Adam turned away, descending into the old torment, remembering how Rook and Toro Canino had slaughtered his father and mother—Rook's own sister—in that storm of bullets. Finally, finally this heinous man would get what was coming to him!

"I'm the oldest son! That land was mine! My own bastard father gave my birthright to your mother—my sister—all because I looked too pale, too god-damned white!"

"You slaughtered my dad and mom—your own sister!"

"Of course I killed to get it back! And I'd do it again!" yelled Rook as he pulled a Glock pistol from a desk drawer, leveling it at Adam. "Hey, if there had been another way, I would have taken it. But your stubborn mom gave me no choice. No fucking choice! Besides, your folks did nothing with it. It was me—me—that built it from a rocky dirt patch into a world-class destination resort!"

Adam reeled. But the anguish was familiar territory, and he had a mission to complete, so he said, "Indian Rock Resort was a front, and a laundering operation for your drug trade?"

"Hey, I admire how you handled yourself figuring that out. And now again, I admire how fast you're figuring out my current operation. Nowadays, to me, a half-billion-dollar property like Indian Rock Resort is small potatoes. But I wanted it to even the score. And for old time's sake. It's my birthright!"

Adam asked, "How's that going to work?"

Rook said, "That's all changed. We grabbed Peace and let you and Tripnee keep running around so you could pay the ransom. Unfortunately, you're all just too smart. I figured as much. And you're way too dangerous. So, to hell with the ransom and getting back the value of my beautiful resort." He shrugged, "With regrets, I'm actually sorry, but you all have to go the Bay Way."

"Since you're coming clean," said Adam, "I'll do the same. This entire meeting has been recorded and streamed to a remote location. Even now, your organization is being rolled up. Resistance is futile. The jig is up. You're busted. I trust you know that if you cooperate from here on out, it will go better for you. So, put down your gun and tell me, where is Peace?"

Rook just laughed, then said quietly, "You're darn good, Adam. Makes me proud. But you're about to discover that I'm untouchable, and you're in deep shit."

CHAPTER 33

EMBRACING WHAT IS

If a guy like Reamer Rook is upbeat when he should be miserable, maybe he knows something. Truth be told, something *was* terribly wrong. Dead-eye and three guards, different men from the gate crew, entered and took up positions along the bayside of the room, their Uzis aimed at Adam. As the minutes ticked by, no choppers, no boats, no teams of state troopers or FBI agents, nothing. Taking no chances and leaving him no opening, they shackled his ankles and handcuffed him behind his back. In an even more thorough search than earlier, they found and removed his bolo tie clasp and zipper pull micro cameras—but not the one in his hair.

As the reality of defeat sank in, Adam looked out Rook's floor-to-ceiling windows at the broad Bay spread out before him. The splendor was there, but now it all felt empty, flat, devoid of meaning.

Rook said, "I'm torn, young man. Frankly, you really piss me off. But you're kin. You've got talent. Hell, you're right up there with me. We could've been an amazing team. But it's time to face facts. You and Tripnee are just too clever and dangerous. It's time to take you off the chessboard."

The older man blew out a long sigh, his back and shoulders slumped, and collapsed into a chair. After several minutes of silent, unfocused gazing into the middle distance, he stood up straight. "People expect the hero and heroine to triumph.

Having you and Tripnee die spoils the story, defies expectations, shatters trust. But people need to adjust. The world has changed. I think everyone feels a profound tectonic shift. They think it's attributable to our deep political divide, or climate change, or growing inequality. But really, it's that there is no order. No organizing principle. La Casa is not exactly coming to the rescue, but we do bring order."

Then a gleam entered Rook's eyes, "The trouble you've caused! Call me crazy, call me mean. We've got a special 'Bay Way Wake Up Call' for couples; it's perfect for you and Tripnee. We won't just drop you in front of a speeding containership so barnacles rake you raw, and then whirling propellers chop you to smithereens. Sure, that's part of it. But to spice things up, to provide a woke experience, we chain you and Tripnee together. You won't believe it! Loving couples all lovey-dovey—get overwhelmed by terror and become subhuman animals, clawing at each other, even gouging out each other's eyes in their final moments. I know, I know. Sounds gruesome. Hey, I don't like to do this sort of thing— well, the truth is, I *do* like it. But the reason we do it is: got to terrify people to keep'em in line. Hey, I just work here. OK, I invented this particular horror. But the basic archetypal shape of things—using fear to control people, to create order—is just how things are done. It's what works."

Adam was not sure if the tiny spyware camera threaded into his hair was working, nor did he know if BC or anyone else was recording the feed, but regardless, Adam resolved to go down gathering evidence. Even if he and everyone he knew went down, somehow, someway, someday, someone had to stop La Casa. Although at that particular moment, it seemed unstoppable.

"You say you create order," Adam asked, "So why bother with messy kidnappings?"

Reamer Rook smiled and said, "Did you know I always wanted to be a writer? Like they say: If you want to make money writing, write ransom notes."

"But seriously," he said, "Kidnapping is a cartel tradition. Very nice income stream—and it's quiet and invisible. People know if they go to the press, we'll Bay Way the whole family. A big plus: a family that's coughed up a ransom never gives us any trouble. They're too traumatized."

Sickened, but hoping against hope it would eventually do some good to get this on tape, Adam asked: "Why Wealth Watch?"

"Are you kidding?" scoffed Rook. "What better way to identify kidnapping targets?"

"Why the Wing Foundation?"

"The Wing Foundation and TED Talks," replied Rook, seeming to revel in the opportunity to talk about his exploits, "give me entrée into the circles of the rich and superrich. Lots of benefits: kidnapping targets and straight out donations! Plus you can't overstate the value of a positive philanthropic do-gooder image, especially with some spirituality thrown in. I didn't want to repeat my old radio preaching. Hell, I was probably already pushing my luck. But with my shorter legs and cosmetic and voice-change surgeries, I'm getting away with it just fine—except for eagle-eyed people like you."

"Why support gun control?"

Rook chuckled. "You kidding? Our campaign for gun control makes the Wing Foundation look socially responsible and woke with the times. And, bottom line, fewer guns in the hands of law-abiding citizens makes the world safer for La Casa! Obviously, unarmed people are one hell of a lot easier to control!"

"Why the name Black Elk?"

"I admire the real Black Elk's wisdom," said Rook. "The

guy's insights into reoccurring dreams and rituals are powerful stuff. Hey, cartel spirituality is not an oxymoron, I like genuine spiritual juju. We're actually bringing accessible, practical spirituality to people."

Rook's openness was amazing, almost unbelievable. Adam realized the man had an apparently insatiable desire to brag about his exploits—especially to Adam, his nephew. Was this Rook's twisted version of familial bonding?

"Uncle Reamer," asked Adam, going for what he prayed might someday be used in court as a key incriminating quote, "Help me understand the full extent of what you're doing. What's your overall plan?"

Rook got up, walked around to the front of his desk, sat on the edge, and looked almost fondly into Adam's eyes. "I'm going to honor this, your dying question. You may be too naive, Adam, to understand. But I'll do my best to explain the deeper wisdom of what I'm doing. I admit the logic is not self-evident. But the reasoning is there. Believe me, I've given it a lot of thought.

"On one level, I'm going for wealth, power and status. Just like any man! But there's a lot more to it. We've already got the FBI, of course, and judges, police chiefs, politicians, you name it."

"Including both Montana and Wagstaff?"

"Obviously," said Rook. "We're perfecting and expanding our traditional profit centers: smuggling, human trafficking, identity theft, sex, drugs, kidnapping, extortion, good old robbery. But we're not stopping there! We're excited about new ventures, including spiritual teaching, extremely profitable 'nonprofits' like the Wing Foundation, and our pilot program in the East Bay—taxing working people twenty percent of their pay. Sure, we've hit some rough spots, but we'll iron out the kinks and then: gangbusters! So far we're mainly just in the Bay

Area, but soon we'll expand throughout California and then to the whole nation!"

"You can't really hope to skim off a portion of everyone's paycheck," said Adam.

"We charge only a 20% tax for protection and order. The combination of federal, state and local taxes adds up to over 30, 40, 50 percent—and still there's only sketchy order! A big part of our plan is to reduce existing government taxes, so overall taxes do not go up. Honestly, Adam, do you feel your current taxes are appropriate and well-spent?"

Adam had to admit that he did not. But of course, Rook was being absurd. "You call extortion, kidnapping, terrorizing, and killing at will 'order'? You're completely deluded, Uncle Reamer!"

Rook sighed. "Every big change, every important evolutionary transition requires sacrifices. Let me explain something to you, Adam. The government has gotten too corrupt, too bogged down to be effective. It squanders our resources without resolving real problems."

"And La Casa could do better? You're all goons and criminals."

"I see your point," said Rook. "I do. Many of our people are goons and criminals—but they follow orders. And we're already putting together teams of the best minds, the smartest people in key fields, to put the twenty percent tax funds to work tackling the real challenges facing our country."

Rook swung his arm westward, as though indicating something huge beyond the Bay, beyond the Pacific. "Hey, look at China. Look how far they've come. How fast. They're going to eat our lunch. I'm not saying our plan is perfect. But gradually switching to a benevolent philosopher-king style government with a firm hand is worth a try!"

Adam shook his head, stunned.

Rook chuckled, "I know what you're thinking: What about democracy and voting? OK, you got me there. There'd be no voting and no protesting. The thing is, most people barely have time to vote, and the average person doesn't protest—and, in fact, finds protesters annoying."

CHAPTER 34

THE BAY WAY

"I'll be honest," said Rook, "for me, the intensity and fun of this Bay Way depends on both of you understanding what's going to happen."

Adam and Tripnee sat naked, handcuffed together, in the far stern of a powerboat racing through the night over rough water. Looking around, Adam saw they were out on the central Bay, speeding toward the shipping lanes.

Rook faced them, perched on the edge of a bench molded onto the back of the cabin. Spread out on either side of him, bundled up in thick jackets, stood Toro Canino, Dead-Eye and three other goons, all brandishing Uzi machine guns. Oblivious to the chill wind and stinging spray, Adam studied the men and layout, desperate for any opportunity, any slight opening, to make a move—but saw none. Meanwhile, a glance forward told him they were closing in on a containership accelerating toward the Golden Gate, barreling out to sea.

"Here's a little preview," said Rook, raising his voice enough to be heard over the engine roar and ongoing swoosh of water racing under the hull. "First, some background: In some parts of the Bay Area, dead bodies on the streets are no problem. But, let's face it, in most places, corpses attract attention, generate press, basically stir things up—and jeopardize our low profile. Whenever possible, the less blood and gore, the cleaner, the better—so I came up with this idea of dropping people at night in the path of container ships speeding out the Golden Gate—the Bay Way. You gotta admit it's kinda iconic, archetypal, damn near biblical. Like getting swallowed by a whale! Right?"

Moments before, Rook and his men had marched Adam up on deck, a blackout bag over his head, wrists handcuffed at the small of his back, and ankles chained—forcing him to hobble in 6-inch steps. As he stood chained and blind, they'd cut off his clothes—every stitch—with big scissors, at times jabbing him and drawing blood. Next, they'd brought up Tripnee, similarly blinded and restrained, and sliced off her clothes as well—bruising and cutting her as they did so. Then, with Uzi muzzles jammed into their flesh from all sides, the cuffs and leg chains were removed—and they were handcuffed together—Adam's right wrist to Tripnee's left. Next, with the bags still in place, the cartel men had used their gun barrels to prod them back onto the stern bench. Finally, the bags had been pulled off, presumably so they could better appreciate Rook's preview of what was to come.

Rook continued, "Container ships average 150 feet wide and a thousand feet long. They have two to four propellers, each 30 feet or so across spinning at, say, one hundred revolutions per minute. Their bottoms are covered with gnarly barnacles, which act like a massive cheese grater," Rook smiled, his tongue darting around, licking his lips. "Time is money, right? So these ships speed around the Bay and out the gate at 20 knots, pushing bow waves 20 feet high."

Rook's words gushed out, "Picture it: The ship's coming fast. There's no escape. No way to get out of the way. You're fucked. You're driven underwater, tumbled and raked along the hull, the barnacles skinning you alive. And finally, at last, the propellers chop you to smithereens!" Aroused by his own words, Rook's body shook with apparent glee, "Like going through a hundred-and-fifty-foot-wide Cuisinart."

Aware that the container ship was getting very, very close, Adam studied the men and the boat around him, racking his brain for some way, any way to save himself and Tripnee, but their situation seemed hopeless.

"No, no!" yelled Rook, glaring at Adam. "I see the wheels turning in your head. You're desperate to escape, but make no mistake, young man. If you make a single false move, we'll shoot both you and your girlfriend through kneecaps and elbows—and still throw you overboard."

Rook leaned back and looked from side to side at his men, "Ain't that right?"

"Oh, yeah!" drawled Toro, sighting his Uzi at Adam's knees and making as though he was about to pull the trigger.

Dead-Eye nodded, his protruding lips grinning, his tongue lolling in view.

"So behave yourself," Rook said. "I like people to begin the Bay Way healthy. It's just better. After all, I'm not a monster."

Rook flipped a cover off a deck button with the side of his thick black shoe, and said, "This first button swings you out over the stern."

Adam and Tripnee sat transfixed, eyes glued to the black plastic button. Reamer Rook's foot descended and the bench lifted! On davits, like a dinghy or lifeboat being launched, the bench swung back off the stern, suspending the ex-Navy SEAL and the FBI agent out over the boat's wake.

Rook and his crew leaned forward, eyes lit up, nostrils flaring, teeth bared. Toro Canino—El Dragón—probably still smarting from his humiliation at the hands of Tripnee and Linda—directed an especially intense, fevered stare at Tripnee, his Uzi shaking in his simian fingers, an animal growl in his throat.

Rook kicked the cover off another deck button, and yelled, "This second button flips your bench upside down."

An idea sprang into Adam's mind. The cartel cruiser would cut across right in front of the bow of the containership and drop them directly in its path. If they could throw off the timing, even by a little, he and Tripnee might be dropped not at dead center, but off to the side—maybe with a chance of swimming out of the ship's path.

Earlier, with his body turned to hide the movement from his captors, Adam had managed to reach down behind the bench to search for a handhold—and had found one: a plastic molded lip or ledge that ran the length of the bench's back. If, when the bench turned upside down, he could grab that ledge with one hand while holding the front edge of the bench with his other hand—if he could do this for, say, just half a minute, he and Tripnee had a chance of survival! Even if they put a bullet through his hand, those seconds would be worth it.

But timing was everything. He'd have to grab the bench at the very, very last moment. Move too soon, and they'd pulverize his knees and elbows...making any move impossible. Wait for it, wait for it....

Rook hovered half-standing, eyes on fire, pelvis thrusting, body writhing as though in orgasm, "Aaahhh! This is it! The moment of truth! Sooo beautiful!"

Time slowed down. The moment arrived. Rook's foot descended onto the deck button. A split-second—an eternity—before the bench spun, Adam's left hand flew down over the bench back and seized the plastic molded ledge, while his handcuffed right hand gripped the bench's front edge. At the very same instant—amazingly!—Tripnee did the same thing. Fantastic! On her own, in an instant, she must have devised the very same strategy! With both of them gripping the bench, they really had a chance!

Except—damn, damn, damn—the bench changed as it spun! The front edge transformed into a slick, ungrippable rounded corner, and the rear ledge disappeared into the back of the bench—like a breadboard into its slot! Rook must have designed the bench to do this very thing—to offer hope, only to destroy it.

Adam and Tripnee, naked and handcuffed, pitched forward and down and plunged dead center into the ship's path. The last thing Adam saw as the black water closed above him was Rook, eyes alight, laughing.

CHAPTER 35

DEAD CENTER

Salt water shot up Adam's nose, stung his pinched shut eyes, chilled and numbed him through and through. Tumbling. Where's Tripnee? A tug on his wrist—it's her! Is she OK? Which way up? Stroke, kick, stroke. Aaaaaaaaaaaa-hhhhhhh! Air, sweet, life-giving air!

The cartel launch was long gone. A wall of foam swept toward them, white, glowing iridescent in the black night. The huge dark oncoming steel cliff pushing it was a towering ship's bow!

Adam went deep inside himself. In emergencies, instead of panicking, the goal was to notice and set aside fear, rather than let it take over. Peace's words boomed in his mind: "You are not your fear. You are simply the place where fear—and a lot more—happens."

It came to him: Tripnee's a river guide; she's at home swimming rapids. I'm a Navy SEAL. Water's our element. So how do we survive an eighty-foot-wide meatgrinder?

Quick! Think! Modern container ships have giant protruding bows below the water line. Big, jutting, underwater, bulbous noses that push the sea aside to make way for the ship. Much of the displaced water streams directly to the sides and down to get sucked through the propellers. But a portion of the water surges up on top of the projecting nose to flow through the twenty-foot-tall bow wave.

Maybe, just maybe, a broad, flat shape—such as two humans hooked together and spread-eagled side by side—could find an equilibrium point dead center in that wave, a balance point where they could stay put, suspended, while the rushing water surged around and past them. The racing sea water would continuously tear them off and away—but at the equilibrium point it would rip them off equally to the right and to the left—leaving them hovering, balanced—battered and crushed—but at least postponing the trip down along the hull into the props.

But how, how? It was one shot in a billion. The advancing ship was upon them. Its towering bow advanced over them, blotting out the night sky. Violent water pressure caused by the onrushing bulbous proboscis compressed his chest. Tripnee's intense grasp told him she felt it too.

He saw from the bow's pointed silhouette against the starlit sky that he and Tripnee were, by some miracle, positioned smack-dab, dead center before the bow. Water around them began to divide, most of it dove to the sides and down, but some lifted up. It was now or never! They had to get into the water going up into the bow wave. Adam started kicking and stroking with all his might. The question was, could he pull both himself and Tripnee up into that current? Amazingly, instead of feeling a drag on his wrist where he was cuffed to Tripnee, he felt lightness and support, even an occasional tug pulling him to stroke faster. What a woman! She must have come up with the same plan: Their only hope was to go up, up, up on top the underwater bulbous bow, up into the bow wave. As one being, they moved together in sync. If there was any tugging, it was Tripnee tugging him, nudging him into longer, stronger, faster strokes.

The ship's underwater nose shot under them. The water around them erupted, tumbling and pummeling, but also lifting the handcuffed pair. Tripnee's river guide instincts had taken over. Just like kicking off rocks in a whitewater rapid, she was using her feet to kick off the gnarly metal surface. Adam did likewise, following her example.

The bow wave churned and exploded in all directions. With the two of them locked together and spread out across the ship's center bow stem, they formed a kind of pancake shape, broad enough to gain a tiny bit of wavering stability. An ongoing avalanche of frigid, foamy sea water continuously smashed, battered, and walloped them not only back into the unyielding steel bow but also up, down and sideways, at times even flipping them upside down. Each shift in position upset their razor's edge equilibrium, forcing them to constantly kick, stroke and somehow body-surf back toward an elusive, impossible-to-maintain balance point.

But our biggest problem is breathing, or rather, not breathing, thought Adam. Continual immersion on whitewater rivers, getting washed down through rapid after rapid, leads to what is called "flush drowning." But this tossing and turning inside a ship's bow wave was worse. Rivers offer breathing spaces between rapids, and occasional patches of solid water provide buoyancy to get to the surface. But this bow wave was pure surging froth, only offering random, rare access to air. Exhausted, pummeled and hypothermic as he and Tripnee were, it was too long—way too long—between breaths. When the tumult of the wave thrust their heads out or there was a gap in the foam, Adam gulped in oxygen desperate not to black out—and prayed Tripnee was doing the same.

Struggling to maintain a steady position in the wave, constantly fighting to keep from getting washed down through the ship's propellers, Adam felt his strength draining. How long had they been in this wave? The ship must have left the Bay by now and steamed out the Gate. But where was the ship now? He had no idea. He only knew he had long since exhausted any remaining energy reserves, and had—at best—a minute or two left. Tripnee must be at the same point. *Well, we've no doubt survived the Bay Way longer than anyone else,* Adam thought, feeling his mouth form a tight smile. But now it was all over. What a way to go! Sorry, Tripnee. We tried.

Then, amazingly, the behemoth vessel slowed and slowed even more, making the bow wave smaller and less turbulent. The ship was going to offload the bay pilot! It would not stop completely, just long enough for the pilot boat to come alongside and pick up its passenger. Then the huge barge would accelerate to full cruising speed again and race out into the wide Pacific Ocean.

Oh, God! Adam's thoughts reeled. This would be their only chance. But even at reduced speed, suction into the props would likely be inescapable. And the trip down to those giant twirling razors would skin them alive. Shit! Fuck! Hell!

Still, again, it was now or never! The odds were terrible, but they'd have just this one chance. Adam caught Tripnee's eye and saw that she understood. He kicked off the bow, and Tripnee came with him, swimming hard in complete sync. Still handcuffed, discombobulated by turbulence, at first they scraped and tumbled along the hull—losing swaths of skin— but soon managed to gain footing, and used their feet to kick off the barnacles. Getting the hang of it—and drawing on their eerily similar experiences in running over rough rocks along river banks—they broke into a sort of run as the barnacle-covered surface slid past. This evolved into a rhythmic kick— kicking off that giant cheese grater. Ingeniously, they angled their kicks to propel them toward the ship's side, away from the propellers. Maybe it was working! Bouncing along, each fierce kick seemed to help, getting them closer and closer to the water, missing the whirling blades. Oops! Oh-oh! Maybe not! But got to keep kicking, kicking, kicking anyway! Fuck, shit, hell! It wasn't going to be enough! Aaaahhh!!!

Well, we gave it our best, Adam barely had strength to think. Probably came closer to surviving the Bay Way than anyone before us. At least soon we'll no longer be starved for air, and the pain and cold will be over. They were caught in a downward rush, unbelievable noise and pressure.

Here come the blades, was his last thought. Then blackness. Nothing.

＊   ＊   ＊

Their angled kicking had moved them far enough. They missed the blades, although just barely. But as he passed within inches of one of the ship's spinning screws, Adam was knocked unconscious. Tripnee, who had been flushed further away from the blade, swam them both to the surface, where, between gasps for air, she yelled for help. But the container ship continued out to sea, and the pilot boat was already accelerating back toward the Bay. At the utter edge of life, Tripnee looked around. There, a hundred yards away, was a light, an ocean navigation buoy! She couldn't believe it! Somewhere she found the strength to pull a blacked-out Adam over to the clanging, rocking beacon, where three sea lions were lounging around, spending the night. Two of the creatures slid off and made a space for Tripnee, who, with her last iota of energy, pulled Adam onto the dank, smelly platform. A third sea lion stayed, allowing Tripnee to position both Adam and herself alongside his sleek body for warmth.

CHAPTER 36

THE SAN FRANCISCO BUOY

Naked, exhausted, scraped raw and barely conscious—but alive—Tripnee clung to the tipsy, clanging navigation buoy while sandwiching Adam between herself and the sea lion. The rotund, nine-foot-long beast seemed to sense their desperation, and miraculously (or so it seemed to Tripnee), the sea lion let Tripnee press Adam into its surprisingly dry fur. Just barely visible low on the horizon, the lights of San Francisco shimmered like some fantasy Shangri La in another universe. The world of the buoy was black and empty, consisting only of windblown waves. Eventually, Tripnee, like Adam, fell unconscious.

Halfway through the night, Adam awoke. Tripnee—who was either asleep, or maybe had blacked out from hypothermia?—felt ice-cold to the touch and shook with convulsive shivering. He switched places with her to gently squeeze her goose-bumped form into the sea lion's warm, pungent fur. Like a gift from the universe, the welcoming critter occasionally moaned, barked softly and writhed to change positions, but overall seemed to accept Tripnee and Adam as fellow denizens on his perch.

The wind died down and the sea calmed. Adam and Tripnee were still oozing blood from their many scrapes. The dorsal fins of what Adam recognized as great white sharks circled the buoy, glistening in the moonlight. As he drifted in a half-dream, the ravenous fish swam through his mind and he had the thought, *That's going to make a swim for shore a bit dicey.*

Suddenly, in the early light of dawn, Adam knew what to do. They awoke, compressed together, his belly against Tripnee's back bone and her front embedded in sea lion fur. It seemed to Adam that the huge dog-like creature understood the gift of a Tripnee frontal embrace.

Later, somewhat recovered, they stood up, holding on to the buoy's superstructure to keep from being pitched overboard; their appearance causing a flock of nesting seagulls to take flight amid a cacophony of wing-flapping and piercing cries. The great whites still circled. Adam counted ten of them. Of course, the area around the Farallon Islands—some eighteen miles distant—was a favored feeding and breeding ground for the species. Coordinating their movements, they climbed up past the clanging bell to the buoy's navigation light, which was about ten feet above water. Adam scanned the ocean for any sign of a boat, anything. But there was nothing, nothing but more sharks.

"Yippee!" yelled Tripnee. She had spied dozens of seagull nests high up on the buoy's superstructure. Buck-naked, still handcuffed, clinging to their tipsy floating metal island, they gorged on seagull eggs, chowing them down, shells and all. Hungry and thirsty as they were, the eggs hit the spot.

"Best breakfast I can remember!"

And sure enough, just as Adam had expected, a dot appeared on the horizon, coming straight toward them out the Golden Gate, growing larger as it drew closer. It was the pilot boat, which delivered expert bay pilots to incoming ships—and picked up the pilots of outgoing ships—right at their buoy.

CHAPTER 37

NAPA RIVER

It's one thing to provide hot food and drink, clothes and a ride to two naked people you find stranded and shivering on an offshore buoy; it's another thing entirely to loan them your money, iPhone, credit card and boat. But that's exactly what happened. Astoundingly, the pilot boat captain, Dimitrios, a bearded young man with wide shoulders, a beer gut, and a hearty laugh, remembered that Peace had helped him overcome dyslexia when he was a little boy, in his grammar school library in El Sobrante. When Adam and Tripnee told the captain about Peace's kidnapping, the cartel and the Bay Way, he had insisted on helping however he could, including loaning them his personal twenty-one-foot Ranieri two-hundred-horse, forty-knot bay boat. Such things don't happen very often!

On the run in from the buoy, Adam used Dimitrios's phone to call BC and then Linda, but neither answered. As soon as they reached the pilot boat dock on the San Francisco Embarcadero, with Dimitrios' blessing, Adam and Tripnee jumped into the Ranieri and raced across the Bay at full speed toward Jack London Square, anxious to make sure BC was OK and to check on Dream Voyager, which Adam had docked there.

As they approached the boat basin at the foot of Broadway, Adam throttled back to glide slowly into the small marina. Both Dream Voyager and BC's classic Chinese junk were nowhere to be seen. Adam and Tripnee's hearts sank. Did the cartel's reach have no limits? The two empty slips a mute scream of great wrong, of heinous evil loose in the world.

Sick at heart, Adam tied up the Ranieri in Dream Voyager's spot. He and Tripnee then went around asking neighboring boat owners if they had seen anything. In all marinas, there are certain people who take note of everyone else's doings, especially comings and goings. Someone had to have seen something. But no one had. Both boats were floating quietly at their moorings at nightfall, but come sunrise, both were gone without a trace.

Adam downloaded the Apple app Find My Mac onto Dimitrios's cell phone. He entered his ID and password to pull up a GPS satellite map, which showed his laptop and iMac together, somewhere up the Napa River. Very likely, still with Dream Voyager.

Adam fired up the Ranieri and they set off. Going forty knots, they sliced out of the Oakland estuary, under the Bay Bridge, and across the growing white caps of the Slot. Then they raced under the Richmond-San Rafael Bridge, past the old whaling station, and on north across San Pablo Bay toward Vallejo and the mouth of the Napa River.

Adam drew Tripnee close. In a comfortable silence, each was lost in thought. Eventually, Adam said, "It seemed like forever, but I just realized the whole Bay Way, from the moment we were dropped into the water to when we missed the propellers by inches took only about 20 minutes!"

They continued drifting for awhile, side hugging at the wheel of the Ranieri.

"I'm still reeling," murmured Tripnee. "Wagstaff and Montana totally played me. Having me go undercover as a life coach to Silicon Valley CEOs was a scam from the beginning. They just passed my reports to La Casa which used them to identify targets for kidnapping and blackmail! And the whole time I was Gaia, thinking I was spying on them, they were just using me to rake in a small fortune on Albany Bulb! I was such an idiot!"

Adam pulled her in for a hug. He said, "We both were naive. Slow to grasp how deep and wide the cartel has penetrated. They've bought off judges, police, prosecutors, politicians, the FBI. They own the Bay Area—who can say how far they've spread?"

"Oro o agua is a powerful tactic few can resist," said Tripnee, her eyes glistening, "Anyone who resists winds up dead." Drying her eyes, she resumed, "OK, an immense monster with tentacles spread far and wide. OK. Politicians and feds and locals feeding at the trough. OK, fucking OK!" An old, intense fire familiar to Adam flared into a full-blown firestorm as Tripnee spoke, venting pent-up rage. "The world is fucking terrified and going down in flames. OK. But, they're not fucking untouchable. We've got to stop these bastards! We've just got to work that much harder! No matter what, we've absolutely got to bring these fuckers down!"

"That's my girl!" Adam gave her another long, tight squeeze.

Already they were streaking up the estuary between Vallejo and Mare Island. The Ranieri squeezed under a low drawbridge, then passed under a highway bridge high enough to accommodate an ocean liner. Ahead, broad shallow waterways blended with a maze of tidal islands and saltwater marshes. Throttling down to fifteen knots, they followed a string of green markers along a narrow, meandering channel. As they penetrated deeper into Napa Valley, the wetlands fell away and they found themselves in a defined channel with levees lining both banks.

Eventually they came to a spot where a thicket of sailboat masts bristled beyond the levee on their left. The GPS showed

Dream Voyager was close by. To scout the situation, Adam pulled in to the bank, tied up to a snag, and climbed the high levee. In the distance, as far as he could see in every direction, were the famous vineyards of Napa Valley. Spread out immediately below him was a large marina crammed with mostly older, oddball floating craft—with a sprinkling of high-end luxury yachts. Sure enough, there in a near corner were Dream Voyager and BC's junk Big Zen, tied to a pier end, floating placidly, with no one around—at least no one was visible.

Adam slid down the steep face of the levee and reboarded the Ranieri. He described the situation to Tripnee and said, "OK, let's get 'em."

Tripnee cast off and pulled in their mooring line. A hundred-foot-wide gap in the levee connected the river to the marina, and they powered on in. Counting on an element of surprise—and luck—they motored straight to Dream Voyager and jumped aboard, quickly positioning themselves to deal with anyone coming up from below—Adam beside the main companionway and Tripnee at the forward hatch. But nothing stirred. Going below, they found no one. Everything was just as they had left it, including the hidden weapons caches.

But Adam sensed they had been observed. Someone was approaching along the dock from the direction of BC's junk. He grabbed a Sig Sauer pistol P226 and Tripnee seized her gun of choice, a Beretta Nano Frame. They took up positions—Adam behind the Nav desk and Tripnee in the galley—from which they could fight off any intruder—or so they hoped.

Someone climbed aboard. "Adam? Tripnee?"

CHAPTER 38

WASHINGTON, DC

A t the sound of BC's baritone, Adam and Tripnee broke into big grins and bounded up on deck. BC looked gaunt and red-eyed. His normally ramrod posture sagged. Instead of returning their smiles, the big man stared down at his hands.

"Good to see you!" BC looked up and cracked a fleeting smile. "The online cartel chatter says you both were Bay Wayed last night. Word is you're both dead and gone."

As they caught one another up on events, Adam and Tripnee learned that although the cartel had found and shut down transmissions from the pineapple, they had not detected something BC had installed remotely on his own via the pineapple: a root kit. Thank God they had not told Wagstaff about it. Like a super-duper virus deep in the base of the computer, the root kit allowed BC to listen in on a portion of La Casa's communications, but to avoid detection, BC had to use it very sparingly.

"When the whole thing was coming down," recounted BC, "I heard they grabbed both of you, and they were coming for me, so I got the hell out of there!"

"How'd you get both Dream Voyager and Big Zen clear up here?" asked Tripnee.

"I used Dream Voyager, the bigger vessel, to tow my junk. Towing a boat that size ain't easy, but I got a remote controller—so I can power and reverse and steer Big Zen from the cockpit of Dream Voyager. Plus, I used some towing techniques Peace taught me." At his own mention of Peace, BC's eyes teared up.

"They're saying you two are fish food," he continued. "But I figured if anyone could survive the Bay Way, it'd be you. So I hid here. Out of the way, but still findable for someone resourceful like you two. If you want to disappear with a boat— or two—anywhere around the Bay, you couldn't ask for a more backwater gunk hole than this."

BC fell silent, his eyes downcast, his big hands rubbing his arms and legs. "There's something else. The cartel put out kill orders on Linda and Peace."

With Peace in cartel custody, they all knew what this meant. Peace was gone. Any sense of joy or relief that the three of them—Adam, Tripnee, and BC—were still alive and would be reunited with Peace disappeared. And God help Linda if El Dragón and the cartel goons got their hands on her.

The exhaustion of the night on the buoy caught up with Adam and Tripnee. Feeling spent, they moved with shuffling steps. Slack, drained and miserable, they crawled into bed and slid into troubled sleep. Tripnee's earlier fire was out, extinguished, kaput. Both were overwhelmed and lost in sadness at the reality of judges, police, politicians and the FBI jumping and fetching at the whim of Reamer Rook, El Dragón and La Casa.

The next morning, Adam felt even worse and knew Tripnee probably felt the same. They didn't say anything. Where do you go, what do you do, to whom do you turn, when the very foundations of your society have turned rotten? When your whole world implodes?

Adam climbed the companionway steps, dropped listlessly onto a cockpit bench and looked around. Morning light glinted off slow ripples lapping nearby boats. Two dolphins—big ones—momentarily broke the harbor surface before continuing on to wherever they were going. The world, he saw, was beautiful. Something Peace used to say came unbidden to mind: "No matter what, you've always got yourself, and that's everything."

At first, the thought did not register. But gradually it did. Something from within coursed through him. He came back to himself. He took deep breaths. The world was still beautiful—and full of potential—and he had Tripnee. His pulse quickened. He sat up straight, shoulders back. No matter what, Peace or no Peace, in misery or joy, you rise up. You keep going.

He walked over to Big Zen and, through an open porthole, told BC that breakfast would be served shortly. He returned to Dream Voyager, gave the same message to Tripnee, and got busy whipping up bacon, fried eggs and tomatoes, fresh brewed coffee, green juice and English muffins with butter, jam and honey. As he cooked, it came to him that they could and would take action—doing just what, he didn't know yet.

Tripnee and BC dragged themselves listlessly to the cockpit table. Slowly, perhaps through osmosis, they also perked up. Ever so gradually, the food, Adam's energy and that indomitable spirit, deep within, brought them around.

Adam said, "We've got to go to Washington, D.C."

BC said, "The root kit chatter says the cartel controls people clear into DC. Who we gonna trust?"

"People we already know," said Adam. "We'll feel our way along, figure things out as we go."

"I know someone," said Tripnee. "My first FBI boss works at FBI headquarters. She's not at the top of the bureaucracy, but not at the bottom, either. I can't imagine her going on the take."

"Excellent," said Adam, "I've also got a couple of friends in

DC. Let's hope to God they haven't gone over to the dark side. Let's get moving."

BC said, "You two go. You have the connections, people you know. Meet 'em face-to-face, to figure out who we can trust."

"I'd feel way better," said Adam, "if all three of us go."

BC said, "Best if I stay here. I'll monitor cartel communications. Alert you to threats."

Adam and Tripnee used Dimitrios's phone to arrange an Uber ride to nearby Travis Air Force Base. During three tours of duty in the Middle East, Adam had made some lifelong friends in the military. One such buddy was piloting an Air Force C5 out of Travis, headed East, later that very day. A nice thing about hitching a ride unofficially was that it kept them off the radar and allowed them to carry guns. They traveled light, with one small bag each. As a further precaution to remain untraceable, they picked up burner phones at a mall in Fairfield and switched to using cash-only by drawing on Adam's Dream Voyager stash.

While waiting for their flight, they made calls using the burner phones. After take-off, when the C5 had leveled off on autopilot, most of the flight crew went into the back of the plane to sleep, and Adam's pilot buddy, whose nick-name was Toast, invited them up into the cockpit. Adam felt his trust and rapport with Toast was as strong as ever, and they all opened up. It turned out Toast was based near DC, his wife worked in the government bureaucracy, and he had a candid, up-close take on the capital.

When they filled him in on their mission, Adam's pal blew out his cheeks, let out a long breath, and launched into a tirade: "Wow! You've got to succeed. There's no other option. The thing is, Washington DC is a mess. Seat of empire. Unbelievable amounts of money and power. Constant networking, dealmaking, back-scratching, and influence-peddling. Every day, every decision, every dollar is fought over in deadly earnest. One really weird thing: it's impossible to tell the good guys from the bad. There's no line between corruption and normal lobbying. Everything is fair game. No holds barred. The place is wild. Dangerous, and wild."

After they landed at Andrews Joint Military Base outside Washington, D.C., Toast drove Adam and Tripnee through morning traffic into the city. Their route took them across the National Mall past the Washington Monument, Lincoln Memorial and the Capitol Building. Sure enough, the whole place reeked of money and power.

Thinking it would provide their best chance of reconnecting deeply with their old friends, Adam and Tripnee decided on separate one-on-one meetings. Tripnee got dropped off at the Hoover Building, the FBI's national headquarters, where she had scheduled a meeting with her former boss. Adam continued on with Toast to the Longworth House Office Building, across Independence Avenue from the Capitol Building. It looked like he was going to be just in time for his meeting with his DC friend, Valerie Zizmor. A friend from his high school public speaking club, Valerie worked for the House member whose district included El Sobrante and much of the East Bay.

Adam had just climbed out of Toast's Chevy Tahoe and was sprinting up the front steps of the Longworth Building when his phone rang. It was Valerie.

"Adam? There's a problem."

"What's that?"

"I can't believe it! When my boss found out about our meeting, he actually ordered me to break off all contact with you."

"Why!?"

"He says it's for my own safety. The guy's paranoid. I'm not going to let him tell me what to do, of course. But I need to meet you later tonight, away from here."

Soon thereafter, Tripnee called to say her FBI friend had not shown up for their meeting. A coincidence?

Adam and Tripnee teamed up for the next meeting. Ty Jeppesen had been Adam's squad leader in Afghanistan, and was now an admiral working with some secretive branch of the NSA. Back then, Adam and Ty had been close in rank, had shared countless missions, and had come to completely trust and depend on one another. Maybe because, in some way, Ty reminded Adam of Peace, the prospect of seeing him again made Adam's chest ache. Above all, Adam knew the man to be a straight shooter, whose only fault—if you could call it that— was that he carried out orders relentlessly, following them to the letter.

Ty's office turned out to be in a nondescript government building in southwest Washington. Black SUVs with tinted windows that concealed their occupants came and went from a gated basement-level garage. Adam and Tripnee entered a small drab reception foyer, where they found two uniformed security guards. When Adam told them they had an appointment with Admiral Jeppesen, the sentries sat up a little straighter and asked them to take a seat. In under two minutes, Ty walked in and, with a finger to his lips, silently ushered them through a massive steel door, which Ty opened by placing his palm on a biometric scanner.

The building was a SCIF—a Sensitive Compartmented Information Facility—a totally secure building where cell phones, eavesdropping surveillance electronics and any sort of spyware would not function. The first room inside the heavy security door was lined with lockers—where Ty asked Adam and Tripnee to leave their guns and phones and other electronics. Next, they passed through a security check where they were scanned and subjected to an intrusive pat-down. From there, Ty buzzed them through a series of secure doors until they came to a nondescript conference room with a big, plain table encircled by chairs.

Once the three of them were alone in the room, with the door closed, Adam introduced Tripnee, and Ty warmly welcomed them both. Ty then got down to business, "I know you asked that just the three of us meet, but based on the situation, I had to bring in the Attorney General. He has the clout we're going to need."

"He's coming here to our meeting?"

"Yes. He's already in the building and he'll join us shortly."

"Dammit, Ty. Are you absolutely sure we can trust him? The cartel has corrupted all sorts of powerful people in California—people who should be above reproach—and we think they've done the same here in DC."

"Shit," said Ty, "The thing is, I wouldn't last a day in this town if I acted on my own, no matter the reason. I've got to work with and take orders from people above me."

The door opened and in walked not just the United States Attorney General but also a man Adam recognized as the President's national security advisor. Both men wore expensive suits and had finely coiffed hair; and something about them did not inspire confidence. But what choice was there? Ty was right. These men had the power to crush and clean up the cartel—provided, that is, they weren't already owned by the cartel. But how could that be possible? These were two of the most powerful people in the United States of America.

Adam and Tripnee had to trust and forge ahead. They laid out the full catastrophic situation, summarizing La Casa's ongoing campaign of killing, kidnapping, extortion, robbery, and sex and drug trafficking. Ty and his superiors listened with rapt attention, leaning forward, riveted. Encouraged by their obvious interest, Adam and Tripnee described in detail Oro o Agua, the Bay Way, child sicarios, the 20% tax, and the corruption of the local FBI—omitting, out of some innate caution, only the root kit, BC and the current location of Dream Voyager and Big Zen.

When Adam and Tripnee had finished, the Attorney General said, "This is incredible. Thank God you survived! It's good you've come to us!"

The national security advisor said, "Yes. We've got to get on this. You've both already done heroic work, but we're going to need your help to wrap this up."

"Yes!" Adam and Tripnee exclaimed almost simultaneously.

"We were hoping you'd feel that way," said Tripnee.

"It's a complicated situation," said Adam. "We'll need to work as a team to bring down this sprawling cartel."

They outlined a plan to take down La Casa, going into a fair amount of detail.

The Attorney General said, "We all have our work cut out for us on this one. Speaking of which, I'd like to adjourn this meeting and get started. I've taken the liberty of calling an Uber for you. It should be waiting out front. In the morning, we'll all fly to San Francisco."

They all shook hands. Adam and Tripnee were exuberant. Leaving the room, they retrieved their guns and cell phones and made their way out of the building.

Outside, it started to rain. The car was waiting, but just as they reached it, another young couple rushed up and claimed it, insisting it was theirs. Tripnee put her arm through Adam's and pulled him away, laughing, "No problem. I feel like walking anyway. The cool rain really feels good." So they happily walked off.

They hadn't gone half a block when they heard a loud explosion. They looked at each other and Tripnee said, "The car! Those poor damn people."

Sure enough, as they stepped out into the street, they could see the Uber in flames two blocks away. Adam called a second, random, real, hopefully safe Uber and they headed for their hotel.

En route, Tripnee tapped her phone to check on her FBI friend. It was the friend's work number, and she talked quietly for a while. Putting away her phone, she sobbed, "My friend! She's dead! Killed by a car bomb this morning!"

Adam, stunned but thinking fast, told the driver to take them directly to the airport.

Then he called his old high school friend, "Valerie? It's Adam. Your boss is right. It's too dangerous for us to meet."

"To heck with that, Adam. You're facing something really big and important, and I want to help."

Adam said, "Just hearing that helps. But for your sake, for now, it'd be best for us not to meet."

"You've got to be kidding!"

"You're wonderful, Val. But trust me. I'll be in touch as soon as I can."

Adam clicked off, wondering if even those last few words put his friend in greater danger. He had no way to protect her. The less she knew and the less contact he had with her, the safer she would be.

Then, Adam got a secure text message from Jeppesen. "Something's terribly wrong. I'm getting zero cooperation, and instead expect retaliation from above. You and Tripnee must go into hiding immediately. Be super-careful. This could take time. I've exhausted my options for now and have to keep my head down and bide my time. Watch out. Stay alive to fight another day."

His old pal was doing him a solid. They'd hit a wall in DC. It was what Toast would describe as a sea of corrupt deep state functionaries, with cartel operatives mixed in. People focused entirely on lining their own pockets—oblivious to the public good—or the dire threat to the Bay Area and the nation.

Well, they'd confirmed the cartel's reach was long and wide. The fact was, they were probably in greater danger in DC than they would be in the Bay Area. Obviously, just barging in full tilt had not worked. They needed to give this a great deal more thought and come up with a sophisticated strategy. In fact, to stay and continue to knock about would likely get more innocent people killed. For now, it was not only best—it was essential—to think of their own safety.

Time to retreat. They shipped their weapons via Fed Ex and used fake IDs—hers from an FBI assignment a decade before, and his from his stint in Navy SEAL black ops—to board the next flight back to the Bay. As they settled into their seats, Tripnee said, "They'll think us dead—just two bodies in a bombed-out car."

CHAPTER 39

I-80 EAST BAY FREEWAY

U pon landing in Oakland, just before getting off their plane, after the other passengers had deplaned and while the flight staff was preoccupied, Adam and Tripnee ducked down and put on rough disguises—a nondescript wig of medium-length brown hair, mirror sunglasses, jeans and blue dress shirt for Adam and a blonde Dolly Parton wig, blue contacts and baggy sweats for Tripnee. These costumes wouldn't stand up to close inspection, but should throw off anyone watching for them at the airport.

They left the plane separately. By prearrangement, Adam hired a taxi at the north end of the airport—and then had stopped briefly on the airport's south side to pick up Tripnee.

They felt relieved—and oddly safer—to be back in the Bay Area—even though it was swarming with people looking to kill them on sight. Eager to make sure BC was OK, they directed the cab to head north along the East Shore Freeway I-80 through Oakland, Berkeley, Albany, and El Cerrito. In Richmond, something caught Adam's eye. Three black SUVs in single file accelerated to match their speed one lane over. Adam and Tripnee's taxi, in the fast lane, was blocked by cars ahead of and behind it. They were sitting ducks. The whole thing unfolded fast, but Adam experienced it in slow motion, like some dystopian ballet of freeway death. As the three SUVs came up alongside, their windows rolled down and gun barrels poked out—all with good angles of fire on the boxed-in taxi. Adam threw Tripnee to the floor and himself on top of her, hoping to protect her, and, in the same instant, yelled out to warn their driver—who, seeing the gun barrels swinging toward him, screamed in horror.

At that exact instant, the strangest thing happened. The vehicle right behind the taxi, a white minivan, sprayed a torrent of lead into the three SUVs, riddling them with bullet holes, instantly ending any threat. Poking his head up, Adam saw that it wasn't just the volume of fire from the minivan, it was the uncanny accuracy. From what he could make out, the would-be shooters in all three SUVs went down immediately. The three drivers, though, were spared and veered away to get out of the withering fire, soon crossing the slow lane and slowing on the shoulder. It had all begun and ended in under two minutes.

Adam reassured Tripnee and the cab driver that it was over. He was astonished when he looked back at the minivan. There, laughing, were the two former cartel sicarios, the boys Vocab and Rasheed.

Deeply rattled from the encounter, the taxi driver gripped his steering wheel with white knuckles and drove erratically. He weaved in his lane, but managed to continue up the freeway, with the minivan following close behind. After several miles, Adam had him get off the freeway, and drive in circles on surface streets to make sure there were no more tails. Figuring the taxi might still be on the cartel's radar, Adam and Tripnee joined Vocab and Rasheed in the minivan. Obviously thrilled to have his taxi empty, the driver, a white guy in his sixties who was now covered in sweat, took off like a shot.

"I'm sorry, Adam," said Vocab. "We know it's bad to kill. We promise not to keep doing it, but…"

"You saved us!" Adam and Tripnee jubilantly thanked and hugged the boys. And then thanked and hugged them again.

The minivan crossed the Carquinez Bridge, did more tail-shaking maneuvers, and took them to the Vallejo ferry terminal. Its driver and owner was another of Peace's ex-lost boys and a longtime friend of Vocab's, but it seemed safest for all concerned to free him up and send him on his way ASAP. He seemed relieved, and sped off, leaving the four of them to arrange with a Lyft driver for an off-the-app, off-the-record ride to the Napa River. At the marina, Adam and Tripnee helped Vocab and Rasheed carry their duffles—now with their AR-15s inside—along the floating docks to Dream Voyager. When they were all out of sight below deck, they again let loose their feelings, hugging and sharing and pouring forth thanks and more hugs.

BC came over, his eyes sparkling, laughing to see them all OK.

Adam said, "You boys are supposed to be safe and sound up on the Kings River!"

"Don't get us wrong," said Vocab, "we love the river!"

"Yeah, we love the Kings…all except the "no wifi" part," said Rasheed.

"Just thought we'd come back and see if we could help ya'll," said Vocab.

Adam glanced questioningly at the duffle bags containing their AR-15s.

"Oh, you remember when you let us each pack a duffle? Well, we sure weren't going to leave our guns behind, with a war still going on," said Vocab.

Tripnee asked, "But how in the world did you know we were flying in, and know to follow us from the airport?"

BC jumped in, "I've been monitoring the root kit. When I heard the cartel had three hit squads set to follow you out of Oakland Airport, I guessed things didn't go so well back in DC."

"Early, early today," said Vocab, "we hitched a ride out of base camp…"

"Yeah, OK, we snuck out," interjected Rasheed.

"…and we just arrived back in Oakland when we FaceTimed BC…" said Vocab.

"Hey, I was desperate, you two were set to die," said BC, looking at Adam and Tripnee, "so I asked for their help."

Both Adam and Tripnee rocked their heads in amazement—and gratitude.

"We were goners!" marveled Tripnee, her cheeks wet, looking adoringly at Vocab, Rasheed and BC. "You saved us!!!"

Adam and Tripnee filled them in on the DC trip. BC, and, clearly, everyone present, felt stunned and overwhelmed by how deeply the cartel's tentacles had penetrated the highest levels of government.

"It's so bad," said Adam, "even telling someone about the situation can get them killed. We don't know the exact extent, but the cartel seems to have almost unlimited sources of information and influence."

As they brought each other up-to-date, Adam recounted his final encounter with Reamer Rook.

BC said, "The micro hair camera probably got washed away in that bow wave, but it recorded and streamed right up until you got dropped in the water."

Hearing this, Vocab and Rasheed exchanged glances. Vocab asked, "We'd like to see that footage!"

BC said, "Sure," and hit a few keys on his laptop. The big screen in Dream Voyager's main salon sprang to life, and they watched Reamer Rook's full rant. There, sharp and clear, big as life, were El Patrón and El Dragón, salivating, doing the Bay Way, El Patrón fulminating about supplanting the government and bragging about the cartel's horrendous deeds.

As they watched, Vocab and Rasheed kept nodding at each other and, at times, chuckled with delight.

When the showing ended, Vocab could barely contain his excitement, "If made into a good video, this footage could be the crowning evidence that could put El Patrón and La Casa away. Maybe get 'm the death penalty. We've made a whole series of videos—about break dancing, street racing, and Peace's wisdom—that've gone viral. Been seen by forty four million people last time I checked. Mind if we make a copy of this footage and have a go at editing it?"

CHAPTER 40

THE JOHN GREY

"You're not going to believe it, but there's something I've got to tell you," said BC. "Something strange over in the far corner of this marina."

Intrigued, Tripnee asked, "What's that?"

"There's an old vessel over there," said BC, "the hundred-twenty-foot John Grey. It's stout enough, and has a big enough bow, to go out to sea. But overall, it has the look of a Congo river boat out of The Heart of Darkness."

"Caught my eye, too," said Adam, "a real classic. But what about it?"

"I've been keeping a low profile," said BC, "as low as you can with two boats that stick out like sore thumbs. I've picked up vibes that this other boat is also hiding, keeping a low profile. I figured most likely it was just sailors who like their privacy. Who doesn't? But privacy-loving or not, most live-aboards are neighborly—not these people...they got a hostile, keep-away vibe."

Rasheed, leaning forward with interest, said, "You've got to listen to your gut, man."

"So, yesterday," continued BC, his voice getting lower, more intense, "I hear two guys from the boat talking in the marina cafe! I swear they've been around Peace, channeling the guy."

"How so?"

BC fiddled with his phone, laid it on the salon table and said, "Listen to this!"

From BC 's phone speaker came a gravelly male voice, "Hey, we deal with all kinds. They're pissed, they're unhappy, they heap scorn. OK. Same ol', same ol'. But this guy, phenomenal! None of that. Hard to put my finger on it, but he's different."

At the sound of another, higher male voice, Adam and Tripnee exchanged glances. Both voices rang a bell.

The second voice said, "The guy listens. He's got curiosity, man, really. Hey, I seen fakes; he's no fake. The guy's learning all the time, and I swear he really just plain appreciates people. I know, I know, it sounds crazy, but he treats everyone like the Messiah."

The first, deeper male voice: "Yeah, yeah, still, you know what we gotta do."

The second voice: "No way 'round it."

Tripnee said, "I've heard those voices before!"

Adam said, "Yeah, me too. But, it's odd, if they're Peace's kidnappers, it's strange they talked like that in public."

BC said, "Big as I am, in my old boat clothes, there's certain people who write me off or don't see me. These guys look tough, like Latino gangster hit men, not like boat people. Definitely not people you'd expect to be talking about listening to and appreciating people."

Vocab said, "I can tell you. Those guys are stressed. They've long since gotten a kill order on Peace. And Peace's days, maybe his minutes, are numbered!"

They rapidly formed a plan.

*　　　　　*　　　　　*

Twenty minutes later, Adam, wearing his wet suit and watertight fanny pack, slid off Dream Voyager's water-level stern platform, and swam quietly through the darkness, glad the backwater marina had few lights. The John Grey, moored alone on bow and stern anchors in a far corner of the boat harbor, had a mostly one-story superstructure, divided into individual cabins—each with a door to the wrap-around main deck. Below the main deck, portholes about two feet off the water, some lit, some dark, dotted the hull on either side.

Moving silently, Adam paused at each porthole to look and listen. The first three were closed and quiet, with no one visible, but the fourth was open. A voice—the deep gravel voice from BC's recording—said, "We got the order a long time ago. Shoulda been done already! We've got to do the deed and confirm it's been done!"

Adam unzipped his waterproof fanny pack, and pulled out his Sig Sauer, careful to hold it above water.

"OK, you want to do it?"

Adam silently pulled up eye-level with the porthole, and peered in to see two men. A smaller man on the left and to the right, a big muscular figure, who at that moment drew a Glock pistol from a shoulder holster. Of course! The voices. Big macho and mini-macho. It was Mack Dowell and Hektor, Rook's Kern River hit men!

Mack Dowell said, "Well maybe I'll check my gun," and started to clean his weapon.

Adam considered putting a bullet into the head of each man right then and there. Clearly, they were holding Peace prisoner. But something held him back.

After a while, Mack Dowell said, "You know, the guy knows what he's doing. Making this darned hard on us."

Mack Dowell continued cleaning his Glock, taking his time about it. Adam judged the time was right to make his move. But still, he delayed.

After a long while, his gun clean, loaded and ready, Mack Dowell finally said, "Hektor, could you do it?"

The reply was slow in coming, but finally Hektor said, "OK."

"Well?"

"Ok. OK."

It was time. With his left hand, Adam pulled himself up eye-level with the porthole, his Sig Sauer ready in his right hand to plug the men. But when he looked in, Hektor was just disappearing through a door to the right. Feeling sick, expecting to hear the report of Hektor's gun any second, Adam kicked himself. 'What the hell is wrong with me?'

But he heard no gunshot, and about ten minutes later, Hektor re-entered the cabin and sat back down in his spot, saying nothing.

After a while, Mack Dowell said, "This is what we've been doing for days!"

"Dithering."

"Waffling."

"Gonna get us killed!"

"You know what I'm thinking? We've known Rook longer than anyone. Have you ever known him to forgive not following an order?"

"Never!"

"Exactly!"

"How he thinks, he'll use us as a fucking teaching moment. And he'll kill us as a lesson for everyone else!"

"Seen it so many times."

"Yeah, you know he will! So, does it make sense? We kill Peace, only to have the cartel kill us? I say we at least let the old guy live."

"We're dead either way!" There was a long, loud groan. "Dammit!!"

"Hey, as long as we're alive, there's a chance. Right?"

"Not really. We'll be fighting the tide, fighting the wind!"

"Insane, man. We're insane!"

The two men just sat there, immobile, undecided. Eventually, their heads hanging down, they fell asleep. Adam circled the ship, and confirmed that the only three people aboard were Hektor, Mack Dowell and Peace. With all three snoring away, he swam to the bow anchor chain, where he quietly called Tripnee and BC to apprise them of the situation and fine-tune the plan.

While Tripnee and BC quietly paddled a dinghy up to the John Grey's starboard side, Adam silently boarded the port side. Moving with great care, Adam checked doors along the wraparound deck. Each was securely locked by a keypad latch and heavy-duty deadbolt, which rendered Adam's lock-picking skills useless. Hektor and Mack Dowell might not be following cartel orders, but they were still running a tight ship.

Tripnee and BC had worked their way around the boat, Tripnee going clockwise, BC in the other direction. They all met up in front of a large door that seemed like a main entrance and probably led to stairs that went down to lower levels of the ship. But there seemed to be no way in, without bashing the door down—and raising the alarm. Surprising these guys in their bunks would be so much safer for Peace! But one way or another, they were going in!

The John Grey's superstructure was one-story high at the stern, but three-stories tall forward. After signing for Tripnee and BC to stay put and cover him, Adam pulled himself up to the second level. Again, he found every door closed and bolted. Determined, he scaled to the bridge on the third level, where again every door was battened down tight.

Finally, Adam discovered a closed but unlocked window on the bridge. It was way too small to fit through, but he was able to reach in and unlock a nearby door. With his Sig Sauer at the ready, Adam entered and made his way down into the John Grey, making sure each cabin was clear of bad guys as he went.

On the level of the main deck, Adam opened the door for Tripnee and BC. With guns drawn, the three of them silently, swiftly made sure the cabins on that level were clear, then descended an interior stairway deeper into the ship. Right where Adam judged it should be, they found a cabin door, behind which came loud snoring. This interior door was unlocked.

With his fingers, Adam signaled the one-two-three order they would enter. Tripnee went in first and swung right, BC was next and swung left, and Adam brought up the rear and took center. Hektor and Mack Dowell continued to snore away in their bunks, each within reach of his Glock. Adam and Tripnee each took a man, while BC covered the whole room, providing backup for both. Tripnee pressed the barrel of her Beretta into Hektor's neck while grabbing up his Glock with her other hand. Adam simultaneously did the same to Mack Dowell.

"Don't fucking move! Stay put and we won't hurt you."

The men woke with a start, surprised out of their gourds. Both reached for their weapons, but, finding them gone, froze.

"Move like that again and you're dead. Nod if you understand."

Both men nodded. Adam and Tripnee backed away, their guns aimed squarely at the men.

"Very, very slowly. Roll over onto your stomachs, arms behind your backs. Do as we say, and you live. Any false moves—any at all—and you die!"

Mack Dowell and Hektor did as directed. Adam and Tripnee cuffed the two with heavy-duty plastic hand cuffs. Interesting. After their initial shock, the cartel men seemed to almost welcome this turn of events. Peace had worked some magic here. Even so, Adam, Tripnee and BC thoroughly searched the men and the room, finding several weapons, including two Uzi machine pistols and a ton of ammo.

Leaving Tripnee and BC with Hektor and Mack Dowell, Adam threw open the door to Peace's cabin and rushed to his uncle. Peace jumped from his bunk, a broad smile spreading across his face.

"My boy! My boy! So great to see you!"

"So great to see you, Peace! Are you okay?"

They hugged and laughed, held each other at arm's length, eyes gleaming, then hugged and laughed some more. Adam was filled not only with love, but also with a new admiration. In the course of finding Peace, he had come to see his uncle in a new light. The guy was no head-in-the-clouds ninny. He was an extraordinary human soul, performing near-miracles right and left. But Peace—and all of them—were still in deep trouble, and had a long way to go!

Adam and Tripnee checked the old man over and found him to be in excellent shape. Then everyone gathered in Hektor and Mack Dowell's cabin.

"I listened at your porthole for awhile," said Adam, indicating the open porthole with a nod, "I know the risk you took defying Rook to spare Peace. What you did took guts. Thanks."

"I'll just add," said Tripnee, "that had you tried to go ahead and kill Peace, Adam would've stopped you dead. Dead."

Peace, looking wonderfully chipper, a twinkle in his eyes, said, "I felt you nearby, Adam, my boy. I was imagining you holding off and giving these men a chance to do the right thing. I'm glad it worked out that way!"

Looking at Hektor and Mack Dowell, Peace continued, "These men have done bad things in the past. But they're showing signs of making better choices." Then Peace cracked a mischievous smile, "At heart, they're not bad men. I think I've gotten them into hot water with their boss."

BC couldn't take his eyes off Peace, his cheeks wet with tears of joy.

Mack Dowell said, "We're all so, so fucked!"

CHAPTER 41

THE OVAL OFFICE

Back aboard Dream Voyager, after outpourings of tears, laughter and more hugs, BC got everyone's attention, "It's only a matter of time—probably very little time—before the cartel finds us and strikes again—probably with overwhelming force."

Little Rasheed said, "We've got a weapon to fight back! You all have to see what me and Vocab put together!"

Vocab had the video cued up, and hit play. There for the world to see, on the main salon's big screen, with skillful editing and clear audio, was Adam's hair micro-camera footage of Reamer Rook boasting about La Casa's killing, kidnapping, narco-trafficking, prostitution and extortion. It showed the man proudly explaining the cartel's use of child hitmen, Oro o Agua, the Bay Way, the 20% tax, and how he controlled police, judges, district attorneys, and members of the FBI. The short film showed Rook and El Dragón and their men salivating and almost ejaculating as they dumped Adam and Tripnee into the Bay Way. And it didn't stop there. With some 60-Minutes-style narration, the video juxtaposed and connected the Attorney General and national security advisor promise to take action with their attempt on Adam and Tripnee's lives. Finally, devastatingly, the video ended with news clips of Reamer Rook partying with the President of the United States!

There was wild applause.

"On social media," said BC, "this is guaranteed to go viral. It will probably bring down the government!"

Peace said, "It would go viral alright…"

Rasheed crowed, "Yeah!"

"…but all you'd get," continued Peace, "is civil war."

Vocab jumped up, "So be it! This ain't no time to pull punches or be diplomatic!"

Peace replied, "Trouble is, the focus would be on blame and acrimony, not on stopping La Casa."

BC said, "So what should we do?"

Then Peace spoke: "The real value of Vocab and Rasheed's video is its potential to convince the powers that be to clean up the Bay and bring down the cartel. If we handle this well, this video will give them no choice but to do the right thing."

BC seemed to take this in and slowly nodded, "But how we gonna do that? You saw what happened to Adam and Tripnee in DC!"

Peace smiled, "I know just the person to call."

"Really?" asked Adam.

"Someone who can get an audience with the president anytime, day or night," said Peace, "Harry Bellacozy."

"You sure?" asked Adam, "He's way too close to Rook!"

"Harry likes to hobnob with everybody," said Peace, "but I know the man. He's a rascal, but he would never condone the cartel."

Tripnee said, "I hope to God you're right."

Peace made the call and, amazingly, soon they were all on their way to meet Bellacozy's jet at nearby Napa Valley Airport, which fortunately had an extended runway. Peace urged everyone to come, including Hektor and Mack Dowell, whom Tripnee had convinced to turn state's evidence. The two, now freed from their handcuffs, were in fact desperate to come, sure they'd be killed if left behind.

Peace led their motley entourage up the steps to the 737, and it was moving and reassuring, Adam had to admit, to see Harry and Peace, two old symposium and Burning Man buddies, reconnect.

"You old coot," Bellacozy said to Peace, "You're in the thick of it again!"

"Who're you calling an 'old coot?'" smiled Peace as he hugged his longtime friend, "You crazy old coot!"

Seeing the palpable trust and goodwill between the men, Adam let out a long breath.

As they entered the private custom plane and passed the cockpit door, they were welcomed aboard by, who else—pilots Ben and Jerry! Then, Harry himself and General Eisenhower, Harry's head of security, ushered them into the plane's opulent main salon.

"I'm guessing with all you've been through, you all could use a good meal," said Harry. "So I asked the chef to whip up a little something." A team of cabin attendants, three women and a man, showed everyone how to activate mechanisms that swung big trays up out of the arms of the salon chairs to create spacious dining tables for all. Within minutes, everyone was digging into ribeye steaks, baked sweet potatoes, steamed broccoli and a fabulous Pinot Noir. As they ate, they again screened Vocab and Rasheed's video and formed a plan.

Upon landing at Ronald Reagan International Airport, Harry's 737 taxied to a secluded corner of the airport grounds, where Admiral Ty Jeppesen stood waiting by a row of black SUVs with government plates. Stairs were rolled into place, and the motley crew filed out of the jet and fanned out into the vehicles for the drive to the White House.

Entering at a side entrance, they passed through an extremely thorough Secret Service security scan and pat-down. Tripnee and Adam had to give up their guns, and exchanged frowning looks as they did so. It was a sad day in America when you're not sure if it's safe to enter the White House unarmed.

It was 3 a.m. when they walked into the Oval Office. Looking only half-awake in his pajamas, the President shook hands all around, including with little Vocab and Rasheed, waved everyone into a circle of couches and chairs, moved around to sit behind his desk, and said, "Okay, Harry, it's the middle of the god-damned night, so this better be good!"

Harry said, "It will be, Mr. President. I suggest we begin by hearing from the people spearheading the investigation: Adam, Tripnee and BC."

Adam outlined the overall situation with enough specific detail to draw a vivid picture. Next, Tripnee and then BC sketched in more of the story from their perspectives. From there, they went around the room. Peace, Vocab, Rasheed and even Hektor and Mack Dowell briefly told their stories. The president seemed to listen intently.

As each person added their chunk, the cumulative effect was devastating. The portrait of Reamer Rook's, Toro Canino's and La Casa's ongoing, relentless, remorseless campaign of murder, intimidation, extortion, corruption, kidnapping, sex trafficking, drug dealing, home invasions, robbery and fake spirituality was just plain overwhelming.

But in case all this weren't enough, then came the clincher—Vocab and Rasheed's video—which made it all chillingly, terrifyingly real. As the video played, the President ground his teeth and his facial muscles quivered.

Before the end, Harry stopped the video and—wisely, Adam realized—said to the President, "None of this video needs to ever see the light of day. That is, provided we take decisive action, with your backing, to stop the cartel."

Harry restarted the video, and when they watched the news footage of the President partying with Reamer Rook, the big man glared at the screen with steely eyes, clenched his hands into fists, and looked royally pissed. But he was probably nowhere near as pissed as he would have been without Harry having said what he did.

The President asked, "How many copies are there of this video?"

Vocab stood up, looked the man in the eye, and said, "As insurance, in case anything were to happen to me or Rasheed or any of us, copies are set to go to the entire media and to all two million of my and Rasheed's YouTube subscribers."

As an experienced player in the social media realm, the President knew in a heartbeat that the video would be unstoppable. If released via social media, it would go viral worldwide, and would undermine, if not destroy, all confidence, not only in his presidency, but also in Bay Area and United States government in general.

Oddly, the President still seemed to be weighing various possible responses. Somehow, this glaringly obvious case of monstrous wrong became difficult to assess in the moral vacuum of Washington, DC. But slowly, eventually, the President did the right thing.

After calming down from seeing the video, the president said, "Blackie's a big donor, and we've had good times. But son of a bitch, Harry, you're an even bigger donor—hell, a much bigger donor—and that's huge!"

A little later, their host mused, "Besides, I hate the Reconquista element of La Casa. The very idea that they lay claim to California!"

And finally he said, turning to his one aide in the room, "OK, OK. We got to OK a real big cleanup of the Bay Area."

CHAPTER 42

THE PENDULUM SWINGS

Harry, looking at the President, said, "I guess you see now why we needed to meet with just you, and none of your inner circle."

The President nodded and, looking at Adam and Tripnee, said, "When you talked to my Attorney General and national security advisor, it's pretty god damn obvious that, instead of taking action or informing me, the rats tried to car-bomb you, and then got the cartel to send those hit squads! It's a miracle you're alive!"

Adam felt encouraged, thinking, 'He gets it!'

"With so many people compromised," continued the President, "we've got to set up a special, separate, secret task force. I'd like you, admiral, to lead it, and the three of you Adam, Tripnee and BC, to be part of it."

An actual plan, not just a Wagstaff ruse, took shape. The special presidential task force would be composed of Navy SEALs, a special forces battalion, the Coast Guard, two Navy destroyers, and military police. They drew on information from Tripnee, BC's spy craft, General Eisenhower, Vocab, Rasheed, Hektor, Mack Dowell and Adam. Secrecy and surprise were crucial. The task force would simultaneously arrest Reamer Rook, Toro Canino, the Attorney General, the national security advisor, and the corrupt people in the FBI—and at the same time round up as many mid- and low-level La Casa operatives and cells as possible. Inevitably, some of the small fry—and perhaps some bigger fish they did not know about—would scatter, but if they locked up the key ringleaders and as many of the other people as they could, the threat of a vast, coordinated cartel undermining the very foundations of law and order would be stopped, they hoped.

Admiral Jeppesen would oversee the arrests in DC, while Adam, Tripnee and BC would take the lead in the Bay Area. To minimize risk to the task force and public, they needed to make the arrests when the men were unarmed and away from any goon squads or fortified compounds.

For the Washington, DC, arrests of the Attorney General and national security adviser, they considered the oval office, but no one knew whom they could trust in the White House. So they decided on the SCIF in Jeppesen's building—the same venue as the earlier meeting—where the two men would be isolated, separated from any weapons and cell phones, easily taken into custody and unable to warn confederates.

As they fine-tuned the plan, the Admiral chuckled in anticipation, "This'll be great! They'll be so pissed!"

Similarly, in the Bay Area, Tripnee would lead a team that would lure FBI agents Mercedes Montana and Judd Wagstaff to a phony urgent meeting in the SCIF in the San Francisco FBI office.

The collaring of Reamer Rook and Toro Canino, on the other hand, promised to be more complicated. A full-out, military-style assault on Rook's fortified Belvedere compound was not going to fly. It would be too dangerous and too full of unknowns for the task force and surrounding Bay. Besides, insisted the President, "Imminent societal collapse or not, you just don't do something like that in a wealthy place like Belvedere. Too many big donors."

So, how to catch Rook away from his house? As the team

studied the situation and pondered options, BC analyzed the latest root kit data. The cartel seemed to be pretty much doing business as usual. The chatter suggested that La Casa was taking in stride the I-80 death of its three hit squads, the all-out manhunt for Adam and Tripnee, and the mysterious disappearance of Peace, Hektor and Mack Dowell. Meanwhile, income—more than ever—was pouring in from drugs, robbery, prostitution, identity theft, ransom, home invasion and extortion. Two more teachers from Peace's elementary school had been Bay Way'd "most enjoyably." Also, Total Embrace was on a roll—and had one of their Albany Bulb mega—gatherings coming up during the next full moon.

Then BC picked up word that Black Elk—i.e., Reamer Rook—would be presiding at the Albany Bulb event!

"That's our chance," said Adam. "Rook's habit is to go by boat!"

They had to avoid a shootout near the Total Embrace crowd, but the boat ride would provide the perfect opportunity to apprehend Rook.

CHAPTER 43

ANOTHER BAY WAY

Adam chose the top of Mt. Livermore, the highest point on Angel Island, as his command post. From this vantage point, he looked almost straight down on all of central San Francisco Bay. Like a football gridiron seen from a skybox on the 50-yard line, the roughly rectangular Slot on the south side of the island from the Golden Gate to Berkeley sat directly under his nose. To the east, the East Bay waterfront, including Albany Bulb, Brooks Island, and Richmond's Marina Bay and Brickyard Cove, spread out before him. To the west, Belvedere, Richardson Bay and Sausalito dazzled as though he was looking straight down into a box of jewels. And closest and most clearly visible of all, between the north side of the island and Tiburon, the erratic currents of narrow Raccoon Strait frothed virtually at his feet.

Because it was the shortest route from the cartel's Belvedere compound to Albany Bulb, Rook's boat ride would likely take him through Raccoon Strait. Halfway through this spectacular narrows, scooped out of Angel Island's steep northern face, lay a deep, tranquil inlet named Ayala Cove. Because it was largely hidden from boats moving from west to east, this cove was the ideal place to ambush Rook.

The Coast Guard had the authority at anytime to stop, board and inspect any boat. The idea was, under the guise of a routine stop, to suddenly surround and completely overpower Rook and his crew and give them no choice but to opt for a quick, bloodless surrender.

There was no way to predict the reaction of cartel sociopaths. Normal people would yield to the overwhelming firepower of two 87-foot Marine Protector Class cutters, each carrying two 50-caliber machine guns, well-armed crews of ten, plus two squads each of Navy SEALS armed and body-armored to the teeth. Also, it seemed likely Rook would yield, because he would assume that he could free himself with a phone call. A call to someone he no doubt "owned" high up on the chain of command. Someone who would not only release him and his men but also make any inspection citations disappear and abjectly apologize for the error and inconvenience. The fact was, however, this guy and his crew followed no rules, and killed on a whim, so it was essential to prepare for the worst.

Trying to anticipate every eventuality, Adam deployed an entire squadron of radar and night-vision-equipped Coast Guard craft, plus two Navy destroyers. The two lead boats—the heavily armed 87-foot cutters—hid deep in Ayala Cove, ready at Adam's command to pop out and surprise the cartel boat. Other Coast Guard cutters floated at the ready near Sam's Dock in Tiburon, Brickyard Cove on Point Richmond, Horseshoe Cove by the Golden Gate, and behind Alcatraz in the middle of the Slot. Three fast, smaller, shallow-draft Coast Guard patrol boats hid behind Brooks Island near Albany Bulb.

Also, two Navy destroyers surveilled the strait from a distance, one from the west, the other from the east. Adam had to admit he was glad Admiral Jeppesen had insisted on the destroyers. Hopefully, Adam's team would bring in Rook without a shot being fired, but if Rook and his gang tried to escape or counterattack, it would be nice to have the option of blowing them to kingdom come—a step for which Adam already had the President's authorization, should he, Adam, at his sole discretion, deem it necessary. With Rook, anything could happen.

All of the boats and all of the people were in place. A few dozen steps from his island mountaintop command center, Adam even had a Coast Guard Sikorski helicopter standing by, with motor hot and a squad of Navy SEALs aboard, ready to take off at a moment's notice. At his side, Adam had a hand-picked team of elite Navy SEAL officers studying the Bay through powerful night-vision scopes.

Nothing was left to chance. Because the one place hidden from view from the command post was the west face of Belvedere, an additional Coast Guard cutter patrolled the downtown Sausalito waterfront, where it continuously kept eyes on Rook's compound and dock.

Adam's team had been in position for hours, and it was still early. With Rook scheduled to speak at 11 p.m. or so, he would probably begin his cruise to Albany Bulb around 9 or 10. The moon was full and the tide was super-high. As the alpenglow of sunset faded into deep twilight, the task force members deployed their night-vision scopes, which turned night into day, allowing them to see details, including people's faces sharp and clear even miles away. From across the water, they could hear the drums of Total Embrace and feel the swelling, pulsating tribal energy.

From his eyrie, Adam checked his squadron. All was good. He tried not to congratulate himself on his preparations for the coming encounter, knowing from experience that pride (cockiness) goeth before a fall. Better to stay humble, stay afraid, and use the fear to stay alert, searching for what might have been overlooked.

Despite knowing better, even as he kicked himself for doing so, he slipped into a reverie. Behind him, in the Slot, the weather was cold, foggy, blustery. But down in Ayala Cove, directly below him, it was lovely, calm, even balmy. No wonder Captain Ayala in 1775 choose to anchor here while his Spanish sailors used his ship's long boats to explore the Bay and create maps showing accurate depth readings that were used for over 100 years.

Uh-oh! Adam had to snap himself out of this. There was a megalomaniac madman on the loose. A man well on his insane way to crippling, perhaps destroying, the nation as we know it.

Suddenly, Adam's headset yanked him into the present. The captain of the cutter on the Sausalito waterfront radioed, "A delivery van is pulling away from the pizza factory!" This was their code for: A boat is pulling away from the cartel dock.

For several minutes, the height and steepness of the Belvedere peninsula blocked Adam's line of sight. Then a long black motor launch came into view, headed south toward the mouth of Richardson Bay. Peering through his powerful night scope, which revealed the scene in sharp, bright detail, Adam recognized Rook's sinister boat with the revolving rear bench. The bench was occupied by two voluptuous women who had been stripped naked—Linda, the school teacher, and Rook's neighbor Magdalena! They must have seen through Rook's Black Elk charade—and the Bay Way was to be their reward.

Each woman sat with her arms behind her back, no doubt handcuffed. Facing the pair were Rook, Toro Canino, Dead-Eye and the usual goon squad. The night vision scope was so clear and the magnification so strong, Adam could see spittle wetting the men's lips.

This was bad. Not just because Magdalena and Linda were in terrible danger, but also because hostages limited his options. Adam could no longer just obliterate the cartel bastards.

Still, from another standpoint, this was a lucky break! At least they had a shot at saving the women!! Adam made a split-second decision to stick with their plan. After all, what other choice did he have?

The thing was that the boat's route would be different tonight. When the cartel launch cleared the southern tip of Belevedere, instead of turning left east into Raccoon Strait toward Albany, it continued straight south toward the foggy, windy shipping lanes in the Slot.

Adam almost threw up. The sick psychos were squeezing in a Bay Way on the way to their spiritual gathering! They were using a double Bay Way murder to goose and fluff themselves, getting themselves aroused and ready for the "spiritual" frenzy of Total Embrace.

Speaking through his headset, Adam alerted his task force to be careful not to injure the hostages, and ordered the entire flotilla to converge on and surround the cartel boat. They would not have the advantage of sudden surprise, and the presence of hostages would limit what they could do, but he had deployed all these boats for a reason—so they could overwhelm Rook's crew anywhere in the Bay—and stop them, no matter what—and that was going to happen damn soon!

Rook and his crew, who were clearly not using night vision, were slow to see what was happening. When the two Coast Guard cutters—one from Horseshoe Cove and the other from behind Alcatraz—converged ahead of the gangsters, blocking their path, the cartel launch at first held its course. Then, when they finally realized what was happening, the cartel goons likely thought—correctly—that their attackers would not shoot because they had hostages. So they pulled out guns and charged straight at the Coast Guard boats. Blasting away with Uzis and pistols, they sent a spray of lead into the two cutters.

Just then, when the goons were focusing all of their attention forward, Linda—on the stern bench behind them—seized her opportunity. Adam laughed to see it! She extended one of her long, supermodel legs and quickly tapped Rook's two deck buttons—which activated the mechanisms that lifted and flipped the bench—plunging the women into the Bay.

The cold water was perilous—but probably felt wonderful, compared to cruising with the goon squad. Rook and Canino glanced back just in time to see the women drop into the waves—out of their reach. Adam chuckled with delight to see the men explode with rage, suddenly denied their hostages.

Adam immediately ordered the helicopter to pick up the women, who he knew would be fighting for their lives, trying to keep their heads above water with their arms handcuffed behind their backs. Within moments, the chopper lifted off and began a fast swooping descent toward Magda and Linda, who were perilously bobbing in the water.

Adam commanded the destroyers to blast the cartel craft to oblivion as soon as they could get a clear shot. Perhaps anticipating this—realizing that without hostages, they'd be blown out of the water at any moment—Rook's boat deployed some sort of nitrous oxide speed booster. Like a bolt from a crossbow, the cartel craft shot between the two cutters. Clever move! While Rook was between them, the two Coast Guard boats couldn't fire for fear of hitting each other. But once the cartel boat was beyond them, the cutters opened fire with a vengeance. The cartel pilot, though, was a skillful bastard who threw the black launch into a series of wild, erratic maneuvers, making it hard to hit.

The task force squadron converged from the east, north, and west. Three fast small craft raced on hydrofoils from Brooks Island, followed by the cutter from Brickyard Cove and one of the destroyers, to close in from the east. Six cutters—led by the first two to engage, followed by others from Ayala Cove, Sam's Dock and Sausalito—swept down from the north. And the other destroyer and a second cutter from Horseshoe Cove moved in from the west. They had Rook boxed in on every side except the south—and that opening would close soon.

Rook's boat was totally outnumbered and outgunned—and had no chance. Except—damn!—it was managing to dodge shell after shell from the destroyers while maneuvering south, dodging and darting ever closer to the foggy, blustery Slot, where an especially dense arm of opaque fog extended in from the Golden Gate. Even if Rook reached the fog, however, there was no way he could evade the squadron's radar or massive firepower.

Still, the squirrelly son of a bitch kept swerving and jumping, and with uncanny luck, avoided the squadron's withering fire by the thinnest of margins. The Bay Way launch sped into the billowing fringes of the fog bank—and was just moments from disappearing into the dense wall of fog.

Suddenly, the swirling fog thinned, revealing a towering steel wall racing from east to west. It was a quarter-mile-long container ship, speeding toward the Golden Gate. The hydrofoil boats, followed closely by a cutter and a destroyer, pressed in from the east, forcing the sinister Bay Way launch to turn west and run parallel alongside the quarter-mile-long behemoth.

What luck! The south door was now closed. Adam's presidential task force squadron finally had the cartel leadership completely boxed in, with no possible escape. The proximity of the containership meant that the squadron had to be very careful firing cannons and heavy armament, but, unless Rook surrendered—which didn't seem likely—a kill shot was imminent.

Trapped and done for, Rook's speedboat ran parallel to the long, straight side of the containership, looking very small next to that behemoth. Desperate, insane, nutty as fruitcakes, Rook and his crew raced along beside the ship, and then, probably hoping to escape off to the south, tried to cut across its bow.

But it didn't work out so well. The move was impossible. It was so beautiful, what happened next!

The cartel boat tipped up sideways on the twenty-foot bow wave for a moment and then rolled over, spilling everyone who was onboard into the water directly in front of the speeding container ship. Although roiling fog partially obscured the scene, Adam saw it all through his powerful night vision lenses. The launch going vertical on the wave, the bodies falling like rag dolls into the foam, the boat and bodies disappearing under that beautiful oncoming container ship bow. Within moments, there was nothing. Nothing but a few—surprisingly few—bits of flotsam and jetsam floating up in the wake of the container ship as it steamed out to sea.

All of this happened in just minutes. Adam swung his scope back to check on Linda and Magdalena. The chopper was hovering right over the water and was just then lowering a basket. After the two women managed to roll into it, the basket was rapidly cranked up to the level of the chopper's open door. As Linda and Magdalena were bundled into blankets and pulled into the helicopter, Adam caught a glimpse of Magda's dancing mole and of Linda's long, strong form. Thank God they were okay!

Swinging his attention back to the squadron, Adam had the boats patrol the area for an hour, scouring the vicinity for any sign of survivors or body parts. But no bodies were found, just a fine sprinkling of boat debris.

After a while, one of the SEAL officers on the mountaintop said, "No one could survive being dumped like that in front of a container ship."

Thinking, what the heck, Adam sent three cutters out to check and patrol around the San Francisco buoy for eight hours. Just to be sure.

CHAPTER 44

JACK LONDON SQUARE

The next morning, Adam woke up aboard Dream Voyager beside a sleeping Tripnee. After raining enough kisses on her neck and shoulders to bring a smile to her contoured lips, but not enough to fully awaken her, he went up on deck. Nothing was stirring over on Big Zen, so he decided to stretch his legs with a stroll.

With the events of recent days whirling in his mind, Adam followed the floating piers to land and began walking along the Oakland waterfront. It was mid-morning and Jack London Square was already alive and throbbing. The foodie restaurants—many with inviting shaded patio terraces—were already packed. On an outdoor stage, a kids' chorus from a local school entertained a delighted audience of a hundred or so with rhythm-and-blues numbers. The kids, who were Hispanic, Asian, black, and white, radiated talent, spunk, and obviously were headed for excellent future careers in the field of music.

One restaurant bar with outdoor bocce ball courts erupted in roaring laughter and cheers every time someone made a lucky throw. Boats big and small came and departed from marinas lining the shoreline. Groups of sea kayakers and standup paddleboarders, like flocks of ducklings following their mother, trailed behind instructors from California Canoe and Kayak, a water sports shop overlooking the estuary. Sculptures of Jack London and Buck, the canine hero of Call of the Wild, induced strollers to pause. Nearby, an Amtrak train disgorged a new wave of exploring souls.

Adam's heart gradually filled and lifted. Tripnee had successfully collared Mercedes Montana and Judd Wagstaff. Ty Jeppesen had brought in the Attorney General, the national security adviser and three key DC FBI honchos. Reamer Rook, Toro Canino and their vast horrible cartel had been brought down. And life went on.

All around him, people of every background and ethnicity dined, conversed, biked, lounged, strolled, shopped, explored and laughed. The true gold of cordiality and kindness was in the air. The world, evidently, was going to be OK.

Walls of art tiles harmonized with the surroundings, and, because life imitates art, were maybe a subtle instigator of those surroundings. The tiles beamed forth sweet messages. One stated, "Live together as brothers, or perish together as fools."—MLK. Another said, "Dear Lord, be good to me. The sea is so wide, and my boat is so small." Others read, "The person who says it cannot be done should not get in the way of the person doing it." "We are all one. Peace on earth. You and me." "We are the universe becoming conscious of itself." "Learn to love yourself." And still another, created by the 1997 class of Cleveland Elementary said simply, "Peace Love Caring Sharing."

A bit mezmerized, Adam marveled at a monumental bronze sculpture of an eagle in full vigorous flight, bearing an irresistible goddess of peace who looked so much like Tripnee, that his heart actually did skip a beat. A little further on, Adam paused to study the weathered exterior of The First and Last Chance Saloon, where Jack London as a kid did his homework every afternoon. Got to do your homework!

Peace came to mind. To his own surprise, Adam had come to deeply admire his uncle. Talk about courage, compassion and wisdom! His uncle had helped—and was loved—by so many. Adam saw it in the eyes of BC, Vocab, Rasheed, Magdalena, Linda, Bellacozy, Ben, Jerry, Ike, and even Hektor and Mack Dowell.

In the final analysis, it was Peace who had played the crucial role in bringing La Casa to light and, by being the key figure they all rallied around, taking it down.

Adam now finally understood Peace's focus on spiritual awareness. Taking the high road and seeing the positive had not been a non-acknowledgement of his grief over his parents' deaths. It had simply been offered as a way forward when the young Adam was ready. Without Adam knowing it, Peace, by virtue of who he was and his flow of wisdom, had buoyed and enriched the youthful Adam. His uncle's steady caring had given Adam his inner foundation, and had enabled his younger self to blossom. So much of who Adam had become—his abilities, his values, his intuition, his curiosity, his joy of life—had been inspired by this man, his uncle Peace.

Adam was reminded of the folktale of the young man who thought his father a fool, only to be amazed, a decade or so later, by how much his father had learned in the interval. Peace had always been there, loving and nurturing, but also giving him the freedom to grow up independent, self-reliant and vibrant. How amazingly lucky he was to have this man in his life!

On a whim Adam climbed to the roof of a tall building and looked around. The beckoning panorama of the Oakland-Berkeley cityscape spread to the east, north and south. To the west, the iridescent waters of the Bay bejeweled by Yerba Buena, Treasure, Alcatraz and Angel Islands and the tiara of the Bay Bridge filled the middle distance, and beyond stood the shimmering City itself. The whole place was a teeming hive of striving, struggling minds and hearts, precious beyond measure, worth defending all-out.

EPILOGUE

A few weeks later, once the full story came out in the media, the task force's work was well-received. The President even got a few days of favorable press. The key cartel conspirators were going to be locked away for a long time. Many of the cartel small fry, especially those who caught wind of the crackdown early, had escaped arrest, but without the ringleaders, the threat to fundamental law and order was removed.

To celebrate and to have some fun, Peace held a garden party. Adam, Tripnee, BC, Harry Bellacozy, Admiral Ty Jeppesen, Linda, Magdalena, Vocab, Rasheed, Ike, Ben, Jerry and the gymnosophists were all there. Even Captain Dimitrios, the Sausalito non-boat-owner Al Capricio, and the former cartel hitmen Hektor and Mack Dowell showed up—the latter two in the company of sheriff's deputies and wearing court-ordered ankle bracelets.

What's more, the President came. How could that be? Was it to curry favor with his biggest donor by far, Harry Bellacozy? Or to portray himself as an ordinary man of the people? Or was it curiosity? Or perhaps the camaraderie? Whatever the reason, there he was, making quite a stir with his entourage of aides, Secret Service bodyguards and reporters. Right there in Peace's creekside El Sobrante garden: the President of the United States!

True to Peace and Harry's symposium tradition, the wine and

philosophizing flowed like a great river. Lively, wide ranging, controversy-laden conversations filled the air. Many who were present took advantage of the opportunity to talk at length with, and share their views with, the President. Here among the redwoods and fruit trees, Adam noticed little of the name-calling, rigid certitude or ideology-based outrage so common in the outer world. Perhaps because these people treated each other, and each other's opinions, with civility and respect, minds expanded, and much common ground was discovered.

It was a motley crew, but they'd all played a role in something epic and valuable. They'd bonded and had gotten to that wonderful level where, despite their differences, they accepted and appreciated each other simply for their goofy, fallible, miraculous, shared humanity.

Someone proposed a toast, "Hey, we saved the Bay!" To this they drank deeply.

Someone else said, "Admit it, we saved the United States of America!" Then they drank deeply again, and again.

At one point, the President said to Peace, "Harry talks about you a lot. Are you enlightened?"

To this, Peace replied, "No, Mr. President. I'm just on the path, like everyone else."

"The hell you say," said Harry.

BC said, "Talk, Peace, talk."

Rasheed and Vocab whipped out their phone cameras and began recording. "A viral video is coming!"

Adam and Tripnee reached for each other, holding hands. They and pretty much everyone looked on, nodding affirmatively, many whose eyes were filled with tears of, what, joy?

Peace, who like everyone else, had been enjoying the wine, let loose. "Well, a little something I've learned is that all of us have within ourselves direct access to the wellspring of universal energy, unlimited awareness, full perpetual access to the creator. Each of us is, now and always, whole, OK and *where it's at!*"

The old rascal paused, beaming. There were shouts of, "Skoal!" and "Amen." Everyone lifted their glass in a toast, then fell silent again, hanging on his every word.

"You don't need to yearn to be fixed or to be anywhere other than where you are," Peace continued. "To have such yearnings is only human, of course. But when these yearnings come up, simply take notice without thinking they are truly from your essence. They may indicate you are sad, or need nurturing, or that it would be good for you to do something for yourself. But you are not the yearning, or the sadness, or the neediness. You are the space these things flow through. You are presence. You are life force. You are the creator. As Rumi says, 'It is your light that lights the world!'"

"Beautiful," enthused Adam, "I'm going to meditate on that!"

The End

AUTHOR'S NOTE

This is a work of fiction set in an actual place, the San Francisco Bay Area. The characters and events described herein are imagined, while the places, with some embellishments, are mostly real. In particular, the Oakland Renaissance, the Kings River—the largest watershed in the Sierra—and the magical Bay itself are wonderfully genuine.

This being said, it is worth noting that gangs and cartels do in fact traffic in humans, use children as lookouts, drug carriers and hit men, and have been known to "tax" teachers and others a percentage of their salaries. Fortunately, at least in the U.S., the level of police, judicial and political corruption is less than portrayed herein. Of course, corrupt officials are the last to reveal they are on the take, and are the first to proclaim themselves anti-crime.

To learn more about the author's other books, visit WilliamMcGinnis.com. The author welcomes your comments at bill@whitewatervoyages.com.

Reviews are the lifeblood of indie authors!

ACKNOWLEDGEMENTS

What a wild ride it has been to research and write Gold Bay! A lifelong adventure, really. The Bay's shores and waters—and the Bay Area's rich, kaleidoscopic cultural mosaic—were my playground, my magic kingdom, growing up. Countless great souls—too numerous to name—provided aid and inspiration along the way and in the actual writing of this novel. But I would be remiss if I did not attempt to single out a salient few:

I thank my son Will McGinnis for sharing his plot and character insights and uncanny knowledge of tech spyware. Given his level of expertise with the latter, it's obvious he's in the CIA, and, per "Company" guidelines, must pretend otherwise.

For awakening my thinking on myriad levels, I thank my dear friend Janet Brown, CEO of FundX and founder of the FundX family of mutual funds. By the way, it is only by pure chance that Janet's spectacular waterfront Belvedere home is nearly identical to that of Magdalena Alvarado in the novel.

My love of the Bay and the creation of Gold Bay were immeasurably enhanced by the companionship and encouragement of my illustrious sailing buddies. Noteworthy among this crew: My older brother Gregor, who died in the East Bay Firestorm of 1991, with whom I shared countless voyages around the Bay in a tipsy sailing canoe that he built. My teenage cronies Bobby, Joe and Norm, with whom I sailed, by dark of night, a leaky eleven-foot raft from Angel Island to Brooks Island. Bud Robyn, owner and captain extraordinaire of the real, original Dream Voyager, a Bruce Farr 73. Herman Haluza, with fond memories of our off-shore cruises to the San Francisco buoy. Al Wallash, may we ever continue our flights of euphoria sailing the Bay and imbibing grog akin to ambrosia of the gods at Berkeley's Rare Barrel Brewery. Captain Mark Kocina, owner of Central Coast Sailing Charters, whose warmth, talent and mastery of the arts of sailing and living make sailing the Bay and the California coast pure joy. And the intrepid boat people at Tradewinds!

I thank Hisham Ali Bob for his friendship, and for sharing his many insights gleaned as the coordinator of Oakland's Youth Non-Violence Program. I salute Dimitrious Fowler of the Oakland Police Department for welcoming me into his squad room and letting me tag along on meth busts.

I deeply appreciate my Bay Area writing pals. My dear friend, editor and mentor Jil Plummer's suggestions, rescues, guidance and tireless assistance kept me going and made the writing fun. Similarly, for their help and encouragement, I thank Nalini Davison, Isabel Allende, Gary Turchin, Hao Tran, Jim Barnard, and Pendragon writers Marjorie Witt, Ken Kerkhoff, Anindita Basu and Wendy Blakeley.

Linda Jay's help with copy editing and ad copy, Joseph B. Lloa's expertise with cover design, and Andrew Benzie's artistry with book and cover design and all phases of modern book production have been a godsend! Jerrilee and Becky Parker Geist and Bryan Lamb of Pro Audio Voices are as this is written doing a fabulous job producing and promoting the audiobook. For their help as cover art consultants, proof readers and much more, I thank Pat and Clay Jensen, Toni Hall, Barbara Blaisdell, Mace Thompson, Doug Stanley, Barry Kruse, Don Stevens, John Walsh, and Karen L. McDaniel.

Lee Foster, Wendy Bartlett, Tamara Shiloh, Tom Joyce, David Kudler, Ruth Schwartz, Judy Baker, Judy Reyes, Arlene Miller, Mara Lynn Johnstone, Tony Hawthorne, Robert Perry,

Lorna Johnson, Scott Calhoun and the other richly talented members of the Bay Area Independent Publishers Association (BAIPA) poured forth savvy guidance and encouragement.

I treasure my gymnosophist sauna cronies whose ongoing philosophizing steadily bumbles along solving the world's problems. To Randy, Robin, Scott, Zuzanna, William, Michelle, Lloyd, Ali, Yuriy, Mace, Fred, Christopher, Russ, Barry, Rick, Marco, Hoc, Ed, Mo, Ron, Hyung, James, Bob, Earnest, John, Claudell, Abraham, Tom, Kostya, Rita, Monica, Lisa, Jordan, Theressa, Vanessa, Saeng, Nadia, Davy, Dave, Bruce, Subhas, Samantha, Wes, Shelly, Art, Arnold, Tony, Phil and all the great souls at the Lakeridge Club—may we continue to enjoy the moment, practice kindness, and soar!

On a deeply personal note, I would like to express my love and appreciation for Will, Alexandra, Mary and Neville McGinnis, Veronica Rand, Ted and Ruth Kearn, Sherrin Farley, Yazheng Song, Luther Stephens and Christopher Brown; you mean the world to me—I am so lucky to have you in my life!!

Last but not least, I would like to thank and praise my dear readers. I appreciate you! To one and all I extend a huge thank you! Please attribute the good stuff in Gold Bay to those mentioned above, and its shortcomings to me alone.

Very best wishes,
Bill McGinnis

ABOUT THE AUTHOR

A California native with a Master's in English literature, William McGinnis wrote two novels and five non-fiction books about whitewater rafting and sailing. His passions include hiking, woodworking, staring into space, audiobooks, and exploring new paths to adventure, friendship and growth. Bill lives in El Sobrante, across the Bay from San Francisco. His author website is WilliamMcGinnis.com.

Books by William McGinnis:

Whitewater Rafting

The Class V Briefing

The Guide's Guide Augmented:
  Reflections on Guiding Professional River Trips

Sailing the Greek Islands: Dancing with Cyclops

Disaster on the Clearwater: Rafting Beyond the Limit

Whitewater: A Thriller (Adam Weldon Book #1)

Gold Bay: An Adam Weldon Thriller

Good News: In *The Cyclops Conspiracy,* the third thriller in the Adam Weldon series, Adam and Tripnee sail the Greek Islands tracking down terrorists intent on smuggling suitcase nukes into Europe and America.